5/12

THE IGUANA TREE

by **MICHEL STONE**

THE

IGUANA

TREE

A Novel

] Michel Stone [

Hub City Press
Spartanburg, SC

Second printing, March 2012

Cover design: Lisa Jones Atkins and Dorothy Chapman Josey
Interior design: Corinne Manning
Author Photo: Carroll Foster

Library of Congress
Cataloging-in-Publication Data

Stone, Michel, 1969-
The iguana tree / Michel Stone.
p. cm.
ISBN 978-1-891885-88-4
1. Families—Mexico—Fiction. 2. Human smuggling—Fiction. 3. Illegal aliens—Mexican-American Border Region—Fiction. 4. Illegal aliens—Crimes against—Mexican-American Border Region—Fiction. 5. United States—Emigration and immigration—Fiction. 6. Domestic fiction. I. Title.
PS3619.T6569I48 2012
813'.6—dc22
2011037779

Parts of *The Iguana Tree* have been previously published as short stories or excerpts: "Beyond This Point," (Raleigh, NC) *News and Observer*, September 24, 2006; "Pollos," (Raleigh, NC) *News and Observer*, January 23, 2005; "Dance of the Coyote," *South Carolina* magazine, August, 2004.

ART WORKS.
arts.gov

This project is supported in part by an award from the National Endowment for the Arts

HUB CITY PRESS

186 West Main Street
Spartanburg, SC 29306
864.577.9349
www.hubcity.org

For Beth and Roy Smoak

Hope is a waking dream.

— Aristotle

prologue

LILIA LINGERED beneath the shade tree and watched her husband leave, though the morning dawned mild, and she had no need yet for the canopy's cool shadows. Héctor slipped from their courtyard, past two brown hens scratching among weeds, down the narrow, dusty lane on which Lilia had always lived, then rounded a slight bend and was gone. She knew he would make his way to the bus stop at the edge of the village, then on to Oaxaca City, and then… Then she did not know what would become of her Héctor, or how far the trip to the border was, or how far beyond the border he would go. She must put these thoughts from her mind now.

Lilia gripped her mug in both hands like a prayer, inhaling the scent of coffee and cinnamon, and watched the sky and buildings to the east color pink then orange. The dark sky to the west remained unaffected. She drifted from the shadows into the center of the courtyard and lifted her face to the rising sun, closing her eyes, basking in its radiance. It was a constant. A familiarity. Cold weather existed elsewhere, not here. America had cold places, but they seemed as distant, as foreign, as the weightlessness of outer space or the sunless floor of the Pacific Ocean. All were places for which she felt ill-equipped and fearful. Héctor viewed

America as The Great Opportunity. Lilia saw it as The Unknown.

Overhead, yellow-headed blackbirds flitted among the tree's dense foliage, flapping wildly as if to distill the perfume of waxy blossoms half-hidden amid wide, verdant leaves.

Beyond her courtyard wall Lilia's village slowly awakened: the crow of a cock and the bray of a burro in reply, the clanking of the fishmonger's wagon winding its way to the pier, and other sounds that were all Puerto Isadore's own, all Lilia's own. She caught a trace of orange incense in the air. Crucita is awake, she thought. Each morning before her coffee, often before dressing, Lilia's grandmother lit an incense stick. Today she burned orange. Yesterday had been orange, too. Or maybe sandalwood. Lilia could not remember.

The western sky had lightened to pastel. A goat pulling a trash cart made its way past her in no hurry. Lilia watched him pass in silence, then walked inside to nurse her infant daughter—an only child—Alejandra, leaving the courtyard smelling of goat and incense.

1

"I WANT to show you something, *amigo*, to be certain you understand."

He looked Héctor in the eyes. He was a man to be feared, confident, calculated, experienced. He knew far more than Héctor. His pulse would not quicken when he stabbed a man to death. He would take no pleasure in the act, nor would it haunt him. His dark eyes gave no indication of a soul. Héctor turned away, watched the passing landscape.

Then he saw it.

"The border, friend," the coyote said.

Héctor looked at the border, then back at his driver.

"You wonder why you need me, heh, friend? You see this simple metal fence, rusted and worn and easily transversible, and you say to yourself, 'This is nothing. I do not understand. One could walk across that line right now and be in America.'"

Héctor said nothing, confused by what he saw, and suddenly wondered if he had, indeed, no need for a coyote after all, if this were all a trick, a scam to lure innocents to the border, to steal their money.

But seeing the border and the desert wasteland beyond it answered no questions. The mystery remained, grew. He saw no guards, no guns, no watchdogs, no border patrol. He saw men, women, and children now, dotted all along the shabby wall. He had not noticed them at first. They waited, watched, though for what Héctor could not possibly know.

"They are *pollos*, chickens, friend," the coyote said, jutting a finger toward a small cluster of men crouching near a gap in the metal. This was a term Héctor had not heard before regarding those heading north. Héctor thought about chickens being led by a coyote. That did not fit. A coyote would devour a chicken.

"They are foolish, and they will cross on their own, or with some cheap, inexperienced coyote," Héctor's smuggler continued. "They will all be back in Mexico within a day. The rare few who are not caught will likely die of thirst in the desert."

He nodded toward a group of six, huddled by another gaping hole in the metal fence.

They seemed to have nothing with them, no provisions, no bags.

"They will need at least two gallons of water a day to survive out there. Look at them," he said in disgust. "They carry maybe a gallon or two among them all. Sometimes the ones who make it deep into the desert find a mesquite tree, hang themselves by their belts, preferring death to come quickly and surely rather than slowly and with uncertainty. Do you know about death in the desert, friend?" he asked.

"I can imagine it," Héctor said.

"No. You cannot imagine it. But I will tell you about it. The heat bears down unlike any you have experienced. The desert has no ocean breeze like you have in your village. The sun scorches your skin and your tongue, and breathing is an agony. Lips crack, bleed. Dried blood cakes in your nostrils, and you ask God why your tongue has grown scales." He stopped, as if he wanted Héctor to consider his words before continuing.

They rode in silence, Héctor dutifully studying the Mexican side of the border, just as the coyote wanted him to do. He had dreamed of it for so long, he could not feel certain he really saw it now.

"Your parched insides curse your mouth for singeing them with each hot breath you take," the coyote continued. "Slowly you realize you will not survive. That the desert is going to win, only it is in no hurry. Then your prayers change, friend, and you no longer pray to the Virgin for water, but for a tree to hang yourself or a rattlesnake to strike your ankle. The trees are few, but the rattlesnakes, they are plentiful," he said, a rising pleasure in his voice when he spoke of rattlesnakes.

He slowed his truck to a stop, and pointed to the desert beyond the six-foot-tall metal sheet that separated the men from America. "A fool's graveyard."

He began driving again, turning the truck around, heading in the direction from which they had just come. His tone remained the same when he said, "You shall not suffer such a fate, friend. You will reach *El Norte*. Your bones will not find their final resting place there," and he raised his chin toward the desert.

Héctor said nothing. He watched the chickens along the border. Most had nothing with them except for a woven sack and a water jug. He saw children, some as young as five and six, crouched near their parents, watching the desert as if it were the ultimate prize. A lump formed in Héctor's throat. He had not cried in a long time, and he would not do so now in this coyote's presence. He felt like a traitor to his fellow country-men when he prayed that the border patrol would catch them before they walked far into their journey. *God deliver you.* Two men slipped through the fence and disappeared.

Within minutes Héctor and the coyote arrived at a small, one-room shack made of corrugated tin. Héctor followed the coyote inside. His eyes took a moment to adjust to the sudden darkness of the interior. A man sat on the floor in the corner smoking a cigarette, his back against the wall. The room contained no furniture, the floor littered with news-paper, bottles, and cigarette butts. The unmistakable stench of urine permeated the place.

The smuggler didn't acknowledge the man in the corner. He said to Héctor, "You will wait here until we cross," and he walked out, locking the door behind him.

Héctor didn't know if the man in the corner was a pollo or a coyote. The man sucked one last drag off his cigarette, then snuffed it out on the concrete floor.

"How's it going?" the man said, exhaling smoke with his words.

Héctor nodded a silent greeting, then shoved his hands into his pockets to still them.

Suddenly the stranger burst into laughter. Héctor's fingernails dug into his palm as he made a fist, unsure if his companion were a lunatic or if Héctor were just missing something terribly amusing. He stared at the floor, not wanting to look at the man in the corner. Finally the laughter subsided enough for Héctor's companion to speak.

"I see why they call us *pollos, amigo.* You look scared shitless, just like a baby chick the hen has left alone in the yard. Ah, but take no offense," he said, lighting another cigarette and offering the pack to Héctor. "I am sure I looked like you when I arrived here. I am Miguel."

Héctor took a cigarette and accepted Miguel's offer to light it. "I am Héctor," he said, still unsure of the stranger's sanity. "How long have you been here?" Héctor asked, blowing smoke away from his new acquaintance.

"Four days," Miguel answered, flicking the match across the room toward a green plastic bucket that smelled like a makeshift toilet. "I may die of cancer from these before we go. Though they are good to help with the waiting. I do not know how long we will be here. Perhaps the coyote was waiting for you to arrive. Maybe now we will go."

Héctor looked about the sparse room, attempted to calculate the many hours of waiting represented by the cigarette butts surrounding him. He wondered about the fate of those who had waited before him, the only hint of their presence here the squashed remains of their smokes and the scent of their urine.

"I am going to South Carolina," Miguel continued. "Where are you heading, Héctor?"

Miguel was a small, lean man, maybe a head shorter than Héctor. His coal black hair was cropped close to his round, dark head, and his broad nose and wide forehead revealed his Indian heritage.

"I have not decided. I have no destination other than America," Héctor said. "I'll see where work takes me."

"A man needs a plan, Héctor. Come with me to South Carolina. My cousin has a house and a good job as a foreman on a tomato farm. He will find us work."

"Perhaps I shall join you, if work is available there. Where do you come from?" Héctor asked.

"My people are from the mountains, the *Tarahumara*."

Héctor had heard of the Tarahumara Indians, but had not known any in Puerto Isadore.

He wondered if they were all like Miguel, in manner and in looks.

Miguel continued when Héctor remained silent. "Most of my people remain in the Sierra Madres forever, preferring not to mix with others. I am an outcast, I suppose." He chuckled when he said this and sucked on his cigarette as if his survival depended on the smoke sinking deep into his lungs.

"I have never met one of your people," Héctor said. "But we are all Mexicans. Your people prefer to stay in the mountains. My people stay by the sea in Oaxaca State, in Puerto Isadore. People are comfortable with what they know, I think." Héctor had not realized how much he missed conversation.

"So, Héctor, you and I, we are not comfortable men then. We are leaving what we know," Miguel said.

Héctor nodded, running both hands through his hair, letting his cigarette dangle from his lips.

The sun descended outside the lone, small window on the western side of the shack, casting shadows across the wall and floor. The men ate nothing, for they had no food. They talked until Héctor could no longer see Miguel's face.

"My people are athletes. We are very strong runners for great distances. When my tribe plays *rarajipari,* I am the best in my community," Miguel said.

"I do not know of this *rarajipari,*" Héctor said.

"You are missing out, Héctor. I will tell you about it. I am not keeping you from something, am I, *amigo*?" Miguel said, and Héctor imagined Miguel's smile, though it was lost in the darkness.

"We have teams, you see, and we play this game in the mountains, running along the slopes, kicking a wooden ball for great distances. We wear *huaraches* on our feet and the matches last for days. My teammates called me a mountain goat. I could go all day."

Héctor said, "I am not much at running up mountains."

Miguel seemed to be turned away from Héctor now, his voice falling distant.

"These cigarettes. I am probably not good at running the slopes any more, either."

Héctor heard Miguel lie down, rustling in his corner, then grow silent, except for his breathing. Their conversation for this day was over. Héctor stretched out on the hard concrete, closed his eyes and thought of mountain goats running wild and free along green slopes. How pleasant to live as a goat with all the berries and vegetation his family could ever want to eat growing where they lived and played, with no worries about the future, with no thought of what may lie beyond their lush, green slope, and no concern with trying to cross difficult obstacles to keep the family fed.

When sleep came, Héctor dreamed not of contented goats, but of a withered corpse swinging in the hot wind.

ONCE EACH DAY the door opened and a coyote delivered sandwiches or fruit with drinking water. During the thirteenth night, Héctor awoke to someone kicking his boot.

"Get up. Get up! Let's move. Quickly now!" a man barked, his voice unfamiliar.

Then Héctor heard Miguel say, "I am awake, mister."

The stranger in the room held a flashlight, and in the shadows Héctor could see Miguel stumbling to his feet, as if he were not quite awake. The room, aside from the narrow shaft of light from the flashlight, remained dark, and Héctor felt certain the morning light was yet hours away. In seconds he and Miguel stood fully alert. He caught a glint of metal across the stranger's chest, no doubt a gun strapped there.

"Follow me. Do not speak, but move quickly," he said. "Piss before we leave."

How strange this all was. The faceless stranger commanded their complete obedience, yet they had no way of knowing who he was. Héctor felt like a schoolboy being told to piss, but both he and Miguel did as they were told. When they finished, they followed the stranger a few meters to a pickup truck. He motioned to the back, and the men climbed in. In seconds they were racing down the road. The wind chilled Héctor, and he pulled his knees to his chest.

Miguel spoke first, "I guess this is it, Héctor. This night we will cross into America." He paused, then added, "Or maybe we are about to be killed. Who can know these things until they happen, heh, *pollo*?" He laughed at his attempt at humor, but Héctor did not smile. He had been wondering if this man with the gun was part of the plan. Perhaps he was a lawman. Perhaps the coyote had been killed, and this man planned to take Héctor and Miguel into the desert and kill them. How could he know? He was a pollo, indeed, a scared shitless little chick, just as Miguel had said when they had met.

The truck slowed and turned into the parking lot of a large, nondescript building, perhaps a warehouse. The driver flashed his lights three times, and immediately the huge door to the building rose. The truck entered the building before the door fully opened, and in seconds it closed behind them.

Miguel prodded Héctor with the heel of his boot and whispered, "Knowing you has been a pleasure, Héctor."

Miguel's face wore no expression, no hint of seriousness or humor, excitement or fear. This Miguel fellow could joke his way through a firing squad to hide his emotions.

Inside the warehouse florescent lights glowed bright. Héctor eyed a large delivery truck and counted fifteen men. Most sat in a group on the floor along the left side of the large, open room. A few busied themselves around the delivery truck, and Héctor wondered if it would deliver him across the border. The building appeared to be a storage facility for toys. Crates and bins of dolls, puppets, toy drums, and other children's playthings overflowed onto shelves along the high walls. Héctor thought of little Alejandra. Perhaps he could keep a doll for her, present it to her when she and her mother arrived in America.

The stranger who had driven them here got out of the truck, and Héctor saw him for the first time in the light. A gun strapped across his broad chest, he looked like the professional wrestlers Héctor had seen in comic books and on posters along the streets in Mexico City. His upper arms were the size of Héctor's thighs, and Héctor thought this man had no need of a gun. He wore canvas pants, black boots, and a green shirt with snaps up the front. His straw cowboy hat, white and spotless, seemed oversized, as if his commanding figure called for a hat bigger than anyone else wore.

"Go over there with the others," he said, motioning to the group sitting along the wall.

Héctor and Miguel did as they were instructed. How strange to be in a room with so many men without speaking. The men who were not seated, the ones in charge, moved quickly and smoothly without any words. Each seemed to have a job to do, and each had done his job many times before. Héctor looked around at the men among whom he sat. He saw in them what Miguel had claimed to see in him just days before. They looked nervous mostly. To sit silently and do as other men commanded was an odd and humbling way for a man to behave. But each of them knew they had chosen to be here, and each would do as he was told in order to achieve his dreams. Héctor felt a strong connection to these strangers. He thought about their ride to America in the back of the delivery truck. Perhaps there they would talk of their loved ones, of what they were leaving behind and of the places they planned to go in El Norte. Perhaps some would become friends, and maybe even settle in the same town in Texas or South Carolina or Arizona. These thoughts calmed Héctor's nerves, and thrill replaced the dread he had felt over Miguel's talk of impending death.

In less than four minutes, the back of the truck had been completely loaded with crates of toys. One of the men slammed shut the back of the delivery truck, and with it Héctor's hopes of riding smoothly into America vanished. So, he and these pollos would not be riding in this truck after all. He felt his shoulders droop.

Then, "Okay, *pollos*. Here, now. Let's go," the man with the gun said.

The men rose to their feet, and shuffled over to the truck where the man stood.

One at a time a worker took a man underneath the truck and came out alone. Héctor could not understand what was happening. When his turn came, he crawled under the bed of the truck with the man. A small hole, no bigger than the lid of a barrel, opened above Héctor's head.

"Climb in, and lie flat. Your head goes that way, your feet at this end. Pack in tight. We have many of you. Now go," he said, guiding Héctor, helping him disappear into the dark underbelly of his deliverance.

2

THEY HAD NOT lain together in far too many nights. When anyone asked her about him, Lilia would say, no, no, I have not heard from him yet. *Yet*, as if a future with her husband were certain.

When the driver slowed to nearly a stop, Lilia slid from the back of the truck and began the short, hot walk home from the agave fields. She passed two pigs, the one with the crescent-shaped, black patch on its back and the other with the odd gait, as if one of its legs were shorter than the rest. She knew them well, and the silly hens, too, who pecked the dust beside her path. Passing the shack of the old widow who lived just down the lane, Lilia smelled the familiar scent of her fish stew on the warm Pacific breeze. Before Lilia reached the courtyard, she heard her grandmother Crucita singing an old tune she often sang when she cooked or worked her clay or swept the courtyard. The music sounded like home. How strange to feel both joy and sadness at once. She kissed the old woman on her brow. "You have been busy." Fresh baked bread cooled in the open window, a pot of soup simmered on the fire, six new pieces of pottery sat on the table, and in the cradle lay Alejandra, cooing as if all the sounds and smells pleased her.

"We have enjoyed our time together," Crucita said, clicking her tongue at the infant.

Lilia scooped up her child, smelling her sweet, black hair. Crucita sliced Lilia a piece of warm bread and poured her some goat's milk. "You had a good day?"

"I suppose," Lilia said.

"Alejandra is awake more often. She is good company for this old woman," Crucita said, sinking into a chair.

The bread was soft and delicious. "Won't you have some?" Lilia asked her grandmother.

"No, no. I have little appetite lately. Little Alejandra's companionship replaces my desire for food. I remember when I first met your grandfather; for weeks my happiness and desire for him replaced all hunger. My great-granddaughter does the same to me now, taking away all needs but my need for her."

Lilia shook her head. A day could not pass without Crucita mentioning her love for her long-dead husband whom Lilia had never known. "The *fiesta* begins tonight," she said.

"Of course," Crucita said. "I hope you will go."

Lilia wiggled Alejandra's toes. "I told Rosa and the girls today in the fields that I will join them."

Crucita said, "Go. Getting out will be good for you. A young girl's mind will grow unhealthy if she stays home with her old grandmother every night. I will keep Alejandra."

THE REASONS to thank Saint Isadore were many: for births, for marriages, for family, for health, for life. Even those who'd lost a loved one during the year could find reason to celebrate the dead's passage to the Spirit World. So Lilia washed the stickiness of the fields from her skin and combed her long hair, recalling how beautiful Héctor found her hair when she wore it down like this.

"Hello? Anyone here ready to have some fun?" Rosa shouted from the courtyard. She wore a bright, fluffy pink skirt and a frilly white blouse and carried a sack in her arms.

Lilia stepped to the doorway in time to see Rosa kiss Crucita's cheeks and withdraw a bottle of mezcal and three small cups from the sack.

"We will dance together in the streets," Rosa said, pouring three servings of the strong drink while her youngest two children giggled and played marbles beneath the shade tree. Lilia felt both ashamed and grateful when Rosa added, "We all have much to be thankful for, Lilia, even in difficult times." She clipped a pink rose into Lilia's hair. Rosa handed a cup each to Lilia and Crucita and said, "The fruits of our labors, friends." She put a cup to her lips, threw her head back, and swallowed the strong, honey-colored liquor.

Crucita and Lilia did the same, and Lilia felt the smoky mezcal heat her throat and gut. "Thank you, Rosa," Crucita said, rising. "You girls enjoy the festivities." She patted Rosa on the back and added, "We do have plenty to be proud of here; keep reminding Lilia of the beauty of her own country." Then the old woman made her way toward the house. Like the goats that pulled the trash carts through their village, she seemed used to laboring, accustomed to being tired.

"Of course," Rosa said.

"She finds Héctor hard-headed, ashamed of his heritage," Lilia said when Crucita was inside.

Rosa poured two more cups. "Is he not?"

"I adore Crucita, but perhaps she is a bit old-fashioned, set in her ways."

"I agree with her, Lilia."

Rosa and Lilia's mothers had been close, and too often Rosa treated Lilia as a child, as if she had an unending responsibility to look after her dead friend's daughter. In no mood for a disagreement but determined to defend her husband's choices, Lilia said, "We cannot be expected to earn a hundred *pesos* a day stringing beads or picking agave."

"Why not? It is honest work." She passed a cup to Lilia. "Another?" How difficult saying no to Rosa could be. But the first cup had warmed and relaxed her. Surely another would only make Lilia feel better and numb her worries about Héctor. Drinking was easier than arguing.

Soon the women walked down the lane, past the widow's marigold petals, strewn about in honor of the woman's deceased husband. Rosa seemed not to notice the widow's tribute, but the sight haunted Lilia, as if foreshadowing her own lonely future.

Music filled the air and excitement surged palpable to all in Puerto Isadore. How foolish Lilia felt participating in the celebration, wearing a rose above her ear. A goat bleated past them, part of a Mexican flag painted on its back, as two young boys chased it with paint, hoping to finish their job. They giggled and yelled to the women as they passed, "Hello, pretty ladies!"

Moments after leaving the lane, Lilia and Rosa became part of the colorful, swirling procession swelling in the streets, moving at a barely perceptible pace, as if all the energy were potential. Men, women, children laughed, danced, swayed, shrieked to music of their own making. Maracas and drums rattled, beat. Rosa's head, thrown back, revealed her every tooth, and a laugh erupted from deep in her belly. She shook all over, clapped her hands, lost in the atmosphere, the electricity of the day, the moment. The procession made its way down to the pier, where soon boats would pass, bright banners, balloons, flowers flying from bow to stern. Those on board delighted in the festivities and homemade decorations honoring their village's patron saint. When they reached the beach, Rosa gathered her children close to the water's edge to catch sight of their father and the red, white, and green streamers the children had fastened to his boat. Lilia bought a can of guava juice from a vender and held the cool metal to her brow a full minute before opening the drink. Standing in speckled shade beneath a tree, she sipped the sweet juice and looked to the sea where a flotilla of boats was forming.

"Is that the beautiful Lilia?"

She turned to see an old, familiar face. "Emanuel! My God, it has been ages. How are you?" The two hugged as old friends do after a long separation. "I am well," he said, smiling widely the way he always had, as if nothing could thrill him more than speaking to Lilia, as if the world were nothing but music and light, and burdens could be dissolved with a grin. "You look as lovely as always, Lilia." She did not turn away or blush as she might have when last they had spoken, years earlier.

"And your grandmother? You and she still live here?"

"Yes, and I have a daughter. Alejandra. I married Héctor two summers ago."

"I had heard about your marriage, but not the child. A daughter! Congratulations, Lilia."

"Thank you," she said, wishing she had Alejandra with her now so Emanuel could see her beautiful child.

"And Héctor? He is here today?"

She lowered her eyes. "No. He has gone to the border, to *El Norte*."

Emanuel frowned. "With a coyote?"

Lilia had only recently learned this term for a smuggler. "Yes. He will send for us when he is settled."

He nodded but said nothing, as if imagining a fate too harsh to acknowledge.

"Are you still living in Oaxaca City?" she said.

"Yes. I am in Puerto Isadore only a few days. I suppose I'll remain in the city, but I will forever be of this village, you know? This is home," he said.

"You look like a city boy," she said, glancing down at his fine shoes.

He grinned. "Perhaps, but I have many wonderful memories of this place. Plenty right here at this very pier." His eyes sparkled as they had in his youth, giving him a look of mischief.

Lilia thought of evenings so distant they seemed more like someone else's experiences than her own. Of twilights melting into evenings spent lying next to Emanuel in the sand, under the pier, looking for constellations, sharing dreams. She remembered the hopefulness, the optimism, the kisses that hinted at waning innocence. How long ago that seemed.

"Lilia," Rosa shouted, "Come on. We are going for a boat ride. Come with us."

"I'll be right there," Lilia said.

"A pleasure to see you, Lilia," Emanuel said. "I won't keep you from your friends."

Lilia did not want to leave her spot under the tree. Emanuel did not hold her there so much as the memories of a carefree life, of a long forgotten weightlessness and belief that all would always be right and under her control. When had she last felt this way? Somehow, Emanuel had reminded her. His presence alone had transported her, momentarily, to a time years since forgotten, a time of abundant possibilities. "Enjoy your visit," she said.

He smiled. "You will see me before I return to the city, Lilia," he said, then turned and walked away.

Lilia sipped her juice and watched Emanuel disappear into the crowd. A light breeze blew across the beach now as the setting sun dipped toward the Pacific. She made her way to the boat where Rosa's family waited.

"Was that Emanuel?' Rosa asked.

"Yes. I have not seen him in years."

"If I recall he was sweet on you, no?" Rosa said, as her husband, José shoved the boat through the white foam.

Lilia shrugged, trying not to grin. "That was years ago. He was too wild, always running with the bad boys, you know?"

Rosa smiled. "True, but he is all grown up now. People change." Lilia said nothing more but waved at the crowd on shore, a peacefulness settling over her. Rosa and her children shouted with merriment as they passed other boats, decorated and filled with families.

Lilia wondered if Héctor remembered this was the day the festival began. He would be happy if he were here. She hoped that wherever he was at this moment he was pleased with how his journey was progressing. But she also knew that if he were here today, he would be considering a way to get beyond this place and Mexico, and he would not completely lose himself in the celebration as others could. Héctor had always longed for more. He was a dreamer, wishing to make life better for Lilia and himself and their family.

The breeze blew in Lilia's face, and she waved at a passing boat. At that moment all seemed just right in Puerto Isadore, and Lilia could not imagine living elsewhere.

LILIA WALKED home alone by the light of the moon. Perhaps Héctor was awake, somewhere safe, pondering the moon, too. As she rounded a bend, she encountered an old man leading a burro so pale it glowed ghost-like in the moonlight. She nodded, and the man returned her greeting with a toothless grin. Neither he nor his feeble burro, a sack of cabbages on its back, made a sound as they traveled the dusty path. The man wore thin sandals, a dingy t-shirt, and baggy trousers. The donkey's eyes were closed, and Lilia wondered if he had eyes at all, and where the two could be heading at this hour. After they had passed, she turned to be sure she had seen them, that they were not spirits. The burro's wiry tail did not twitch, but lay against his white hind-quarters perfectly still, as if all the animal's energy were necessary for walking. Lilia watched them disappear around the curve in the road and wondered if burros experienced emotions. If so, she imagined he felt like a weak soul being led nowhere.

As Lilia neared the courtyard, the sound of Alejandra's crying startled her. Crucita never let the baby get so worked up, and the wailing disturbed Lilia. "Crucita?" Lilia called, scooping up the child from her basket beneath the tree in the courtyard and whispering, "There, there" and clicking her tongue in the way she did to soothe her.

Stew, bubbling unattended, boiled over and caked on the pot, and Lilia's foreboding turned to panic. Clutching Alejandra, she dashed to pull the pot from the coals, and in the midst of shouting her grandmother's name, tripped over a crumpled Crucita. Dizzy and horrified, Lilia nearly dropped Alejandra as she knelt by her grandmother.

"Crucita. Crucita. Crucita!" She was screaming it now, as if the old woman were asleep and deaf and only the loudest shouts would rouse her. Alejandra began to cry, but Lilia ignored her, placing the child on the floor beside her. Lilia took Crucita's face in her hands, gently at first then with more force, squeezing her cheeks. Her skin was cool and her apron and dress seemed too big, as if they were the oversized costume of a child pretending to be a grandmother. How thin Crucita looked. She did not move. Tears streaked Lilia's cheeks, blurring her sight so that all seemed distorted. She continued to caress Crucita's face, her brow, her arms, her hands, repeating her name countless times.

The awkward twist to her limbs, the angle at which her neck bent, all told Lilia her grandmother was in no pain. She knelt, stroking Crucita. She raised her into a sitting position, held Crucita close, rubbing her back gently as Crucita had done to Lilia since birth, to make things better.

The moon passed across the kitchen window, and, still, Lilia sat on the floor, the pot of burnt stew long cold. Crucita's head fell awkwardly onto Lilia's shoulder, not as Alejandra's often did, as if seeking solace, but like something spilled, wayward.

When had Crucita's weary head last sought a shoulder? With her fingers, Lilia combed her grandmother's disheveled hair, then slowly unraveled the familiar, gray braid, now loose and damp from Lilia's tears. She reworked the long strands like ribbons into a tight, beautiful braid, fingering the now-respectable plait until her thumb grew numb, and her tears ceased. Alejandra had long since fallen asleep, but when she began to stir, Lilia held her, too. Clutching her dead grandmother to her side and her infant daughter in her lap, Lilia felt a stranger to herself. She knew her life would forever more consist of three periods: time with Crucita, this day of Crucita's passing, and the future without her.

HÉCTOR TRIED to imagine the words he would use to describe this to Lilia. His chest could explode any moment from the hot air in the cramped compartment, the smell of other men's sweat, from both oppressive heat and palpable nervousness. When the last couple of men crawled in, Héctor's chest tightened with panic. The space simply could hold no more. The boots of the men on either side of him brushed against his ears. He tried to remain motionless out of courtesy, to avoid scraping the ears of the heads on either side of his feet. The already dark box in which they lay became seamless as the coyote closed the hole. The unmistakable sound of welding torch hissed beneath them, Héctor's fate now literally sealed.

At each stage of his journey, Héctor had felt more committed, like he could not turn back, but now, his emotions were different. He imagined screaming, pleading his change of mind. Likely his screams would be ignored if they were even heard at all. And what if, somehow, the coyote were to hear him and open the sealed underbelly, then what? He would undoubtedly take Héctor out back, shoot him, and dump him in the day's trash. Each man must surely have been thinking the situation through as Héctor did.

The roar deafened Héctor when the idling truck engine shifted into gear. The truck shook and rumbled and began moving, and Héctor was surprised that he could not tell, could not remember, if the front of the truck were to his right or to his left. He tried to breathe deeply, to slow his heartbeat, to relax. Mere centimeters separated the tip of his nose from the ceiling of this compartment, and he wondered what happened if a fat man were to seek a coyote. A fat man could never fit here, but a man of great girth would have no reason to leave Mexico. The poor, lean, hard-working men, however, had reason to head north. Héctor wondered, had he been fat, if the coyote would have accepted him.

Héctor had no way to mark the passing of time, no radio, no sights, nothing save the occasional turn left or right, deceleration or acceleration, the feel of a dirt road compared to pavement compared to gravel. These variations were the only changes in the infinitely black undercarriage of the truck.

No one spoke. Héctor had heard tales of men, wrongly presumed dead, buried alive. He understood how such a man felt. He could scratch at the floor or the ceiling until his nails were gone, his fingers bloody nubs, his voice hoarse, his throat raw, but nothing would help him. His situation would be unchanged from the effort. *But I have hope, I have hope,* he said over and over to himself. The words became his mantra, his silent lips forming the word *hope, hope, hope,* for what could have been hours, or minutes: all sense of place and time and reality had been sealed off with the final flames of the welding torch.

Héctor had no way of knowing whose head was just beyond the feet brushing his right ear, but after a while—he could not know how long —he discerned words rising above the rumbling of the truck, prayers uttered in the darkness. The anonymous voice floated soulful, desperate and crying. Soon others joined in until the incessant rumblings of the truck's engine mixed with the desperate prayers of ten strangers in unison. Men cried, but the rhythm was soothing, somehow, with the repetition of the Hail Marys along with the vibrations of the truck. Maybe the comfort sprung from the act of ten strangers reaching out to their god in the most sincere and desperate way.

Héctor felt trapped somewhere between life and death, suspended among the souls of others, suffering similar fates. *Ave Maria*. Hail Mary, full of grace, Hail Mary full of grace. Hail Mary full of grace.

Would they be here days or merely hours? Héctor's thoughts shifted between surreal images of purgatory and the very earthly thoughts of relieving himself. The acrid scent of urine permeated the musty air, mingled with sweat. The first of the men had pissed, maybe from fear. Héctor had heard of men doing so, or maybe he simply had to go and could wait no longer. Why wait? If he were going to be here for a day or more he'd have to go at some point. The smell of the men sickened him, their shared air hot, stagnant. Soon the odor changed to vomit, an unbearable stench, except what choice remained but to bear it? Go some place? Escape? Curse the men who pissed, who vomited? He breathed the smell of desperation. Héctor closed his eyes out of habit, to seal himself off from this place, these smells, the sounds, but doing so changed nothing. His dark surroundings remained the same whether his eyes were open or shut. He hoped he could go a long while before he wet himself. He wondered how long that would be, and he considered that this was a place where a man could die.

The truck slowed, then stopped, but this time was different. The engine cut, and the silence now frightened Héctor as much as had the deafening roar. Instinctively the men fell silent, their prayers ceased to be voiced though surely each prayed his hardest now, in silence. Muffled voices rose just beyond the compartment where they lay. Perhaps daylight shown now, though this was impossible to know. A knocking sound began at Héctor's head then moved to his feet then under him, and he wondered what could possibly be happening outside. Perhaps this ride was a trick, perhaps they were at the border at a checkpoint. What would that be like? The patrol must be checking this delivery truck. He heard the sound of the doors opening and muted noises as the men rummaged above. He dared not whisper, though he longed to ask his compadres what they thought was happening. He imagined border patrol checking the cargo, looking for drugs in the boxes of dolls and toy maracas.

When the truck's engine roared, the sound startled Héctor and emotions again welled in him. He knew not if he should be relieved. Had they passed an inspection? Were they now rolling onto American soil? Were the toys packed with cocaine? Was the truck being confiscated, impounded, sent to be demolished with Héctor and the men underneath never to be acknowledged again? Were the coyotes, right this moment, in the back of a police car, keeping silent about the men in the belly of their truck, in hopes of avoiding further punishment? The truck moved fast now, and Héctor knew they were on a highway. For the first time on the journey, someone spoke.

"I think we are across, men." The voice was faceless, nameless, but it recognized the bond among these strangers who had prayed together in the darkness.

The men, like Héctor, seemed eager to believe the words to be true. Another said, "Then soon we shall drink water, breath fresh air."

A third said, "Yes, you fellows stink," and Héctor recognized the voice as Miguel's.

The few who spoke now seemed optimistic, as if any moment the truck would stop and a coyote would pop open the hole in the bottom, help them out, and say, "Welcome to America." But that did not happen, and for hours more the truck rolled on. It stopped once again, but only briefly, and when the noise and motion resumed, someone said, "Maybe we had to fill up with fuel."

Another man vomited after a few hours and the stench permeated the small space, leading to further retching among the men. Héctor's clothes were soaked through with perspiration. The underside of the truck—the floor on which Héctor and the men lay—had reached an insufferable temperature, assuring Héctor the roads they traveled were hot, and the sun shone outside.

Then a man far away from Héctor, perhaps the first one to have crawled into the box, began ranting, speaking nonsense, begging to get out, banging his fists, his feet, his head on metal. This was the kind of behavior Héctor had feared, either from himself or from another, the behavior of a man seized by panic. The cramped space allowed no room for such movement and the effect was like a wave rolling across the men, each being shoved and forced to move when no place existed to go. The man got louder and the sounds of his own screams incited him into such a frenzy one of the others yelled, "Someone knock him out!"

Someone else shouted, "I cannot. I cannot get a fist to him."

Héctor knew then they would die. The man screamed for his mother and for a woman, Esperanza, and uttered gibberish Héctor could not understand. Héctor fought the natural reflex to clench his hands into fists, to tighten his body into a mode for fighting, for protection, because there would be no protecting himself in any way other than remaining prone and cramped. He could move nowhere. Finally the shouts stopped as if the man had exhausted himself. Had the coyotes heard the screams? He could not possibly know. So much was impossible to know and all a man could do was realize his fate was in the hands of God. That knowledge was only briefly comforting, because then Héctor would consider that it was not God driving this truck, but the coyote, and maybe God had turned his back on men such as these.

The truck slowed and pulled to a stop. The men collectively held their breaths, and Héctor felt sure their prayers were as his: that the panicked man would not resume his fit.

Someone dared to speak, barely a whisper. "We must remain silent, fellows. We have come far. Keep your faith."

Héctor recognized the voice as the one who'd recommended punching the ranting man earlier, and he considered this man to be their faceless leader.

There they waited, and waited, and waited. They remained longer here, still in silence, than they had spent riding. Again new doubts filled Héctor's heart. Had they been abandoned? Were they deep into America now, or had they gone the other direction? Maybe they were back in the warehouse; maybe something had gone terribly wrong. For hours the men lay in their sealed compartment. They could not guess if daylight or darkness were beyond the walls of their metal box. Someone began snoring softly, and Héctor thought *what a blessing sleep would be now*. Sleep was like sunshine and fresh air, something beautiful and unattainable.

4

THE COYOTES reopened the hole in the bottom of the truck. Not until Héctor took his first breath beyond the confines of the secret compartment did he realize just how thick, how putrid, the air inside had become. A new coyote hustled them from the truck, which was once again in a warehouse. This one was larger, a garage of some sort. Two dump trucks sat in the rear of the building and mechanic's tools filled the shelves and walls. Héctor saw generators, tires, and compressors. He wondered why this place would not be a toy warehouse, too. Where would the toys within the truck go? Not for the first time Héctor felt as a child: innocent and curious and uncertain. He inhaled deeply over and over again as he watched his fellow pollos climb out of the truck. He assumed this was American air he breathed, but he could not be certain. Nor could he be certain if he should feel immense relief, or the dread he'd become accustomed to.

As the last man disembarked, the new coyote turned to them and said, "*Bienvenidos a Estados Unidos de América.* Welcome to America."

Héctor smiled for the first time in memory. The other men smiled, too, though no one cheered, none of them spoke. They were indeed pollos, and Héctor wondered if this feeling would ever completely subside. His new position as an illegal American struck him, that from this moment forward his fate would be determined by this status he'd created for himself. He would always have that fear and knowledge that someone somewhere was more powerful than he: both coyotes threatening his family and norteamericanos bent on sending illegals back to Mexico. Perhaps a mixture of fear and joy would always dwell within him.

The coyote led the men into a small office within the warehouse, pointing out a water fountain and a restroom for their use. Héctor fell in line behind others waiting for a drink. Never had water tasted and felt so refreshing and necessary. Héctor believed he could stand before the fountain and exhaust its supply. He splashed it on his face and the back of his neck and drank another sip before relinquishing his spot and moving into the office where the others gathered.

When all the men were present within the office, another smuggler spoke to them. This one, young and hard-faced, held a file box. Héctor marveled at how efficient this system ran, how each coyote had a role and knew it well. The coyotes barely spoke to one another, as if they had done this procedure a thousand times. The vastness of their system impressed Héctor and he wondered if America held pockets of Mexicans living together, like little communities, little Mexican villages. Or did illegal immigrants keep their distance from one another, not wanting to gather, afraid to call attention to themselves? Did only the big American government discourage illegal immigrants, or did the gringos despise them, too?

The young coyote said, "Here I have identifications for you all. We will move fast. I will call out destinations, and you raise your hand when you hear yours. These identification cards are American driver's licenses, issued from various states. When I say the state you wish to go, you will move over here, and we will find you an identification card that most resembles you. You will then study it. Memorize it. Find a partner and test him on the facts. This will be your new identity, and if you slip up, even slightly, your asses will be back in Mexico. You will want to have something better made when you get where you are going."

He began calling states' names. Some sounded familiar to Héctor.

He glanced at Miguel and listened carefully for South Carolina. This is where we part, where our destinies diverge, he thought, looking about the room at the other illegal immigrants, and he wondered if he'd ever again see the men who chose identity cards for Arizona, Colorado, Florida. Where were all these places? Perhaps these men had family in these states, or perhaps they chose their destinations blindly, at random, with no more to guide their choices than a pleasant sounding name.

"Alabama," the coyote called out.

No one raised a hand for Alabama. Alabama sounded pretty. Héctor mouthed the word: Al-a-bam-a. Maybe one day he and Lilia and Alejandra would visit Alabama.

"South Carolina," the coyote called.

Héctor and Miguel stepped forward, raising their hands. A third pollo joined them, and they followed the man with the file box to a corner.

The coyote studied Héctor's face a few seconds then flipped through a file marked "SC." He pulled out a card, held it up to Héctor's face to compare their images, then dropped it back into the box and searched for another. Héctor worried that the box contained no cards with his likeness. Then what? And where did these cards come from? Had they been stolen from the persons whose faces adorned the cards? Were the people pictured on the cards dead?

The coyote was holding a third card now beside Héctor's face. He nodded, said, "This will work, no?" and handed the South Carolina license to Héctor for his approval.

Héctor studied the face on the card. The man in the photo had much longer hair than Héctor's. Isadore Ramírez, 2400 Palmetto Blvd., Apt. 12, Columbia, South Carolina.

How could Héctor memorize the card when he couldn't understand the words' meanings?

Before he could ask, the coyote handed the other pollo his South Carolina card and said, "Pay attention. I will explain this to you."

"Here," he said, pointing with a long, stained nail, "Is your name. Here, your street, here your town, and this is your state." He studied them a moment, to be sure they understood, before he continued.

"You are Isadore Ramírez. Whatever name you have always answered to . . . that man is dead. You have never heard of that man before. If you are to be an American, you are to be Ramírez. When you get on a bus, Immigration will likely board, and they will approach passengers at random. Such is what they do. Their actions mean nothing but that they want to intimidate. A guilty man is easily identified when he will not look at the officers, when he cowers and stares at his shoes. You will not do that. When the officer boards the bus, you look at him in his eyes. You have nothing to hide, and you want him to understand that. Likely he will pass you by, but if he does approach you, you will show him your card, and you will answer his questions with confidence."

Héctor looked into the eyes of Isadore Ramírez and considered the soul behind the face on the card. Héctor imagined slipping into Isadore Ramírez's ghost and making the spirit behind the photograph whole again, into man. I am Isadore Ramírez now, he thought, and he envisioned his own soul fading, merging with one he would never know. He considered his new name a good sign, as Isadore was the name of his village and its patron saint.

A pay phone stood outside the warehouse, and one by one the men stepped outside to make calls. The day burned hot, dry, and nothing of importance surrounded this place. Tall, half-dead weeds grew beside the metal building, and Héctor hoped prettier places existed in this country. Somewhere nearby, traffic rumbled along a highway.

When his time came, he fished a calling card from his wallet and pushed each number on the phone with great concentration. After fifteen rings he hung up. The others had to make their calls. Héctor shoved his hands into his pockets and returned inside. When they had all finished, Héctor tried once more. After five rings a man answered, and Héctor recognized the voice as the shopkeeper Armando. How near he sounded.

Héctor knew he must speak quickly; the coyote instructed the men to keep their calls brief. "Armando. Could you send a boy up the lane to my Lilia at Crucita's house? This is Héctor. I must speak with her."

Armando said, "I cannot leave my shop now, Héctor. No one is here but me this morning, and I see no one nearby to fetch Lilia for you. Where are you? I heard you left Puerto Isadore."

"Can you get this message to Lilia? Tell her I have crossed into *Estados Unidos de América*, and I will call again when I am able. Tell her this, Armando. Tell her I am safe. Tell her I made it, and I will call again soon."

"Sure, sure. I will do this. I must go. I have customers here. Take care, Héctor."

Héctor replaced the receiver and went inside to find Miguel, to learn how they would get to this tomato farm in South Carolina.

5

CRUCITA'S CHEEKS looked waxen. Was this the natural look of death, or had the women who'd prepared her body applied something to the skin? She lay in a simple casket inside the house, and Lilia sat in a wooden chair beside her.

The old widow from down the lane arrived with a small boy. Lilia recognized him as one of the children she'd often seen chasing mongrels and chickens around the village. The woman tottered with a cane, and her right cheek sagged severely from an unnamed ailment. Her eye was like a dying fish's eye, bulging a milky blue. Lilia thanked God Crucita had died with her grace and beauty intact until the end.

The old woman pulled from her dress a pocketful of dainty, white lilies with stems too short for a vase. She did not speak but nodded to Lilia as she offered her the flowers with a shaking grip. With one hand on the boy's shoulder, she leaned over Crucita, studying her face for several moments. The old woman ran a finger along Crucita's stiff knuckles, then turned, nodded to Lilia, and with the boy beside her, hobbled from the house.

Lilia smelled the pale, waxy flowers from where they lay in her lap, a strong scent from such tiny blossoms. She placed them on Crucita's breast, so she could enjoy them on her journey to the afterlife.

Rosa handed Lilia a small cup of mezcal and a dish of cake and said, "Eat and drink, Lilia."

The girls who sold fruit and juice beside the pier entered the house and spoke to Rosa's husband in the kitchen. Glasses and dishes clinked and music played from a cassette player in the courtyard. Maybe the music had played all afternoon; Lilia could not be certain. She tasted a small bit of cake, sweet and so delicate it dissolved in her mouth before she chewed.

"Crucita would like this," Lilia said.

Rosa smiled and stepped to the kitchen to refill her cup and to greet the orange seller and his wife who had just arrived. They handed Rosa a basket filled with limes and three small green melons. The orange seller remained in the kitchen, but his wife came to Lilia.

"May I?" she asked Lilia, opening her leathery hand to reveal a shiny, green lime.

"Of course," Lilia said.

The orange seller's wife placed the lime beside Crucita. "Your grandmother always liked our fruit. She used to say our limes were her favorite."

Lilia smiled and nodded in agreement about the quality of the limes.

The orange seller's wife stood squat and round with oily cheeks and a mouth that always smiled. Lilia wondered if the deep creases beside the woman's eyes were from her constant grinning or from many years of tending fruit in the severe sunshine.

"Your grandmother looks at peace," she said, as her husband called to her from the kitchen. She patted Lilia's shoulder then went to her husband.

The shy girl from the fields—was her name Veronica?—stood in the doorway, a paper sack in her arms. The girl wore a thin brown dress, and sunlight shone through the gauzy fabric, revealing her slender legs. When she approached Lilia, she said, "I have brought you a fish." Her golden eyes had flecks of dark in their irises; they were pretty eyes, but they were sorrowful as well. The girl paused only a moment, when Lilia thanked her, then turned away. Lilia wondered if the girl considered another's passing, perhaps her own mother or a sibling.

Lilia watched Veronica leave, grateful for the many who had come today to mourn Crucita's passing. Rosa's daughter Rosita appeared from the bedroom, carrying Alejandra. Rosita placed her hand on Lilia's shoulder. "I think she is hungry, *señora*."

Lilia stood to take the infant from the girl. Alejandra sniffled, red-faced and agitated in Rosita's arms. Lilia's nipples prickled at the sight of her hungry baby, and she felt her milk letting down. "Thank you, Rosita."

The girl nodded. "Can I do anything for you?" she said.

"No, no, please. Go eat. You are very good with Alejandra, Rosita. Thank you for helping me today."

"Of course," Rosita said. "I'll join Mama in the kitchen, but fetch me after you have nursed."

Lilia took the baby into the bedroom and changed her quickly. By the time she'd secured a fresh diaper on Alejandra, the child's whimpers had turned to wails, her face as wrinkled as a newborn's in her frustration, though she was nearly six months old.

Lilia unbuttoned her dress, milk already streaming from her breasts, and pushed her left nipple into Alejandra's mouth. The baby hungrily sucked, barely able to keep up her gulping with the flow of Lilia's milk.

Lilia's shoulders relaxed. She closed her eyes and wondered which of them comforted the other more: she or Alejandra. Never had Lilia felt as fulfilled or as needed as when she nursed her child. Never had she experienced such a connection to anyone. She considered her own mother and how Crucita had once been a smooth-skinned new mother, too. Lilia imagined a young Crucita, her breasts full and rounded with milk, cradling Lilia's mother in her arms, nursing her as Lilia now nursed Crucita's great-grandchild. The circle of life and the passions it aroused bewildered Lilia. How odd the swings of human emotion could be: only moments ago Lilia had grieved with plentiful tears beside her grandmother's corpse. Now she wept tears of joy at providing sustenance for her infant.

When Alejandra had emptied Lilia's breast, Lilia burped her and put the infant to her right breast. The child soon lost interest, her hunger satiated. Not wanting to change clothes, Lilia pulled a butter-yellow shawl from her dresser to cover the small wet circles of milk on her dress. She kissed Alejandra's brow, then carried the child into the front room where Crucita's casket sat.

Lilia saw through the kitchen window the village priest in the courtyard, speaking with some men who played cards beneath the shade tree.

Rosita came to Lilia to take Alejandra from her. "You have more visitors," she said, reaching for the child.

Rosa had followed Rosita over to Lilia and placed another chair beside Crucita's casket. "The priest has arrived and no doubt he will want to visit with you. Are you going to eat your cake?" she said, motioning toward the small, square table where Lilia had placed the dish and her cup.

Lilia shook her head and handed the plate to Rosa.

"Keep that cup and sip from it, girl. This is a celebration of your Crucita's life," Rosa said.

"A festive occasion, a time of celebration of a full earthly life," the priest said as he approached Lilia. When she stood to greet him, he motioned for her to sit.

"Our Crucita now dances in heaven," he said, placing a candle beside the casket and lighting the wick with a match. He was an old man and had been the village priest Lilia's entire life. Lilia had not often attended services, but the father had baptized her, presided over her quinceañera Mass, her marriage to Héctor, and Alejandra's baptism.

The music in the courtyard grew louder, and Lilia heard Rosa tell someone to find some dominoes.

"Thank you for coming, Father," Lilia said, her voice a whisper, though she'd not intended it to be so. As the priest took a seat beside Lilia, she imagined the hem of Crucita's dress swinging as she danced with her long-dead husband, white lilies tucked behind both ears.

"Tell me, child, what is your fondest memory of your grandmother?"

He leaned back in his chair, crossing his arms and legs as if preparing to listen for a while. Lilia had not spoken more than a few words all afternoon, and the question unsettled her.

She hesitated. "Crucita raised me. She became my mother the instant her daughter, my mother, died bearing me. I have many happy times to recall."

The priest smiled. "Yes?" he said, raising his bushy eyebrows over eyes like golden marbles.

Rosa approached them in silence, eager to fulfill her duties as hostess. She handed the priest a cup of mezcal and tipped the bottle over Lilia's cup, replenishing the half she'd drunk.

"My grandmother spoke her mind. That is not a specific memory but an openness I admired in her." Lilia took a long sip so that she could stop speaking.

The priest did likewise and said, "Can you recall a time you particularly admired her straightforwardness?"

Lilia took another sip, hoping the mezcal would make this easier.

"My grandmother took great pride in her heritage. She made beautiful pottery. She put care into all she did, and she had little regard for those of a different mindset."

The priest nodded, shifted himself in his chair. The tilt of his graying head and the slow way he blinked his amber eyes like an ancient tortoise comforted Lilia.

"My husband has gone to *Estados Unidos de América*, and Crucita could not understand that." Lilia drained her cup and sucked in a deep breath.

"I see. Do you understand why?"

Lilia exhaled and ran her fingers behind her ears as if tucking away loose strands of hair.

"I love and respect my husband and understand his purpose, but I value Crucita's experience, her wisdom. I admire her fierce pride. I cannot easily reject my past because my Crucita has instilled her values in me."

"Go on," he said when she paused and picked at a callus on her thumb.

"I suppose my favorite memories are more like images. I have a picture in my mind of Crucita making pottery, a look of contentment brightens her eyes and colors her cheeks. When I think of my Crucita, this is what I see. Her beautiful pottery."

He nodded, examining the bottom of his empty cup. Turning to Crucita, he smiled.

"You have lived well, Crucita. Your child here is a vessel for your worldly experiences, your tribulations, your labor. She accepts all you have given her. You may rest in God's house and rejoice in the peace you will find there." He brought his fist to his lips to stifle a belch.

"Father," Lilia said. "Do you think I will disrespect my grandmother by going to my husband, by leaving the place of my ancestors? "

He took Lilia's hand in his thick, warm palm. "Let us pray a *novena* of mourning, child."

Lilia found more comfort in his touch than she'd anticipated, and she held tight, concentrating on the words flowing fast and soft from the priest's mouth.

"Heavenly Father, be with your servant Crucita on her journey. Keep her close to you so that she may be a source of guidance and strength to those she has left behind. Help her granddaughter Lilia to feel Crucita's spirit guiding her choices, giving her self-reliance. Strengthen Lilia's faith in herself and in this world and the afterworld, and fill Lilia with peacefulness and renewed strength."

"Amen," Lilia whispered.

The priest stood and pulled from his pocket rosary beads. He placed them in Lilia's hand and said, "Say your *rosario* for nine days and always on the anniversary of Crucita's death." He squeezed Lilia's fist in his and, blinking his eyes slowly, added, "You will be all right, child."

She looked into his confident, yellow eyes, and said, "Maybe," and the tears she thought she'd cried dry choked her again.

The priest lifted Lilia by her elbow so that she stood facing him. "Death will not weaken the bonds between you two."

Lilia nodded.

"Family is eternal. Bones crumble to dust, but love overcomes the decay, child."

Lilia smiled through her tears and welcomed his gentle embrace as he bid her farewell. She walked with him to the door where deep shadows in the courtyard announced the end of this day. How often she'd stood in this doorway as a child, waiting for Crucita to return from the market after a day of selling her pottery. Rosa hummed in the kitchen, washing a dish. Music and laughter filtered into the house from outside, somehow more ghostlike than silence.

"I am sorry Emanuel was not here." Rosa said, drying her thick hands on a kitchen rag.

"Nonsense. He has no business coming to mourn Crucita," Lilia said.

Rosa filled her cup and one for Lilia, sloshing mezcal in the sink as she did so. "Not to mourn Crucita, silly girl. But to comfort you."

"You have comforted me. My friends have been here all day. I do not know Emanuel anymore. He is like a dream to me now, so distant is my friendship with him."

Rosita entered the kitchen. "The baby is asleep now," she said.

"You have been good help to me today, Rosita. Please go on home now and rest," Lilia said, squeezing the girl's hand.

"Yes," Rosa said. "Run along home. I'll be there in a while."

The girl nodded to her mother and left, saying nothing more.

Rosa swallowed a gulp from her cup, shaking her head. "You need a man to comfort you, a reliable man. You do not have that. You have me, José, and our children. We are like your family, but we cannot be for you what Emanuel could be. What your Alejandra needs. José says Emanuel asked him about you. That boy has always had a fondness for you, Lilia. I know this talk bothers you, girl, but with Crucita's passing you must consider your options. You should believe that Héctor is gone."

José entered the kitchen from the courtyard, his face flush from drink.

"Oh, poor Lilia. Come join us. Listen to music and play cards with us. Oh, and here for you is a note from the shopkeeper Armando. He stopped by but could not stay. He asked I give you his condolences." José pulled from his pocket a small scrap of paper, folded in half. He handed the message to Lilia.

"Thoughtful of him to stop by," Lilia said, fingering the folded paper.

"Come play cards, Lilia," José said.

"This day has been long. Perhaps I will watch you play," Lilia said.

"My God," Rosa said, flailing her hands in the air. "Crucita is with God now. She has no pain. And you mope so for Héctor. Be strong, girl. Lift yourself up, Lilia."

Someone in the courtyard called for José. "Come out, Lilia," he said.

"She'll be along in a moment. I need to finish speaking with her the way her own mother would have spoken to her," Rosa said, motioning her husband out the door.

"That old woman lived a long and rich life," Rosa continued, jerking her head toward Crucita's corpse. "She died happy, cooking. Your own mama died giving you life, a life she anticipated with great joy. But you . . . I suspect your constant sorrow is as much about Héctor's leaving as Crucita's passing. Crucita and Héctor are gone. Drink something. Laugh a little. Dance. I guarantee you that is what Crucita is doing in heaven now with your own mama, perhaps with Héctor, too."

"No, Rosa," Lilia said. "Not Héctor."

Rosa spun on her heel splashing golden liquor from her cup onto the floor and Lilia's sandals as she marched to Crucita's casket.

"Crucita," Rosa shouted at the dead woman's face. "I cannot get through to Lilia. She cannot even celebrate your life without depressing me. Give this child a sign that Héctor is there with you, if he is not in hell for abandoning his family." Rosa took the cup of mezcal and poured it into Crucita's casket. She then tossed the cup in at the old woman's feet.

"Enjoy yourself, Crucita. Someone in your family should." Rosa turned and glared at Lilia.

A rage exploded inside Lilia. "Never speak Héctor's name again! You are crazy."

Rosa shook her head. "And you are a fool," she said, brushing past Lilia.

Lilia grabbed a kitchen rag and went to Crucita, dabbing at her grandmother's burial garments. The music outside stopped as Rosa barked at the card players in the courtyard. The white lilies had fallen from Crucita's dress into the casket, and Lilia returned them to her grandmother's breast, their perfume lingering, despite the mezcal's strong odor. The drunken voices in the courtyard faded as the card players' party moved elsewhere.

Lilia fingered the cream-colored lace on her grandmother's pale blue dress until long shadows overtook the room. When finally she stood, her shoulders relaxed for the first time in hours.

She walked to the courtyard and sank to the ground beneath the tree, fishing in her pocket for a handkerchief to blow her nose. She felt a scrap of paper. What was that? Oh, yes, the shopkeeper's note of condolence. She would read it tomorrow.

She clutched her knees to her breasts and listened to faint laughter somewhere down the lane. She ached, tired from mourning, from visitors, and she welcomed the courtyard's familiar solitude this evening. No hint of stew drifted on the thick air, no scent of Crucita's incense permeated this place. And how could that be? Who, but God, knew if Héctor were dead, too? And maybe even God didn't know some things. Some mysteries remained unsolved, complicated, and senseless.

Slats of moonlight fell into the courtyard through the shade tree, shaping silhouettes of leaf and limb, light and dark, illuminating a small white crescent, perhaps a child's sock or a crumpled bit of paper. The slight object glowed in the moonlight near the center of the courtyard. Lilia rose to fetch it. She bent, caressing the leathery strip between her fingers, uncertain of what it could be. She lifted the thing to her face, examining it in the soft moonlight. Then she recognized the shell of an iguana's egg, curled and dried, and she wondered what had become of its insides. How often she had seen the iguana sunning on a low limb, constant company for her and Crucita in their courtyard.

She considered the egg's innards, long gone, once swelling from liquid into a living creature inside the opaque shell, life coming from life, something substantial from something less. Perhaps one of the yellow-headed blackbirds that often scattered leaves and droppings and petals

from the limbs above had pecked this egg, had drunk the slick ins.
If so, the egg would never become an iguana, would never become whaι
the mother iguana set out for it to be. The egg had served, perhaps, as
sustenance to a bird. The bird—careless, distracted, and indifferent—
soon flying off to other trees, other courtyards.

Lilia stretched her arms, leaning against the wall of the courtyard,
the remnant of eggshell in her fingers. She thought of Héctor's dreams,
of the mother iguana's dreams, the yellow-headed blackbird's dreams.

And Héctor, she considered, like the life-giving substance within the
eggshell, existed to provide for his family, to nurture his and Lilia's future
children and Alejandra's future children, but perhaps he, too, carried a
fate like the unformed iguana, a slippery yolk destined to be destroyed
for the sake of others. Perhaps Rosa had spoken truthfully.

The thoughts unsettled her, and she held the shell up before her eyes,
turning it in the moonlight.

She whispered, "Is this my Héctor? Is he dead?" Lilia pictured Héctor's
white bones unmistakable and jutting from his corpse, a vulture pecking
his flesh in the hot desert until the winds came and blew sand over what
was once her Héctor, covering him, dissolving him into the earth like
a raindrop, and he would be gone, save for the memories of those who
knew him. "Can this be Héctor, Iguana?" She shouted the words at the
limbs above, "Tell me, Iguana! I must know."

The iguana's response came as words spoken by the breeze rustling
the leaves above, and the words of the breeze blew foreign and indecipherable, and Lilia understood the iguana would offer no answer this
night. She closed her eyes, her head against the courtyard wall, and
hoped sleep would come soon.

"Lilia?"

She heard her name as in a dream.

"Lilia."

Someone stroked her hair. Lilia opened her eyes. A red shirt.
Emanuel. Crouching beside her. He smelled of soap. A trace of sotol on
his breath, but his eyes were clear, gentle.

"Girl. Sweet Lilia. What a day you have had. Let me help you inside."

and Lilia felt his hand gently lifting beneath her elbow. he said, and let him help her to her feet.

ght of you. Worried about you," he said, as they entered

n a lamp.

"Do you need anything? Have you eaten?" He helped her to a chair.

Lilia waved his questions away, yawning. "So much food, Emanuel. Rosa acts as if I am dying of hunger, always pushing food at me." She motioned to the table, piled with tins of sweets, and she smiled as she spoke, despite her tiredness.

"I am sorry I am so late. I see the wake celebration has ended." He sat on the floor beside her chair. How young he looked, how much like the boy Lilia had known in school. When he reached for her forearm, his warm fingers gliding to her hand, she did not pull away.

"You did not need to come, Emanuel."

He smiled. "You have been my friend for years."

She tightened her hand around his and whispered, "Thank you, Emanuel. You are thoughtful." She wanted to say more. To tell him not to leave her. To ask him to sit beside her and keep her company. She wished to say that she felt Crucita's presence so heavily within these walls that at times she became frightened, and that Héctor's absence left a void within her that she could never explain. She wanted Emanuel to know that Alejandra, who slept soundly in her cradle, might be all Lilia had left, and that her allegiance to the child burned within her breast, the incredible responsibility, the immeasurable love filling her in a way that nothing else seemed worthy of her emotion.

He squeezed her fingers, then cradled her hand between both of his. He lifted her fingers to his face, to his cheek, then pressed them to his warm skin.

She wanted to tell him of Rosa's drunken harshness, of her cruel words, of the drink now soiling Crucita's burial dress. Perhaps Emanuel would agree with Lilia that Rosa was crazy.

Lilia felt herself falling, letting go in a way she had not been able to do. Her fingers skimmed Emanuel's cheeks and lips, and he kissed her fingertips.

So many emotions rose within her, but mostly a need for Emanuel to be right here for her now, for someone who knew her, really knew her, to hold her, to love her, to tell her all would be fine again. Rosa did not understand; Crucita was gone and had never understood fully.

She placed her hands on either side of Emanuel's face, pulling him toward her lap. Lilia caressed his hair with her fingers as if he were a child in need of comfort and she his mother. He rested his cheek on her thigh.

Emanuel slid his hands beneath the hem of her skirt, grabbing her ankles tight and lifting his head from her lap, looking into Lilia's face. His eyes burned bright, and he looked more alive than anyone Lilia could recall.

"I could take care of you," he whispered, his breath hot.

She said nothing, unsure of anything. His left hand slipped up her leg to her knee, and with his right hand he pulled her chin to his. He kissed her gently on the lips and Lilia did not pull back, longing to be held, to be loved.

Emanuel raised himself to his knees, lifting the hem of Lilia's skirt. He bent to her, kissing her ankles slowly, then moved to her calves, kissing one, stroking the other. His touch was more than she could bear and she leaned to him, pulling his face to hers. Her mind tumbled, blurring right and wrong. She pressed her lips to his.

The world twirled slowly, gentle and good for the first time in too long. Emanuel parted his lips, his hard, probing tongue pushing into Lilia's mouth, his hands too tight on her forearms, pushing down on her, confining, trapping, and the world sped up, spinning uncontrolled and wild and wrong, and Lilia sat upright, pushing him away, her hands firm against his shoulders.

"No. I cannot do this," she said.

He stared at her.

"Oh, God. I don't want to do this, Emanuel." She leapt to her feet, her hands at her temples.

He sat before her on his haunches like a dog caught stealing a chicken bone from the kitchen. "Lilia," he said, half asking, half commanding.

"No," she said.

He shook his head, wearing the unmistakable expression of disgust, of disappointment.

"Foolish Lilia. You make life difficult. Things could be simple for you and your child, you know. Almost easy."

"You should go, Emanuel," she said.

He stood, staring hard at her face as if he could will a change of mind.

"Please, go," she said.

The waning hope in his eyes flashed to anger, and he shook his head in utter disbelief, as if discovering something unexpected and repulsive in Lilia.

"Now," she said when he made no movement to leave.

"You will regret this, Lilia," he said.

She said nothing but followed him to the door, and then watched him walk into the night. Heat lightning illuminated the far sky, and Lilia wondered what caused the flash. She'd learned in school about storms and electricity, but science could not fully explain such momentary brilliance in the black heavens. She imagined her soul as a dark mysterious place, and longed for a flash of light there, just a quick moment of lightness and clarity, of relief. She watched the skies a few moments longer, but no mysteries revealed themselves in that black expanse, and so she slipped inside, hoping sleep and dreams of distant places might help her restlessness.

Lilia unbuttoned her dress, and as was her habit checked her pockets before tossing the garment across the back of the lone chair in her bedroom. Lying across her bed in her underwear, Lilia opened the dirty scrap of paper. Scrawled in pencil were the words, *Héctor called. He is across the border and good. He will call you later.* Then in black ink across the bottom the words, *Sorry about Crucita. But she is with God now, so that is good. Armando.*

Lilia clenched the paper in her fist, laughing and crying. "Here is your sign, Rosa," she shouted, waking Alejandra. Lilia laughed louder, scooping the infant into her arms, pulling her close. An old t-shirt of

Héctor's remained in Alejandra's cradle where Lilia had placed it that morning. Lilia grabbed it, clutching the fabric to them both.

"Do you smell that shirt, Alejandra? That is Papa's scent, and he is safe, my baby. You will know your beautiful, brave papa."

HÉCTOR AND MIGUEL shared a hard bench beside a soda machine and waited for Miguel's cousin to arrive. Outside, the air had smelled of diesel and exhaust fumes from the buses, but here, inside the terminal, Héctor breathed the sterile scent of cleaning fluids and air conditioning, institutional odors he hardly knew.

Miguel picked up a newspaper from the floor beside a trash bin at the end of the bench.

"Can you read any of that?" Héctor asked.

"Not too much, no, but I can look at the photos."

Héctor waved him off. "You cannot learn news from photos."

"I see they are playing baseball here," Miguel said, flicking a picture of an angry first baseman and an umpire, nose to nose. The player pointed at the base while the umpire pointed at a player from the opposing team, a cloud of dust at their feet.

Héctor laughed. "They get just as pissed about bad calls as we do."

Miguel nodded, flipping pages. "Looks like they had a big storm somewhere beside an ocean."

Several pictures of a nasty squall filled the page Miguel held: waves crashing under houses along the shore, boarded windows, a sailboat toppled like a toy.

"That doesn't look like this place," Héctor said.

"Let's see," Miguel said, running a finger along the foreign newsprint a moment before, "Ha! Our new home. This says South Carolina and North Carolina here."

Héctor stared at Miguel. "And that is where we are heading? That is not so good."

Miguel laughed, tossing the paper back to the floor at the base of the trashcan. "My cousin Pablo has said nothing about this storm. You know how newspapers do; they make shit up."

"No, they don't," Héctor said, studying Miguel's face.

Slight lines ran from the corners of Miguel's eyes to his temples always, giving him a fixed look of mischief, like the faces of wayward boys in church when the priest looked away.

Miguel shrugged and glanced at the clock on the distant wall.

"Your cousin must be a good man to drive this far for us," Héctor said, following Miguel's gaze and wondering how much longer they must wait for Pablo to arrive here for them.

"Sure, he is my blood, isn't he? But I have not seen him in years. He went to America when I was a boy. We have spoken, of course, but he has never returned to Mexico."

"And his wife?" Héctor asked.

"I know nothing of her except he met her here, and she, too, is from our country."

He pulled his shirt tight across his chest. "This manufactured air chills me. I am not used to it."

The coyote had brought them to the bus station hours earlier. The idea appealed to Héctor because so many people milled around this place, coming and going. The station seemed a safe spot to wait for Pablo. The two had spent the day eating crackers from the vending machine, reading the arrivals and departures board, and napping on benches.

"I don't much like the cold in here either," Héctor said, standing.

"I need to move my legs. Too much stillness the past few days, you know?"

Miguel stretched out on the bench. "Lying down feels good, too," he said, closing his eyes.

Héctor stepped to the water fountain and then made his way around a corner to the men's room, nodding a greeting to a withered old man slowly sweeping the floor there. Moments later as Héctor rounded the soda machine, he stopped, unsure whether to proceed or to run. An official wearing a uniform and a gun strapped to his hip, stood over Miguel. The officer reached down, tapped Miguel on the knee.

This was the end; they would be back in Mexico in an instant. Miguel sat up so slowly, too slowly, and Héctor cringed at his friend's ignorance. Did he not understand the stranger was a lawman? With a weapon? At once Héctor realized his own foolishness, standing motionless like a dead tree in the middle of this place, staring at Miguel and the official. He turned with a cough and revisited the water fountain, pretending to drink as the water splashed off his lips into the bowl. When he had bent over the fountain as long as he could bear the wait, he glanced toward Miguel's bench. The official had joined Miguel on the bench. Héctor retreated to the men's room where the withered janitor remained, now bagging trash and humming.

Héctor felt foolish returning so soon to the toilet, but the man nodded at Héctor as if he'd not seen him there only minutes earlier. Héctor went into a stall, locking the door behind him. He would count. When he reached one hundred— no, two hundred— he would emerge and check on Miguel. But what if Miguel needed him now? How could Héctor possibly help Miguel? Héctor must count, wait.

When he reached two hundred, the bathroom was silent, and he knew the old janitor had left. Héctor counted again, this time to fifty, indecisive and desperate for more time, believing the officer surely remained with Miguel.

But a new panic set in. What if the officer had hauled Miguel someplace? Héctor would not be able to find him. And what would he do if he could find Miguel? No, if Miguel were gone, Héctor would have to proceed to South Carolina without him. But Héctor did not know Pablo. How could they identify one another when Pablo arrived? Would he agree to take Héctor after Héctor had let Miguel get caught? But Miguel's capture was not Héctor's fault. Sweat rolled down Héctor's chest despite the cold air; he had to emerge from this stall, go to Miguel.

He stopped at the water fountain again and took a slight sip before turning toward the bench.

To his surprise, Miguel remained, and the officer had vanished. Now Miguel stood laughing and chatting with another man. Héctor stopped and watched as the two nodded, smiling, patting one another on the back.

"Isadore," Miguel shouted, waving Héctor to them. "Pablo," he said to the man, "This is the fellow I told you about. Isadore. Isadore, my cousin, Pablo."

Confused and weak in the belly, Héctor shook Pablo's hand.

"You men ready to roll?" Pablo said, pumping Héctor's hand, beaming a wide grin.

He resembled Miguel in features, but his belly was rounder, softer, and Héctor imagined Pablo's having a wife made the difference there.

"Let's get the hell out of here," Miguel said, a hint of urgency in his voice.

When they were safely in the car, Miguel's smile faded and he closed his eyes. "Shit, Héctor. You will not believe what happened to me when you went for your little walk. Jesus," he said, shaking his head.

"Who was that man? A lawman?" Héctor said, leaning toward the front seat from the back where he sat, his belly settling now as the distance between themselves and the bus station grew.

Pablo stared at the road but said, "You boys have got to be careful. Especially in Texas, man. Doubly so near the border. This place is crawling with folks like you: people here without the proper papers. Don't let your guard down." Then he began to laugh, a family trait perhaps, laughing when no one else knew the joke.

Miguel began to laugh, too.

"What?" Héctor said.

Miguel turned to face Héctor. "We got lucky when that officer approached the bench where I sat, I smiled at him and motioned for him to sit if he'd like," Miguel said.

"You are crazy. I have suspected this all along, but now I know. Your cousin is crazy, Pablo."

"So," Miguel continued, "He says to me in Spanish, 'How's everything going, friend?' and I say, 'Life is okay, except for that big storm in my home state. So much damage there.'"

Héctor looked at Pablo. "Are you this smooth under pressure, Pablo?"

Pablo ran a hand through his hair and snorted. "I wish so."

"Go on," Héctor said, punching Miguel in the shoulder.

"So, he says to me, 'Oh yes, you must be from Florida,' and I say, 'No, never been to Florida. I am from South Carolina, a beautiful place. I work on a crew for a sailboat, but I left to get away from this storm. Heading back today.'"

Miguel tapped the seat beside Pablo. "That is when Pablo arrived at the bus station. I could see him across the place looking for me. The officer says, 'Do you have identification and a bus ticket?' and I say, 'Oh yes, sure, I have identification, but no ticket. I am meeting my cousin here.' Then I shout at Pablo, 'Hey Pablo, it's me, Juan, over here.' I say Juan because that is the name on my new identification. Pablo is quick to understand because he has the great intelligence of all the men in my family, hey, Pablo?"

Pablo said nothing, but shook his head, grinning, and slapped Miguel on the back.

"So Pablo walks up, and I embrace him and say, 'Pablo, this officer and I were talking about the recent storm back home,' and I fish my identification from my pocket and pass it to the man as we speak."

Pablo glanced back at Héctor. "I said to the officer, 'Nasty hurricane. Made a mess of the farm where I work.' The whole time I'm smiling, but I'm wondering what kind of identification this fool of mine has handed the lawman. Then, just like that, the lawman hands it back to him, and wishes us safe travels back to South Carolina."

"Oh, man," Héctor said. "I would have vomited right there on the man's shoes."

"I got lucky. But you know I did as the coyote said. I looked the officer in the eye like I had nothing to hide. Plus, my identification is a decent likeness." Miguel tossed the card across the seat to Héctor.

Héctor studied it, and in an instant noticed the striking resemblance. "You just walk through life as one lucky bastard, don't you, Miguel?" Héctor pulled his own South Carolina driver's license from his pocket. "Look at mine."

"This cat looks some like you," Miguel said before he jutted the card into Pablo's field of vision.

"Not bad," Pablo said, passing the card back to Héctor. "This is passable. If you had not eaten in days."

"And you grew your hair," Miguel added.

"And slid your left eye over just the slightest bit toward your right one," Pablo said, laughing.

"And flattened your nose. Not much, you understand. I could give you a good, quick pop and fix that, no problem." Miguel laughed now, too.

Pablo lowered his window and pulled on to a wide highway.

Hot breeze blew Héctor's face. "Thanks," he shouted over the rushing wind. "You fellows comfort me. Truly you do. I'll be most confident if an American lawman ever asks to see my identification."

The highway sliced through a mat of dry, brown grass as far as Héctor could see, and a brief twinge of longing for his lush village struck him.

Miguel turned in his seat, smiling. "I cannot believe we are here, Héctor."

Héctor reached to his friend, clasping his hand across the seat. "We are here," he said.

Héctor shoved his identification into his pocket and watched the passing landscape, considering his good fortune to have hooked up with Miguel.

PABLO SAID, "You need to understand the mentality here, not so much among the folks you'll meet on Edisto Island, but among others. The politicians and the city dwellers. And those who work for the government."

Pablo had driven all night and much of this day, with only three brief stops, unwilling to let Héctor or Miguel take a shift. They traveled through the states of Louisiana, Mississippi, Alabama, and Georgia, though darkness had cloaked much of their passage through Louisiana and all of their travels through Mississippi and Alabama. Perhaps Héctor could one day return to those pretty-sounding places to view them in daylight.

With his right hand on the wheel and his left elbow propped in the open window, and a gift for easy conversation, Pablo conveyed a confidence and wisdom that comforted Héctor.

"Like that officer at the bus station?" Miguel said.

Pablo glanced at Miguel. "You don't realize how lucky you were back there. You should be in Tijuana by now."

"I understand enough to know I never want that experience again," Miguel said, lighting a cigarette. He pinched his spent match between his fingers and let the wind pull it from his grasp out the window.

"We are going to an island?" Héctor said, the talk of immigration officials unnerving him. Hot wind blew through the car, and he had to shout to be heard.

"Yes, but Edisto is big, you know? You cannot see the ocean from all parts. The island is bordered by both river and sea," Pablo said.

"So that hurricane in the Texas newspaper did great destruction here?" Miguel said.

"No, not so much here. You know, strong winds and a few downed trees; the real damage occurred up the coast, closer to North Carolina. But you don't yet know your American geography, eh?"

Pablo smiled, and Héctor felt childlike in his ignorance, his unfamiliarity with this place.

"You'll learn," Pablo said.

A couple of hours earlier they had passed a large, green sign: "Welcome to South Carolina; Smiling Faces, Beautiful Places." Pablo had translated the words. The nearer their destination became, the more Héctor believed the slogan to be true, at least the beautiful places part.

"That river is so wide, so beautiful," Héctor said, thinking of Puerto Isadore and wondering if, far across that water, Lilia looked out from the beach and thought of him.

"We're almost there now. Once we cross this bridge, we'll be on Edisto Island," Pablo said.

Their windows had been down since Texas, but the air here left his skin stickier than it had in Texas. Moist and salty.

"What's that smell?" Miguel asked.

"The tide, the marsh. The mud there is rich, black," Pablo said, jutting his chin toward the riverbank below them.

"It stinks," Miguel said, fanning the air. "No matter how pretty the scenery is."

Four boats dotted the water, one with a tall, white sail, the other three, smaller motor boats. The wide waterway snaked between two lush banks of tall green marsh grass, their colors primary and bold, like those in a child's artwork. This view from the bridge brought to Héctor's mind the bright hues of his village.

"Welcome to Edisto Island, South Carolina," Pablo said. "We're just a few minutes from my house. Maritza will prepare us a good meal. I bet you've not eaten decent cooking in a while."

"No, not even bad cooking," Miguel said.

When Pablo turned off the highway onto a narrower road, small piles of debris littered the shoulder.

"That's leftover mess from the hurricane. Not a lot of real damage, you know? But enough to cause a few folks problems. A tree farmer down the road, Lucas, is probably going to hire one of you. He had serious trouble from the storm, and he'll be needing a man at his place. The other of you can likely work for my boss. The two of them are pretty close, grew up together on neighboring farms."

"I'll take what I can get," Héctor said. "They are good men, these bosses?"

"They're fair. They value hard work, and they're not above getting out in the fields, sweating, and getting dirty. They pay fair wages. They are decent people. I have never had trouble with Jasper, and I have been his foreman for six years."

Pablo slowed, turning into the driveway of a square, white house where three small children played with toy trucks in the sandy dirt.

"Home," Pablo said, cutting the ignition.

The children ran to the car, shouting, their toys left in the dust. "Papa! Papa's home! Papa's home!"

Pablo opened his door, sweeping the three into his arms. A plump woman in faded blue jeans and a red t-shirt emerged from the house, a yellow dishrag in her hand. She smiled and leaned against the door-jamb, watching her children greet their father.

Héctor exhaled. "Home," he whispered.

7

LILIA SHOOED the stray goat from her courtyard with her broom. From somewhere down the lane boys' laughter caught on the breeze, and Lilia imagined what amused them. She wondered if the young men's entertainment stemmed from something innocent such as a silly, harmless joke, or if a more sinister pleasure sparked their enjoyment. How ridiculous that she questioned the goodness and intent of faceless passersby these days. With Héctor's departure, so much in her world had become odd and uncertain.

"Get from here, you pest," she shouted at the goat nibbling a sprig of grass.

The animal bleated and trotted away, and Lilia swept its droppings to the side where she would not step.

"Are you speaking to me?" The voice was Emanuel's. "I accept the title, if so."

Lilia continued sweeping. "I was speaking to a goat."

"You may call me a goat, Lilia. I have no doubt others have declared me a dirtier beast."

She stopped sweeping. The clarity in Emanuel's eyes and something in the shape of his lips this morning hinted at a gentleness he'd lacked the previous evening.

Lilia placed the broom inside the open doorway and said, "Emanuel, I am weak in every way. My head aches with worry and fear for Héctor. I cannot be distracted."

"Distracted?" he asked, folding his arms across his chest, but not moving any closer to her. His eyes searched Lilia's.

Lilia studied him a moment before she spoke. "Yes," she said, her cheeks warming.

"Do you understand I would never leave you if you chose to remain in Mexico with me?" His voice remained soft.

"Do you not understand that I am married, Emanuel?" she pleaded.

"I do, and where is that husband of yours? He is gone from here, gone from his daughter and his wife."

Flashes of Emanuel's frustration and anger from the previous night came to Lilia, and she wished him gone from this place.

"Why are you here? To torture me? What must I say to you, Emanuel? I love Héctor. I am committed to our plans. Go from my house."

"I'm sorry; I did not come here to anger you."

Lilia shook her head and blew a loose strand of hair from her face. "You are maddening," she said. "I came to you this morning to be certain you understood my feelings for you, Lilia. To be certain your commitment to Héctor is as steadfast as you say."

"You can be sure that my devotion to my husband is true," she said.

"Then I want to offer you help in getting to America."

"What?" she said.

"I am not a bad man, Lilia. Just an honest one. You have a good soul; I could not feel about you as I do if that were not true."

Lilia jammed her hands into her hips and studied Emanuel's face several moments before she spoke. "I have never thought you were a bad man, Emanuel. Your company has always pleased me, but now that I am married, now that we are older, everything is different. I know you are good, but I also know…I also know…"

"What do you know, Lilia?"

"I know you have tempted me," she said, her cheeks flaming. "I have not been tempted before you, and my weakness, my frailty, frightens me. I don't know myself."

"I understand you, Lilia. Your life is uncertain now, and while I know I could bring you stability, I'll not tempt you again."

Emanuel's arrogance both repulsed and attracted Lilia, and her resistance to him strengthened her. She said nothing, as she had nothing else to convey to him.

"My uncle is a coyote," he said. "He is making a trek to the border soon, and he is very good. I will make arrangements with him on your behalf, Lilia. This should demonstrate to you my sincerity. If I cannot have you for my own, then at least I wish you happiness. I wish for you to be with those who make you happiest."

She stared at him in silence.

He continued, "And you are not frail in the way that you describe yourself. You are stronger than you realize."

"I cannot afford to go yet. I must wait for Héctor to work enough to send me the money."

"Would you like to leave earlier than that, to be out of this place with your little girl, to start your life in America sooner instead of later?"

"I suppose so, yes."

"Then do not worry about the money. I will get you to America."

"I am not sure how to take you, Emanuel."

"Tell me you believe I have the most sincere intentions. I want your respect if not your love, Lilia."

"You want me indebted to you," she said.

"No. I want you happy."

"Having my family together would make me happy," she said.

"That is clear. I know that once you are gone to America, we shall never see each other again. So your being indebted to me means nothing. You will be gone."

Lilia sat in a chair and motioned for Emanuel to sit as well. "I don't know what to say. What to do. First I must speak with Héctor." Lilia brought her hands to her lips. "I will repay you, Emanuel."

"That smile is a large down payment, Lilia."

Alejandra stirred in her basket.

"And my baby? Can your uncle accommodate one as small as she?"

"He has a woman he employs. Her specialty is babies."

A familiar gloom edged into Lilia's hope, and she questioned her reasoning, her emotions, her ability to think logically. "I will discuss this matter with my husband," she said.

"Certainly you will. I must go, Lilia. We will speak soon." He rose and left Lilia and Alejandra alone again.

Lilia retrieved her broom and swept the courtyard she'd already swept, her mind a thousand miles from where she stood.

8

AFTER A MEAL of pork and beef and eggs and fried potatoes, Maritza served the men sweet custard and brought out a pillow, sheets, and a foam mat from somewhere in the back of the house.

"One of you can sleep here," she said, dropping her armload to the floor. "The other can sleep with the boys in their bedroom. Two beds in there; the boys can share one. The baby sleeps with us."

Maritza's round cheeks glistened.

"I'll stay with the boys," Miguel said. Then, turning to the children who greedily ate their custard from green plastic plates, he added in a loud whisper, "You will thank me later. You don't want this fellow anywhere near you." His eyes widened as he glanced at Héctor, and he fanned his wrinkled nose.

The boys giggled, the younger one spitting custard.

Maritza popped the child across the shoulder.

"Sorry," Miguel mumbled, though Maritza's jaw twitched as if she were suppressing a smile.

Héctor scooped up his bedding. "Thank you," he said.

Maritza hauled the youngest child to her hip. "Get to bed, boys," she said to the older two, before disappearing into the bedroom with the toddler.

Pablo stood and shooed the children to their room. "The night's late, and I'm weary from the driving. You fellows need anything more?"

"You've been very generous, cousin," Miguel said.

Héctor stood and nodded. "Thank you, Pablo."

Within minutes the house grew silent except for a box fan whirring in the hot kitchen.

Héctor slipped off his shirt and spread the mat and sheet on the floor in the corner of the room, beyond the table where they had dined. Though he'd had but two beers, a peaceful drunkenness washed over him. He would call Lilia tomorrow, after he met his boss and learned of his new job. Then he would have promising news to offer Lilia. His full belly and the soft pallet beneath him overwhelmed Héctor, and though he wanted to lie awake and imagine his family's future on this island, he slept within moments of turning off the lamp.

HÉCTOR WOKE to the smell of coffee and toasted bread. He turned to see Maritza in the kitchen, her smallest son at her bare feet, sucking milk from a purple cup. These people had not bargained for Héctor, but for Miguel only. Surely Maritza wanted Héctor gone from her home, from her floor where he lay.

The clock on the wall above the television read six o'clock. What was the time in Puerto Isadore now? He believed the current hour to be earlier in his village but he could not be sure how much so.

The child in the kitchen threw his cup, the bang bringing a swift but hushed scolding from Maritza.

Héctor tossed the thin sheet back and sat, stretching his arms above his head. "No problem, I am awake. Don't keep quiet because of me, please."

Maritza wore the same jeans she'd worn last night. What shirt had she worn yesterday? Héctor couldn't remember, and he did not care, but he remembered the pants because he thought how rounded her belly looked in them, soft and fat: the belly of a mother. Lilia did not have that belly yet, and he doubted she ever would. Her skin stretched tight across her lean body. She would never bulge the way Maritza did.

"This child always throws his cup when it is empty, his way of asking for more milk. This is a game to him." She pointed at the boy as she spoke, and the child laughed.

Though her words were spoken in frustration, Maritza's eyes hinted at a playfulness. The child understood his role as the baby of his family. Héctor suspected that boy would continue tossing his empty cup for a while yet.

Pablo, Miguel, and the other two children emerged from the back of the house where they had slept: Miguel and the two older boys in one bedroom, Pablo, Maritza and the youngest boy in the other.

Héctor washed his face and slipped on a work shirt Pablo had given him the previous night.

"Jasper will be here soon to take one of you to meet Lucas, the tree farmer. Which of you wants the job?" Pablo said, opening the front door, revealing soft, early morning light.

Héctor looked at Miguel, letting Miguel choose. Miguel shrugged.

"Your call," Héctor said.

"The other of you will work with me for Jasper on the vegetable farm," Pablo said.

"I'll stick with Pablo," Miguel said. "You can work on the tree farm."

"Very well," Pablo said. "Héctor, Jasper will take you to meet Lucas this morning, and I'm coming along to translate. Sound okay?"

"That's too easy, Pablo. Thank you," Héctor said, amazed at the ease with which his new life was falling into place.

The men took their coffee outside. Héctor and Pablo sat in plastic chairs beneath a large oak tree while Miguel pitched a ball to Pablo's oldest son.

"He's got the spirit of a boy himself, that one," Pablo said, nodding toward Miguel, who laughed and whooped when Pablo's son smacked his pitch across the yard into some bushes.

"I'm glad I met up with him before I crossed. He kept me sane, though I thought he was a madman the day we met."

Pablo smiled and pointed down the road at a vehicle approaching them. "That's Jasper," he said, then shouted across the yard as the truck pulled into his yard, "I'll be back soon to pick you up, Miguel."

Miguel nodded and pitched another ball to the boy.

The two slipped into the cab of the truck, the finest truck Héctor had ever seen: spacious and comfortable with so many knobs and dials. A jet plane could have no more controls than this vehicle. Lilia would not believe this fancy pickup truck.

The truck's driver wore a thin green shirt and kept both hands on the wheel as he greeted them. His eyes matched his shirt, pale and soft, a contrast to his tan, wrinkled skin and the tufts of dark hair revealed under the edges of a grease-stained cap. A slight belly protruded above his belt, but the rest of him—other than those light eyes—looked tough, weathered, a man accustomed to the elements.

Pablo rattled off English words to Jasper, punctuated by the word Héctor. At the mention of his name, Héctor smiled and nodded at the American, who extended a hand. The men shook, and Héctor felt the rough, callused skin along the man's palm. Pablo had spoken truthfully: this American knew something about laboring, and his eyes revealed goodness.

Pablo and Jasper spoke rapidly and with ease. Héctor had never before known anyone fluent in two languages. He decided then, watching and listening to these two speak, that he, too, would be able to speak like this soon.

Within minutes, Jasper turned off the paved road onto a narrow dirt lane winding through a thick stand of trees.

"Lucas and his wife live down here. His tree fields are that way, beyond those woods." Pablo pointed.

An unexpected nervousness crept into Héctor's gut. He nodded to Pablo but did not speak. Pablo had said this Lucas was fair, but Héctor was illegally in this country. Did the gringo know this? Would he care? Of course, Pablo would not direct Héctor to a boss who took issue with Héctor's lack of proper paperwork, yet Héctor's gut flipped.

They rounded a bend and a large house, wooden and white, appeared. Jasper parked beside a truck much like his own. The farmer's wife, a thin woman in a straw hat, must have been waiting on the porch; before Jasper reached the second step, she stood at the top to greet them.

Jasper shouted something to her, motioning toward Héctor.

The woman smiled, waved, and came down the steps to greet them. She wore a loose dress but her neck and arms revealed a sinewy body, fibrous and lean, as if she were composed of nothing but muscle, bone, and gristle. Her smile exposed perfect teeth, and though Héctor could not call her beautiful, he enjoyed the sight of her, the way she descended toward them, unrestrained, like a carefree child.

A man followed her but moved more slowly, with crutches under his arms. Then Héctor saw the fellow had but one leg. Héctor glanced at Pablo, but Pablo spoke to the woman and Jasper in English, smiling and nodding in a familiar way. The American woman hugged Jasper and said words Héctor believed to be "Thank you," before she turned and watched her husband make his way to them.

The man, seemingly tall like his wife, stooped over the crutches in such a way Héctor could not be sure of his full height. He wore a work boot and a plaid short-sleeved shirt, partially tucked into brown work britches, and he did not smile.

The two gringos shook hands like old friends, but the maneuver looked awkward as the one-legged man kept his crutches firmly planted in his armpits.

Héctor understood their small talk had ended when Jasper motioned toward Héctor, then Pablo, his tone turning businesslike, serious. Héctor felt Lucas sizing him up, so he stood tall and smiled, eager to look strong and pleasant, the perfect employee.

Lucas's hair was the color of a guinea fowl, sprinkled with bits of black and white and every shade of gray in between, and he spoke to Héctor in words Héctor did not know.

Pablo said, "He asks if you're up for the job of pruning and fertilizing trees."

"*Sí, Sí.* Yes," he said, nodding and grinning at Lucas and feeling proud he knew the word yes.

Lucas again rattled off a question to Héctor, and Pablo said, "He wants to be sure you have a way here each day, and he says the pay is seven dollars an hour."

"Seven dollar, *sí*, is okay," Héctor said, already figuring how quickly he could get Lilia and Alejandra across if he saved his wages.

The sky had turned pink in the distance, forming tree silhouettes at the edge of the yard.

Lucas nodded as he spoke to Jasper.

"You're all set," Pablo said to Héctor, turning and following Jasper to the truck.

"Thank you," Héctor mumbled, wondering how this first workday would proceed without either of the men knowing a wisp of the other's language.

When Jasper and Pablo had driven away, leaving Héctor standing with the American couple, the woman pointed at her chest, smiling, and said with words loud and deliberate, "I am Elizabeth! E–liz–a–beth!"

"Elizabeth," Héctor repeated.

"Yes, good. This is Lucas! Lu-cas!" she shouted. Perhaps she was hard of hearing.

"*Sí*, Lucas. Elizabeth *y* Lucas," he said to her, reassuring her he was a quick study. The man Lucas said nothing but leaned on his crutches, tired and heavy, as if this were the end of the workday and not the beginning.

The woman turned to her husband, grinning, and spoke to him. She turned back to Héctor, "Do you speak English, Héctor?"

"*No mucho* English. *Un* little English," he said, anxious to get on with his job, more confident in his ability with manual labor than in the learning of a foreign language.

"Jesus," the gringo mumbled at his wife, who shooed him away with a flick of her wrist and headed back up the steps.

"*Jesús, sí. Comprende Jesús*," Héctor said, making the sign of the cross in the air between them, assuring them he, too, was a religious man.

"*Adiós*, Héctor," Elizabeth called from the top of the steps, giggling.

"*Adiós, señora,*" Héctor said, wondering why she laughed but believing her to be good-natured and not mocking him in some way.

"*Adiós,* Lucas," she grinned.

The man shook his head, but gave no other reply as he hobbled to his truck. "Come," he grumbled, not looking at Héctor.

He fished the keys from his pocket and fumbled with getting his crutches in the gun rack behind his seat. Héctor reached up and eased the crutches into position for his new boss.

The señora lingered at the top of the steps, an odd expression shaping her face. She appeared both satisfied and concerned, as if she were at once pleased and worried by her husband's departure. Lucas turned the key and put the truck in gear, and as he pulled from the driveway, his wife turned and entered the house.

Héctor wished he could speak to his boss. Tonight he would ask Pablo about a dictionary, and he would learn to communicate with Lucas, and he would impress the gringo with his efforts.

9

WHEN THE ONE-LEGGED gringo drove the truck into his field of trees, Héctor wondered if this was where he'd spend his days. He scanned the rows and rows of trees, some with small, colorful blossoms, others with large, waxy foliage, and all different than the trees of his homeland. He would learn the names of each of them and amaze Lucas.

The jungle surrounding the field on three sides stood thick and dark, and Héctor considered what strange animals lurked within that place. The back end of the field was bordered not by jungle but by a river, wide and fringed with marsh. Héctor hoped he could one day fish that water. This lush place reminded him of home, so very different than the dry terrain he'd crossed in Texas. Lilia and Alejandra would like life here.

The gringo parked the truck beside a shed at the edge of the field, and Héctor hopped out, eager to get started. Along with various tools, some familiar, others foreign, stood the biggest grass cutter he had ever seen. Parked beside that was a smaller tractor with three huge spades— as long as Héctor's legs—attached to its front. The gringo hobbled into the shed, to one of the posts supporting it.

"Key," Lucas said as he removed the key from a nail.

"Key," Héctor repeated.

His boss pointed to the tractor with the key, and raised his eyebrows, saying words Héctor could not comprehend. Héctor took the key from the man and pointed at the ignition then at himself.

Lucas shook his head and again raised his eyebrows in a questioning expression.

Héctor understood the man wanted to know if Héctor could drive the tractor. "*Sí! Sí, señor,*" and he grinned, knowing this was a job he could do well and please Lucas.

Héctor sat in the tractor's seat and slipped the key into the ignition. After two tries the machinery cranked. He looked at the gringo to be sure of his instructions. Lucas pointed at the knee-high grass and weeds growing between the rows of trees, then pointed at the mower, again saying words Héctor could not understand.

Héctor would do this, and he acknowledged so with a quick nod of his head.

Lucas flicked his wrist toward the field suggesting Héctor get started. Héctor backed the mower from under the shed and headed toward the first row of grass, careful not to bump the trunks of the trees with the wide mower.

At the end of the first row, Héctor glanced up to see Lucas leaning against the hood of the truck, watching him, but when Héctor rounded the end of the second row, Lucas and his truck were gone. Pleased that the man felt confident to leave him alone, Héctor took a deep breath of the salty breeze coming off the river and hummed to the drone of the tractor's engine. What a beautiful field this could be. The trees looked healthy and well cared for, but the place needed tidying up a bit. The one-legged man needed Héctor, and Héctor would make certain Lucas would soon realize as much.

Héctor wondered how Lucas had lost his leg. Perhaps the gringo had had an accident with a mower like this, or maybe his leg had been diseased. But in America the doctors would heal a disease of the leg, and so surely Lucas had lost his leg in an accident. The man, though his hair was graying, appeared too strong and healthy to have possessed a diseased leg. Héctor would discover the answer eventually, he decided.

The longer Héctor mowed, the finer the field became, but the more gnats and mosquitoes he churned up. The insects swarmed about the tractor, and Héctor closed his eyes on the straight-aways to keep the bugs out. A flock of pelicans flew over the field and Héctor smiled. Much of the plant and animal life here were foreign to Héctor, but some sights reminded him of home, and the world shrunk at those moments, and Puerto Isadore and Lilia were not so far away. Héctor imagined the pelicans eating fish here beside this field today and splashing in the bay by his village tomorrow. How simple life could be if one were a wild animal instead of a human.

Sunlight flashed on Lucas's windshield in the corner of the field, and Héctor wondered how long his boss had been back, watching him. When he'd finished the last row, Héctor drove to the edge of the field and cut the engine.

The gringo did not smile but nodded approvingly as he surveyed the field. "Looks good," he said in a low voice then added, more loudly and slowly, "Good work."

Héctor understood the word "good" and he said, "Thank you, *señor*."

Lucas pointed at the mower, then at the shed, and Héctor nodded that he understood. He cranked the tractor and drove it to the shed to park it, but instead of driving it straight in as it had been parked, he backed it in. Lucas watched and a slight smile cracked his lips, before he looked away and pulled his cap down on his brow. This man liked Héctor, but he didn't want to seem too pleased. Héctor decided he'd make the man smile before the week was out.

When Héctor climbed down from the tractor, the gringo called him over to the first tree on the first row. The firm ground lay uneven where tractor tires had rolled on a wet day, and Lucas traversed the distance slowly and with uncertainty. Again Héctor wondered how long the man had been without his leg because of his tentative handling of the crutches.

"Crepe myrtle. The name of this tree is crepe myrtle," Lucas said.

Héctor repeated the words, and his boss nodded.

"Crepe myrtle," Héctor said again, to feel the way his tongue formed the words, and to seal the sound in his memory.

The gringo pulled clippers from a worn leather pouch attached to his belt, and with them pointed to stray shoots growing from the base of the plant. "No good," he said.

Héctor smiled because he understood these words, and he mimicked his boss, "No good."

With only one leg and with both arms clinging to the crutches awkwardly, Lucas could never squat to prune the new shoots from the trees in the necessary way. Héctor took the shears and cut the new growth from the base of the first tree, then looked at Lucas for his approval.

He nodded at Héctor, saying words Héctor did not know, but the nod encouraged Héctor, and he moved on to the next tree. The field was not so large for a healthy man or two to cover, but for this one-legged gringo to work alone, or with maybe just his wife, the tasks would be very difficult if not impossible. Héctor would ask Pablo about this man's situation tonight. Héctor moved from tree to tree on his knees, hunching over each one with care, cutting each sprig with precision. By the end of this day his back and legs would know they had worked, and Lucas, Héctor hoped, would sleep soundly, confident in his new laborer.

PABLO TOSSED his son into the air, catching the shrieking child and protesting only briefly when the child begged for more.

"So Lucas's leg. What happened to him, Pablo?" Héctor said, twirling the portable phone in his hand where he sat, leaning against the shade tree in Pablo's yard, his back already tight from his workday.

"An accident earlier this summer." Pablo set the child down, and the boy ran to his tricycle where he'd left it beside the house.

"How?" Héctor asked.

"Chainsaw. A big hickory tree fell across one of the back farm roads. The thing was half dead anyway and the winds just toppled it one night. Lucas went out by himself to dispose of the debris. When he didn't come back home for lunch, Mrs. Elizabeth went looking for him. Found him lying among the limbs in the middle of the road."

Héctor shook his head, picturing Lucas like that.

"He lost a lot of blood. Nearly lost his life. Apparently, while he was sawing through a thick limb, the saw popped up, chewed deep into his shin." Pablo rubbed the spot beneath his own knee as he spoke.

"Looks like he's doing well enough now," Héctor said.

"Maybe so. Something's changed in him, though. Jasper talks about Lucas sometimes, you know? I pick up on things. Seems he has been down, speaking of selling his place."

"Why?"

"I guess he's worried he cannot keep up with it."

"Maybe he can't. I suppose that is normal," Héctor said.

"No. This land has belonged to his people for generations. Gringos are more tied to ownership of land than are our countrymen, I think. When Lucas started talking about selling, Mrs. Elizabeth and Jasper knew he couldn't really feel that way."

"Is that why I'm working for him?"

"He needs a man on his place. No one wants to see him lose the land he loves, you understand? That's how the old farmers are around here. They feel a connection to their people, their history."

Pablo's son had returned, holding a ball, and stood beside his father, one bare foot on top of the other, his toes squirming in the sand.

"You want Papa to play ball with you, boy?"

The child nodded and Pablo rose, following him to the grass patch beside the house.

Héctor gulped a Styrofoam cup of water and fingered the buttons on the phone. He had anticipated this moment all day. After two rings Armando answered.

"Hello, Armando. This is Héctor. Could you send a runner up the lane for my Lilia?"

"Greetings, Héctor. You have called at a good time, as Lilia and her baby left here only moments ago. Wait a moment, and I'll fetch her."

Héctor's breath caught in his throat, and he placed his cup of water on the ground beside his feet. This would be the day, the moment he heard his Lilia's voice, and his hands vibrated with unexpected tremors of anticipation. He imagined the phone dangling in its booth there beside Armando's shop, Armando loping down the street calling after Lilia. And beautiful Lilia, sweet Alejandra strapped across her breast, would turn absentmindedly to Armando's voice and wonder what she'd left behind.

How long this was taking. Perhaps Lilia had walked elsewhere instead of down the lane toward home. Maybe silly Armando was mistaken; perhaps Lilia had been at his shop an hour ago, not minutes ago. Maybe she had not been there at all this day.

"Héctor?" Her voice was doubtful and breathless.

"Lilia. Oh, my Lilia. Your voice. My God, it's you."

"Héctor. Are you okay?" Her voice was an angel's.

Héctor turned his back to Pablo and the children playing nearby in the yard. "Lilia, I am better at this moment than I have been in a very long time. God knows how I miss you."

"Tell me you are safe."

"I am safe, Lilia. I am okay."

"Alejandra sleeps with your clothing each night, Héctor; she will know your smell when you hold her again. She is growing so much, Héctor. She is beautiful like you. Oh, Héctor. I have missed you so, and worried more than I can say. I have been crazy with fear and doubts." Lilia's tears flowed freely, and Héctor heard her sniffles as if she were lying next to him.

"Lilia, I am in South Carolina, in a beautiful place, an island called Edisto. The trees are plentiful, and they say the ocean is nearby, too, though I have only seen the river. I am staying with the family of a man who crossed with me. I have a job, Lilia."

"I have needed to hear your voice, to know you are well. I have craved this as I have air and nourishment. What is your job? How did you cross? I have so much to ask you, to tell you. Oh, God, how could I not say this to you before: Crucita has died, Héctor," she sobbed.

"My God," he said. The weight of Lilia's burden fell on him at that moment, and he considered how difficult her life had been since his departure. "Oh, dear Lilia. I am so sorry."

"I have needed you, Héctor, and now I have you because you are still on this earth, and I am hearing your voice. We will be together again. Tell me of your job in South Carolina."

Héctor told her of the one-legged gringo and his field of trees. He told of Miguel and Pablo, of his trip in the belly of the truck, and of his wages and how he would save every coin to pay for Lilia and Alejandra to cross, even if he had to save a year or more to afford a decent coyote.

As he fell asleep that night on a thin mat on the floor in Pablo's house, Héctor's muscles ached and blisters throbbed on his thumb and palm from pruning trees. He could not recall a happier time.

10

FAT MOSQUITOES danced along the windshield, evading Miguel's jabbing thumb.

"They've been thick since the recent rains," Pablo said.

One buzzed in front of Héctor's face, and he clapped it between his palms. "One fewer now," he said.

The drive to Lucas's field took just five minutes from Pablo's house, and already they had killed six of the biting pests. "They'll thin out when the day heats up," Pablo said.

"This day is already heating up," Miguel said, looking to the cloudless, early-morning sky.

"How's work on the tomato farm?" Héctor asked.

They rounded a sharp curve in the road, and Pablo jolted to a stop as a doe and her speckled fawn darted in front of them. "They're everywhere," he said, as the deer crashed into the low bushes, disappearing as quickly as they had come.

"I'll take them over these mosquitoes," Miguel said, pinning one against the glass, leaving a small black and red smear.

"So, I should tell you both, Jasper has been in talks with developers. Between him and Lucas they own a long stretch of riverfront property. The big city investors have been hounding them both the past few years."

"Why?" Héctor said.

"Valuable land, not just for farming."

"For what else?"

"You know, fancy condominiums, homes for rich Americans who want a pretty view," Pablo said, waving his hand toward the river, just coming into view through the trees.

Miguel wrinkled his brow.

"Was a time I'd say you have no worries about your job, Héctor. Lucas hates the developers, calls them greedy and stupid. Jasper has been less resistant, always willing to talk to them. Gave one a tour of his place the day before I met you fellows in Texas."

"You say *was a time*?" Héctor said.

"Just before his accident, Lucas ordered a large shipment of a new variety of tree, a type of magnolia, recently developed at the agricultural college, not even available retail yet. Called a 'Moon Jewel' Southern Magnolia or something like that. His farm was to be one of the first in the Southeast to grow the trees. Jasper said Lucas is considering canceling his involvement, though the trees are scheduled to arrive within a month, I think."

"Why cancel?" Héctor asked. Much was difficult to understand in this place besides the language. People's motives. This attachment to land. Sometimes Héctor felt he had been shaken like a maraca then set down and told to walk a straight line.

Pablo pulled into the field. "His leg. The accident. Too much of a burden, I guess. And this was a big deal for a small nursery like Lucas's. An opportunity to make money, to expand."

"Folks always want tomatoes," Miguel said. "Let's hope Jasper holds onto his place."

"I am hoping," Pablo said.

"*Nos vemos en la noche*," Miguel said through his open window, as Héctor got out.

"See you later," Héctor shouted in English.

"Ah," Pablo laughed. "Very good, Héctor. You are a quick study. See you tonight."

"If that means, *let's drink cold beer this evening,* then I must learn these words," Miguel shouted in Spanish as Pablo drove from the field.

Héctor did not watch them go but turned to the first row of trees, slipping on a pair of work gloves as he walked.

The previous night Maritza had found a weathered Spanish-English dictionary for Héctor and gave the book to him after supper. He had lain awake well into the night, looking up words by lamplight. With a pen, he had written in tiny script on the inside back cover the words he most desired to learn. Now, this morning, though he knew at least twenty-five words, his eyes itched from lack of sleep.

He bent and tugged a tall shoot of grass growing close to the trunk of a crepe myrtle. The mowing had improved the look of the field, but the weeds too near the base of each tree remained untouched, and he would pull each by hand until Lucas arrived and gave him further direction.

As Héctor made his way down the second row of trees, something dashed beside him. He stood as three deer darted in front of Lucas's approaching truck, their white tails flashing bright beside their dark haunches. Lucas stopped with a jerk, shouting angry words from his window. He did not seem to notice Héctor until he heard his laughter.

"Good morning, *señor.*"

"Not good," Lucas said, opening his door, pointing at his shirt and pants, damp with coffee.

"How you say?" Héctor asked, pointing at the spot where the deer had slipped into the pines.

"Goddamned deer is how you say," he paused, staring at Héctor. "Deer," he said again.

"Deer," Héctor repeated. "Deer."

"*Sí,*" Lucas said, his first effort at speaking a Spanish word to Héctor. "*Sí,* deer."

"What is *goddamned, señor?*"

Lucas looked at Héctor. "Goddamned means no damned good. No good at all. Bad."

"No good?" Héctor asked, hoping his questions did not annoy his boss but demonstrated his eagerness to learn.

"No good. Eat my trees." Lucas leaned on one crutch and with his free hand pointed toward a row of young oaks in the field. "Eat," he said. "And rub the trees."

Héctor squinted. He would make sense of this. "What is you say?"

Lucas moved his mouth in a chewing motion. "Eat trees," he said.

Héctor brightened with comprehension. He nodded. "*Comer, sí!*"

Lucas handed Héctor a crutch, and with his free hand, fingers spread wide above his own head, fashioned something like an antler. Then he bent at the waist toward the crutch Héctor held. He scraped his hand hard and awkwardly against the crutch. When he stood he said, "Deer rub my trees. Hurt trees."

"*Sí, señor,*" Héctor said, holding up a finger, signaling he needed to consult his dictionary, before pulling the book from his back pocket. He looked up these words *rub* and *hurt*. If they related to the trees, he must learn them.

When he found the words, he understood, and he smiled at Lucas, nodding. "Deer is no good, goddamned," he said, pointing to his dictionary to demonstrate his ability to comprehend anything if given a moment.

"Come," Lucas said. He hobbled to the shed, looking more agile on his crutches than he had the previous day. Under the shed he tapped a big, yellow spray tank with the tip of his crutch, and nodded approval when Héctor went to it and lifted the thing, fitting its two straps over his shoulders. The tank, empty and light, had three large, red X's written in ink across the top.

Lucas motioned toward a thick metal can on a shelf in the back of the shed, and Héctor lowered the container, heavy and nearly full.

Lucas said, "Poison."

Héctor studied the container.

Lucas repeated, "Poison," and dragged his fingers across his neck in a slicing motion.

"*Sí,*" Héctor understood. "Is for deer, *señor?*"

The American's face softened then into something close to a smile. "No, no," he said, poking a tuft of tall grass by the shed post with his crutch.

"How you say?" Héctor asked, pointing toward the grass clump.

"Weeds," Lucas said. "Goddamned weeds."

"Goddamned weeds is no good, *sí?*"

"No good at all," Lucas replied.

"Is bad, *sí, señor?*"

"Yes, Héctor. Weeds are bad," Lucas said, motioning for Héctor to follow him.

"Come."

Héctor carried the sprayer and the can of weed killer and walked with Lucas to a spigot with a hose attached, and with Lucas's guidance, the two mixed the poison and a proportionate amount of water in the tank. Héctor hoisted the tank into the back of the truck before Lucas drove them to the far corner of the field.

Héctor studied the jungle beyond the last row of trees. He would like to take a walk through those deep woods, to smell them, to hear the sounds in the darkest parts. A place could never feel like home until a man knew such details.

A woman sang a song on the radio, and Lucas hummed along to the tune, driving slowly and examining each tree they passed as if he had no other plans for this day, as if each leaf were significant. Héctor's boss seemed at ease, at home here on this farm. Though Héctor could not be certain, he imagined that somehow, at this moment, his boss was as close to his former self, to the two-legged Lucas, as he had been since his accident.

Lucas parked the truck in the shade and walked over to the nearest nursery tree.

Héctor grabbed the poison from the back of the truck and followed.

Lucas pointed at a beautiful purplish-blue flower dangling from a slender vine at the base of the tree. "Morning glory," he said.

Héctor attempted to mimic the sounds, but they were too many syllables. "Say what is, *señor?*"

"Morning glory," Lucas said, slower this time.

"Morning glory," Héctor repeated.

Lucas nodded. "That's right."

"How you say tree?" Héctor asked, gently shaking the sapling by its trunk.

"Holly," Lucas said. "This is a holly tree."

The morning glories' tendrils curled around the base of the meter-tall hollies, engulfing their thin trunks with vine and delicate, conical blossoms. The flowers looked too pretty to be a nuisance, and Lucas must have read as much in Héctor's countenance.

"Weed," Lucas said, leaning over the young tree and tugging the tenacious vine from the foliage. "Poison the weeds. Poison the damn morning glories."

Héctor gave a tentative squirt with the nozzle, afraid he'd kill the holly along with the weed.

"Is okay?" he asked, looking at the small tree.

Lucas nodded then ranted about what must have been the nuisance of the weeds.

Héctor detected the words *weeds* and *yes* and *damn* in the tirade but the rest of his boss's words fell impossibly lost on him. As if at once realizing their language barrier, Lucas wiped his brow on his sleeve and said simply, "Good. Okay, Héctor. *Sí.*"

He left Héctor there with a full tank of poison and many long rows of saplings wrapped in the twisted vines. What a pity to sell a place like this, to fill it with buildings for rich people to sit inside and look out from behind glass windows at the beauty. The prospect of growing a new type of tree here, one not grown elsewhere, appealed to Héctor, and he hoped if he worked hard enough, diligently enough, the American would stick with his plans for the new magnolia trees. That name, *magnolia*, rolled off the tongue much like the state called *Alabama*. The tree sounded lovely, and Héctor spent his morning imagining a field of magnolias, though he had yet to see one.

11

LILIA REPLACED the receiver and mulled Héctor's words. Out of habit she bounced Alejandra, who slept in a pouch draped across her, and fingered a rack of brightly colored woven purses.

"They are nice, those bags," Armando said.

"Oh, yes, fine," she said, wondering how long Héctor would save to afford her crossing.

"I have more in the back if you'd like to see them," he said.

He had moved close to her, and Lilia bumped his shoulder with her elbow when she turned. Perhaps he had been that close all along, listening to her conversation with Héctor. "Oh. No, thank you, Armando. Not today."

"How is our Héctor? All is well in America?" Armando's round face glistened, and he smiled widely, revealing several missing molars. Always eager to hear news, good or otherwise, from anyone willing to entertain him, he leaned toward Lilia, his hands folded across his belly. His shirt lacked a button just above his navel. Lilia considered mentioning this flaw to him just as an old man entered the shop.

"Yes, all is well. See you, Armando," she said, slipping out the door before it closed from the old man's entrance.

Outside the shop in a tangle of weeds, a mother dog nursed a litter of squirming pups, wet-gray and glistening. The weary mongrel's coat hung loose over her ribs as she lay motionless, her young writhing for her milk in the hot dust. Lilia stopped and stared at the puppies, barely an hour old, she guessed. Something about the dogs struck her, demanded her attention.

A dead puppy lay beneath its mother's slack jaw, its tiny belly splayed like a ripe melon, while its blind siblings slithered over and under its lifeless body. The mother dog dipped her head and gently lapped the slick entrails, the pink innards glossy in the sun.

Lilia's stomach lurched, and, pulling Alejandra tight, she turned and hurried down the street.

She tried to reason what she had witnessed. Perhaps the dog was starving, or perhaps eating the puppy was her way of cleansing the area for her living babies. Lilia hardly noticed folks she passed on her journey up the lane, half-nodding greetings when the gesture seemed necessary.

That evening, as she rocked Alejandra, nursing her to sleep, Lilia recalled how the once-painful act of nursing now soothed her as well as her daughter. She considered her fissured nipples, the searing pain when Alejandra latched on those first few weeks, and how Lilia felt like a little girl herself back then, insufficient and unprepared, playing the role of mama. Those days she doubted her abilities, even when Héctor had praised her. How she yearned then to have her baby back inside her womb, safe, where Lilia could not harm her, could not mess up this strange, new job of protector.

She rose slowly to place Alejandra, now asleep, into her cradle. At that moment she understood the mother dog, and her disgust melted to empathy. Had she, too, not longed to ingest her offspring when the infant's eyes, dark and wide, locked onto Lilia's face, as if Lilia were the answer to all questions? *I understand that mongrel*, she whispered, covering Alejandra with a blanket. How I wanted to eat you, to keep you safe from burden and cruelty, to put you back in my womb. How I, too, wanted to lap you up into my belly, where my heart beat was yours again.

She knew then she would accept Emanuel's offer. She would do what she must to have her family together sooner rather than later. To save Héctor the money he would spend for their crossing. This would be her contribution, her way of doing right by her child. Héctor would understand this, and he would be grateful. She prepared herself for sleep, and she did not think of the mother dog again.

12

HÉCTOR MADE his way to the last sapling on the last row and with the weed spray drenched the morning glory vines that entangled it. He'd had to refill the tank twice before the job was completed. Now he unloaded the tank from his back and stretched his arms to the sky, surveying the long row before him. The pretty flowers and their tendrils looked healthy, but he imagined the poison invisible and already seeping into the plants. He wondered how long the process would take. Perhaps tomorrow morning he'd arrive to withered blossoms and leaves hanging loosely about the base of the young trees.

Héctor replaced the tank onto his back and hauled it to the shed at the other end of the field. Working alone like this suited him, and he hoped the gringo approved of his performance so far. He hung the tank on a hook and wondered if he should empty the remainder of the poison and rinse the tank. He would wait and ask Lucas. Where did Lucas go when he left the field like this? Perhaps he had other fields, other business to oversee. Much Héctor simply couldn't know yet, but in time he would settle into life here, into America. Lilia and Alejandra would arrive one day, and Edisto Island would then feel like home for them all.

When the gringo returned to the field, his wife arrived with him. She stood taller than any woman in Héctor's village, with pale brown eyes flecked with gold, and dark hair streaked gray beneath a wide-brimmed straw hat. She possessed an honest face Lilia would surely like instantly.

"*Hola*," she said to him as she stepped from the truck. Unlike Lucas, the *señora* seemed eager to learn Spanish. Héctor took her to be a soothing woman, friendly and outgoing.

"*Hola, señora*," he said.

"You get them all sprayed?" Lucas said, frowning, looking toward the rows at the far side of the field. "All done?"

Héctor nodded, "*Sí*, is good trees. Is no more weeds goddamn."

The señora laughed until she snorted with her nose, and then she laughed more. The gringo mumbled something to her and waved her off as if she were a nuisance, but she laughed still. Héctor understood her pleasure was good-natured, though he could not understand the source, and he smiled at her happiness, knowing, somehow, that her laughter was not directed at him,

"Come, Héctor," Lucas said, walking to the large machine beside the grass mower beneath the shed. "Today we'll dig trees. Willows." Then he repeated, "Dig trees," as he made scooping motions with his hand and pointed at some nearby trees with thin green leaves.

Héctor circled the machinery, examining each part and guessing at its purpose. Attached to the front were three large, triangular spades. They were curved, and Héctor guessed their purpose was to slice into the soil around a tree and unearth it. Héctor knew he could drive the machine, but this tree digger attached to its front end baffled him.

Lucas would have to teach him.

Lucas spoke to the señora with words flowing fast and low, and Héctor marveled at the difference between his own mother tongue and theirs. Some days Héctor held his head high because he sensed he was a quick learner, but at other times, such as this, when Lucas's communication with his wife sounded impossibly indecipherable and foreign, Héctor felt an insurmountable difference in their ways of communication.

The señora's soft expression hardened into one of serious attention. Héctor understood the time for work had returned when the señora climbed into the seat of the machine and cranked its loud engine.

She backed out of the shed slowly, but with confidence and familiarity, then turned toward a row of feathery-leaved trees. Lucas and Héctor followed her. When she reached the row, she cut the engine.

"Willow trees," Lucas said, pointing. "The name of that tree is willow."

"Willow. Willow." Héctor repeated.

"Yes. I need twelve trees. Twelve willow trees," Lucas said, and he held up ten fingers, then held up two again. "Twelve."

"Twelve, *sí, señor*. Twelve trees." Héctor had studied numbers up to the twenties. But reading them in a book and hearing the sounds of the words were different experiences entirely. He liked when the gringo taught him words.

The señora joined the men as they stood at the end of the row, and again Lucas spoke to her with words Héctor could not comprehend. She nodded, then walked up and down the rows of willow trees with a roll of orange tape in her hand. Occasionally she stopped and studied a tree, and, sometimes, she'd tie an orange piece of tape to a branch. Héctor realized her purpose was to choose the twelve trees for digging. While the señora paced the rows, Lucas led Héctor behind the shed to a mountain of large wire baskets.

"For the trees," he said. "Need twelve," he said, pointing from the baskets to the row of willows.

The crutches rendered the gringo worthless at hauling anything, and Héctor lifted as many baskets as he could carry over to the tree-digging machine. After several trips, he'd transported the necessary twelve, then rejoined his boss at the shed.

Lucas motioned to a box, also behind the shed, beside the wire baskets.

"Burlap," he said.

Héctor said the word, "Burlap," but he didn't understand the meaning, only that the gringo wanted him to say the sound.

"Need twelve," Lucas said.

Héctor opened the box. Layered inside were rough, brown squares of heavy cloth. He lifted one, running his thumb across the coarse fabric. "Is burlap, *sí*?" he asked.

"That's right. Yes. Burlap. I need twelve."

Héctor counted out twelve squares and followed Lucas back to the willows where the señora and Lucas spoke and examined the foliage and girth of the trees she had selected. The señora went to the shed and returned moments later, her arms filled with gray straps that looked like seat belts from an automobile. After dropping them in a heap on the ground beside the burlap squares, the señora ascended the machine again, started its engine, and drove down the row to the first tree marked with an orange stretch of tape. Héctor and Lucas moved closer to her, to watch her every move. She worked the levers expertly and the machine never lurched or jolted as she positioned the three, large, triangular spades around the base of the willow tree. With the shift of another lever, the blades sliced into the black soil, cutting a ring. Another shift of the lever, and with increased power and noise, the blades slowly rose, tucked beneath the tree, plucking the willow plant from the ground as if it were a child's toy. When the señora had raised the tree as high as a man's head, she hopped down from her perch and grabbed one of the metal baskets.

"Goes here," she said deliberately to Héctor, lifting the basket with purpose as if explaining a process to a child or to one mentally ill-equipped to grasp the instructions. She lowered the basket into the hole then lined it with a burlap square. This señora was a patient teacher. She looked at Héctor before climbing back into the machine's seat to be certain he understood, and Héctor nodded. This would not be so difficult. With another lever pressed, the tree slowly descended into the burlap-lined basket.

The gringo pointed at the clump of dirt and root now enclosed in burlap and said, "Root ball. The tree's roots are there. Root ball," he said again.

Héctor mouthed the words softly before repeating them aloud. "Root ball?"

"That's right," Lucas said.

The señora again dismounted the machine and pulled one of the gray straps from the pile at the men's feet. She motioned for Héctor to step in close to the tree as she threaded the strap through the metal basket, securing the burlap and basket tight around the soil encasing the tree's roots.

She turned to Héctor, a bead of sweat on her forehead. "Understand?" She said. Then she asked in Spanish, "*Comprende?*"

Héctor did understand. They would repeat this process eleven more times and then Lucas could sell his twelve trees. Héctor imagined this couple doing this work side by side each day. They would do a full day's work with barely a word necessary. How difficult the situation must be for Lucas, unable to contribute in the ways he was accustomed.

After the second tree had been dug and secured in its basket by the señora, Héctor took over the role of depositing the wire baskets into the holes and lining them with the burlap cloth. The process proceeded smoothly, with the señora never having to dismount the machine. Lucas hobbled along supervising Héctor with each aspect and nodding approval or voicing an occasional instruction.

When they were halfway down the row, the señora motioned for Héctor to replace her in operating the loader. "You learn," she said. The gas and the brake were not so different from equipment Héctor had driven in the agave fields. For ten minutes he watched her work the levers, raising and lowering the trees, engaging the spades.

"Understand?" she asked.

He nodded. He could do this.

When her husband waved for her to let Héctor take over, she climbed down and assumed Héctor's role with the wire baskets and burlap.

Working a machine like this came easy to Héctor. He had seen others manhandle heavy equipment, and knew how to be gentle, to shift carefully, to refrain from jolting and jerking. He eased the lever forward, slowly lowering the spades, encircling the base of the tree. Another shift of the levers and the blades plunged into the black soil. One more pull and Héctor plucked the tree from the earth as if it were a weed snagged by a child's hand.

A comfortable breeze had kicked up this late afternoon, and Héctor glanced toward the river, the direction from which the wind blew. The orange sky, streaked with pink and red, foreshadowed a beautiful sunset, and Héctor knew they would not finish bagging the tagged willows before nightfall. The moon would be full tonight, and Héctor wondered if the Americans would work by the light of the moon. He lowered the tree into the hole and waited as the señora secured the root ball. Something odd beside the river caught Héctor's eye. He studied the thing, dark and frightening, and pointed from his perch on the machine. The Americans followed Héctor's gaze to the riverbank just beyond the field's edge.

"What is it?" The gringo shouted over the drone of the machine.

A white seabird flew low across the water.

"The gull?" Lucas shouted.

The señora flapped her arms like a bird and yelled, "Seagull."

"No," Héctor said, jutting a finger lower, toward the shadows of a massive tree that hung out over the water.

Then the Americans saw the creature, motionless and longer than two men. "Oh," Lucas shouted, mouthing something to his wife and pointing.

"Alligator," Lucas shouted. Cupping a hand beside his mouth, he leaned toward Héctor and repeated the word, "Alligator."

"Is ok? Is life?" Héctor asked, standing on his toes to improve his view.

"Oh, yes, he is alive," the gringo said, giving Héctor a thumbs up sign.

The snout and head on the animal appeared longer than a man's arm. Because Lucas and the señora seemed unaffected by the beast's presence, Héctor tried to do the same, but the sheer size of the animal unnerved him.

"Is no bad? Is no eat man?" Héctor asked.

The señora must have read the worry on Héctor's face, and she motioned for him to cut the engine. She spoke to her husband. When he replied, she turned to Héctor and said, "It's no problem, Héctor. He is far from us." She stretched her arms wide and said, "Alligator is far. Far is okay." She moved her index and pointer fingers back and forth like a person walking, then pointed at the alligator and said, "No walk near alligator. Near is bad," She moved her hands close together and repeated the words, "Near is bad."

She stretched her hands wide, pointed at the beast, then to the spot where Héctor stood.

"Far," she said. "Far is good."

Héctor asked again, "Alligator eat man?" and he snapped his hands together imitating an alligator's jaws.

Before the señora could answer, Lucas said, "Yes. That gator ate me," and he wiggled his stump of a leg. He shouted, "Chomp! chomp!"

The gringo's expression did not change as he spoke of the beast eating his leg, and for a moment, Héctor wondered how Pablo could not have known this. How could such a terrible accident have happened to this man?

Lucas's eyes widened at Héctor's silence. "Chomp! Chomp!" he shouted again, wagging his stump as if it were the tail of a dog who'd been given a scrap of juicy meat.

"Is very bad alligator goddamn!" Héctor said.

The señora's laughter erupted, and for a brief moment Héctor believed a squawking sea bird had landed on the tree digging machine.

She whooped until a snort came from her nose. What was amusing her? Lucas's face cracked and a smile split his weathered face.

"Lucas!" the señora spat, then snorted again, before a fresh spasm of laughter overtook her.

Now Lucas laughed, and Héctor laughed, too. They laughed until tears traced the Americans' cheeks.

The gringo waved Héctor down from the machine as his wife laughed and snorted until she had to wipe her eyes on her dirt-smeared sleeve. The señora stepped to Héctor and patted his back while shaking her head at her husband.

"Lucas teases you, Héctor."

Though he could not understand the words, Héctor understood the message, and he pointed at Lucas, smiling, and said, "Bad gringo."

Lucas laughed harder, and his wife said, "Yes, Lucas is a bad gringo, Héctor. He likes to tease."

"What is to tease?" Héctor asked.

"He teases about the alligator, Héctor. The alligator did not eat Lucas. No eat Lucas."

Lucas placed his right crutch in his left hand and extended his right hand to Héctor. Héctor took the hand and the men shook to acknowledge a good-natured ribbing.

Lucas looked at his watch, then spoke words Héctor missed.

He tapped the face of his watch with a finger. "Long day," he said. "Supper time."

Lucas moved his hand as if he were eating, and Héctor understood the man wanted to stop for the day.

Most days, Miguel or Pablo arrived by this hour to carry Héctor home, but neither had arrived. He would walk, and perhaps they would meet him on the way, but, if not, he would walk fast and arrive at Pablo's house in twenty minutes.

Lucas seemed to know Héctor's thoughts. "Come," he said to Héctor, pointing to his truck. "To your house."

The Americans slipped into the truck's cab while Héctor climbed into the back. Héctor hadn't realized how his back ached until he sat. Lucas always listened to the same radio station as best Héctor could tell, and now the tunes drifted faintly from the cab through the open window. Darkness had descended enough for Lucas to use his headlights, and Héctor was thankful for the ride. The moon rose low over an open field as they neared Pablo's house. This was another night Héctor would sleep a deep and dreamless sleep. When they arrived, Héctor hopped out and the gringo handed him an envelope through the truck's window.

"Your pay," the American said, then added, "You want to work in the morning? To finish up those trees?"

Héctor said, "Work in morning? *Sí*, is okay. Work in morning, *señor*."

Lucas nodded. "*Adiós*, then."

"*Adiós*," Héctor said to him, then "*Adiós*," to the señora, who waved goodbye and repeated, "*Adiós*."

Tonight Héctor would call Lilia and tell of the funny gringo's joke, of the alligator who lived beside the beautiful river beyond the trees, and of the señora's skills in driving the tree-digging machine. He'd describe the colorful sunset and the way the pale full moon rose above the field just as it rose in their village. He'd tell her of the optimism brimming inside him, his confidence in their future, in the reality of his dreams for them.

His first workweek in America was ending, and Héctor had succeeded in his goal of making the stern gringo smile. The Americans liked Héctor; he could tell by the way the señora had stroked his shoulder after her husband's joke, and also by the warm, firm handshake of the gringo. Yes, Lilia and Alejandra would like this island and these people very much.

Maritza fried meat and onions and peppers on the stove and the scent made Héctor's belly grumble as he entered the house. She cooked for the men and the children each evening and never voiced complaints in front of Héctor. He wondered if she had friends, other women with whom she could speak about whatever women spoke of when men were not among them. When he could, he would leave her and Pablo's place and find a home of his own. Miguel said he'd heard from another field-hand of something becoming available soon. Together Miguel and he could rent the place until Lilia and the baby arrived.

Héctor slipped the calling card from his wallet and pushed the buttons on the phone. He looked at his watch; he'd told Lilia he would call at seven this evening. He was a few minutes early, and he hoped she'd made her way down the lane to the phone booth. After two rings she answered.

"Hello, Héctor?"

"Yes, Lilia. How are you? How is everything there?"

"All is very good. I miss you so. Is all still well on that island?"

"My work fills my days. You and the little one fill my heart. Everything I see and do I want to discuss with you. The old gringo laughed today."

Héctor could hear Lilia's giggle, faint and sweet. "That is good. You make people happy. I have some good news for you."

"Tell me, Lilia."

"You and I will be able to discuss your work face to face sooner than you may believe."

"How so?"

"I have found a way to get to you. And to get Alejandra to you. To America." She giggled in a way that relayed her pride and excitement about this knowledge.

"I will get you here, Lilia. We have discussed this. I received my first wages today. I'll save all I can and one day, when I can afford a decent, safe coyote for you, I'll send for you both. You know that," he said.

"Emanuel has offered to help us cross now. His uncle is a coyote, Héctor. Isn't this wonderful?"

Héctor could not speak. Had Lilia gone mad?

"Did you hear me, Héctor?"

"I heard you. I cannot believe you are serious. Your old boyfriend? That Emanuel?"

"Are you not thrilled? Do you not want us there together as a family as soon as possible?" Her voice sounded like a child's.

"Why would Emanuel offer such a thing? He is not your husband. And that uncle of his, have you met him? Is he a drug runner? I cannot understand how this has come about, Lilia." He felt his voice rising, and he inhaled and exhaled sharply to steady his temper.

"He has been my friend for many years. He is kindhearted and wants to see me happy," she said.

"Lilia, you have no idea of the dangers in crossing. You are child-like in your enthusiasm. You are naive in your understanding of coyotes and the border. The border is much farther from Oaxaca than you imagine."

"Childlike and naïve?" she said, her voice higher now.

"I am your husband, Lilia. You and Alejandra are my responsibility. You will come to America when I can get you here in a safe way. Emanuel should know that is how life is between a man and his wife. Do not believe he is sincere, Lilia. I do not trust him."

] 89 [

"You are being too prideful, Héctor. Emanuel is a good man. He will do right by me and Alejandra. I am sure of this."

"Will he? What will he charge you for those services, Lilia? Or have you already paid him something I cannot possibly offer him?" He knew he spoke too harshly before the words left his lips.

"My God, Héctor. How dare you speak such words to me? All I want is to get to you, and this is your crazy reaction? How could you question me on my faithfulness? Have you forgotten me this quickly?" She shouted, choking on tears as she spat the last words.

"Lilia. My Lilia. I am sorry to upset you. I do not question your faithfulness, but I do question Emanuel's intentions, his motivations. You are a special woman and men know that about you. You are beautiful. Emanuel is not blind."

Pablo waved to Héctor from the front door, signaling that dinner was waiting.

Lilia said nothing but sniffled.

"Be patient with me, Lilia. I want nothing more than to have you here beside me. You are my reason for all I do," he said.

"Then you must also trust me, my judgment."

"We will speak of this next time, Lilia. I must go now. I will call you in one week, at this same hour. And you have Pablo's number if you need to contact me."

"Yes, Héctor. I have the number," she said. "Alejandra and I have survived here without you. I am capable, and I am no fool, Héctor. You would do well to remember this. I make wise choices."

Later that evening the slumber Héctor had anticipated eluded him, and by four o'clock the following morning he rose and dressed for work by the light of a heavy and distant moon.

13

HÉCTOR WALKED the road, listening, wondering, certain of nothing but his boots on the pavement. An owl sailed low overhead, soundlessly, except for a quick swish of air. A thousand frogs sang their grek-grik grek-grik from ditches and ponds hidden in the darkness. When Héctor reached a dip in the road he knew he was nearing the field, and he smelled the mud of the creek that flowed nearby.

The farm road lay invisible in the waning darkness until Héctor was beside it, and he turned off the blacktop and walked down the gray dirt road into the field. Lucas and Elizabeth would not be here for hours, when they would arrive ready to finish the work with the willows.

Héctor climbed onto the tree-digging machine and cranked it on the first try. Half of the orange-tagged willows remained to be dug, bagged, and secured, and Héctor made his way to the next one along the row. He worked the levers, and the blades sliced into the soil. Another turn and the tree lurched from the ground. Héctor hopped down and lined the hole with a basket and burlap before he lowered the tree. He secured the root ball with the thick gray strap, then cautiously moved down the row, repeating the process.

When the Americans arrived, they discovered Héctor moving among twelve bagged willows, making certain each strap was tight. Elizabeth opened her door, then stood beside the truck, shaking her head. Her face was shadowed beneath her straw hat, but Héctor imagined a smile there as she surveyed his work. Lucas slid off the seat, wrangling a crutch out behind him. He watched Héctor a moment and said something to Elizabeth.

"Good morning!" Héctor shouted, and he could not help but grin, hoping the Americans were pleased. "Is okay I finish trees?"

Lucas said, "Yes, that's okay." He smiled, nodded. "That's just fine." He looked at his wife, and she smiled, too, and shook her head again.

The Americans walked toward Héctor as he tugged the last strap. "What time did you get here, Héctor?" the señora asked, tapping the watch to illustrate his question.

"Four thirty in morning," Héctor said.

Beautiful yellow wildflowers bloomed like flames licking the ditches and the edges of the forest. Elizabeth pointed at Héctor's yellow t-shirt and then at a swath of the blossoms behind him. "You look like one of those bright flowers," she said.

"How you say?" he asked.

"Goldenrod," she said.

"Gol-den-rod," he repeated. "Is nice flower."

Lucas moved among the trees, inspecting the root balls, occasionally leaning down to touch the burlap.

"All is very...how you say *pull*," Héctor assured him.

"Tight," Lucas said.

Héctor nodded. "*Sí*. Is trees root ball is very tight strap."

"You have done a good job, Héctor."

"Ah, thank you very much, Lucas."

"Four thirty is early," Elizabeth said, smiling and feigning a yawn and stretch to imitate one just rising from bed. She gave him a thumb's up. "Good and early."

"Early," Héctor repeated. "No good sleep at the night."

Lucas studied Héctor's face a moment before he spoke. "Everything okay?" he asked.

Elizabeth stood beside Lucas, her expression darkening.

"How you say my *esposa*?" Héctor pointed at his chest, his heart. "My *señora*."

"Your wife?" Elizabeth asked, pointing at Lucas then at her wedding band.

"*Sí*, yes. Wife," Héctor said.

"Is she sick?" Elizabeth asked, holding a hand to her forehead as if she were checking for fever.

"No, no sick," Héctor said. "My wife she want—how do I say—come to America," he said, aware of the lines between his eyes deepening. He tried to sound confident, calm.

Lucas said, "That's okay. Maybe one day she'll get here." Then, turning to Elizabeth, he said something about more trees and showing Héctor how to do something else with the loader.

"A man is coming to get trees on Monday morning, Héctor. You understand Monday? Today is Saturday. Tomorrow is Sunday, then Monday. Understand?"

"Yes, Monday. Understand."

The three walked to the loader where Héctor had parked it beside the last willow.

Together, like a stage act, Lucas and Elizabeth showed Héctor how to remove the tree spade from the machine and how to attach the boom and the hook that would lift the trees from where they sat and transfer them, one by one, to the end of the field beneath the shade of tall pines where sprinklers would keep the roots moist.

Explanations went quickly now with their growing mutual understanding of language and signals. Elizabeth and Lucas left Héctor to the task of transferring each tree to the shade, while Lucas drove his truck slowly up and down the rows, and Elizabeth got out occasionally to tag the prettiest, shapeliest trees for a few remaining orders.

A landscaper in Charleston had requested fifteen hollies with trunks two inches in diameter. Héctor watched the gringos going about their jobs while he drove the loader down the field, transferring the willows, one at a time, the repetitive nature of his own duties soothing him.

Elizabeth eyed each tree, checking some with the caliper to be certain of their girth. As she tied orange tape to an especially tall holly, Lucas pointed to Jasper's truck kicking up dust, approaching them from the far end of the field. Héctor deposited the last willow under the pines and parked the loader beneath the shed. He walked over to Lucas and Elizabeth just as Jasper arrived.

When Jasper stepped from his truck his face wore an expression that foretold important news: a weak smile and tired eyes.

"Elizabeth. Lucas," he nodded to them. "Got something to tell you both," he said, his hands shoved deep in the pockets of his workpants, stained with diesel fuel and the everyday grime of a farmer's life. He noticed Héctor then, standing beside Lucas's truck.

"*Que pasa*, Héctor?" he said, his face serious.

"Good morning, Mr. Jasper," Héctor said. He looked around the field, eager to resume work, uncomfortable standing idle, and hoping Lucas would direct him.

Elizabeth crossed her arms. "Everything's okay, I hope."

"Oh, no, nothing's wrong, nothing bad," Jasper said.

The dialogue that followed fell indecipherable on Héctor's ears, but the body language, the tone of the three Americans, and the few words he could make out, signaled Jasper revealing important news to his friends.

Lucas asked something about money. Héctor bent to the insignificant weeds growing on a nearby row and plucked them. Elizabeth stood silent, staring at Jasper, as if eager to hear his slow response.

When Jasper finally spoke, he broke eye contact with Lucas, and stared at the tips of his own boots.

Lucas rubbed a palm across his mouth, shook his head, and whistled.

Elizabeth laughed and bellowed pleasant sounding words. Héctor understood *happy* and *friend* and *wonderful news*. She stepped forward and squeezed Jasper's arm.

Jasper's lips split into a wide smile of relief, and Lucas stepped forward and shook his hand. Jasper said something about life being crazy, and Héctor knew that to be true.

Jasper nodded toward Héctor. "Héctor, how are these Americans working out for you?"

His words came louder than anything else the three had spoken, and Héctor understood the words were intended for him. He stood and smiled at Jasper, appreciating the wording of his question. Others might have asked the *bosses* how the Mexican was working out for *them*. "They is okay, Mr. Jasper. I keep them," he said.

"He's a hard working S.O.B." Lucas said, looking at Héctor.

"What is you say *essohbee*?"

Elizabeth rolled her eyes. "It's one of Lucas's silly words. Stupid words, Héctor."

Jasper laughed, reaching for his door handle. "Be good," he said, noticeably more at ease than when he had arrived. As Jasper drove from the field, Lucas called Héctor over to him.

"Jasper there," he said, jutting his chin toward the rising dust churned up from the departing truck, "he is selling his land, Héctor." Lucas rubbed his thumb and forefinger, the universal gesture for dinero.

What would Pablo and Miguel do? Would Lucas and Elizabeth sell their place as well? These thoughts crossed Héctor's mind like thunderclouds.

Lucas continued, "Do you understand?"

Héctor nodded. "Yes, he sell his land?"

"Yes," Lucas said. "To developers, for a marina. Where is your dictionary?"

Héctor fished the book from his back pocket and passed it to Lucas. Lucas explained *developer* and *marina*. "For big money," he added.

Héctor recalled Pablo's description of developers, how Lucas considered them stupid.

"Developer is *essohbee*, goddamn, *sí*?"

Elizabeth covered her eyes with her palm. "Do Jesus," she mumbled.

"That's right. No developers here. For Jasper it's okay. For me, not good."

Then Héctor understood his job to be secure, at least for now, and he smiled and said, "Is good for me, *gringo*. No developers goddamn!"

"Goddamn, right." Lucas spat over his shoulder and laughed. "Let's get back to work."

14

ALTHOUGH SHE and Rosa had not spoken since the night of Crucita's wake, Lilia had to tell her old friend her plans. Rosa, like Crucita, held steadfast opinions. Lilia would not please her, but out of respect for her own mother's friendship with Rosa, Lilia would make the effort to explain herself before she left for America. Perhaps Rosa, if she had not been drinking, would apologize to Lilia for her harshness. She had possessed the decency to attend Crucita's funeral, but she left without speaking to Lilia. The children had hugged Lilia but followed their mother from the funeral without a word.

With Alejandra strapped across her belly, Lilia walked to Rosa's house in the bright morning sunshine. The arrangements between Emanuel and his uncle had come together quickly, and Lilia marveled at Emanuel's graciousness in organizing her journey to the border.

The sea beyond Rosa's house glittered like a million shards of glass, and Lilia wondered if the sea in America could possibly be so beautiful. Rosa sat shelling beans on a wooden bench beside her house while her black chickens pecked in the dust near her feet.

"Good morning, Rosa." Lilia spoke first, though Rosa had watched her approach.

Rosa nodded a silent greeting and continued to shell her beans. She wore a bright yellow dress and a green apron, and she looked like she belonged there among her bougainvillea and roses, cheerful and radiant.

"I am leaving today, Rosa. Alejandra and I are going to join Héctor. He has crossed."

Rosa studied her fistful of beans before dropping them into her basket. "I have heard as much," she said.

The two remained silent a full minute before Lilia said, "You have always been in my life. We have different minds on the subject of going North, but I am a grown woman now with a child and a husband. I respect you and what you have done for me. I respect that you were my mother's closest friend. Out of that respect, I have come to tell you goodbye, Rosa."

"How can you pay for this, Lilia? Was it not Héctor's plan to send for you after some time?" Her words fell soft, almost motherly. "He's been away barely a month."

"Of course, he intended to save, to pay, but the wait may be a year or more," Lilia said.

Rosa ran her fingers through the beans like a rake through dry sand, and she watched the beans roll and part. "Patience, Lilia, often reveals much. Life is uncertain. Sometimes rewards come from restraint rather than from haste."

"What could I possibly reap from sitting here, my baby not knowing her father, and Crucita gone? Emanuel has offered to fund my crossing. He has connections," she said, straightening her back.

"You are rash, girl. What does your husband say of this?" Rosa continued to gaze into the basket of beans, as if she drew her surprising calmness from what she saw there.

"When I tell him, he will rejoice, of course," she said, wondering if this were true. "I am helping him achieve a dream he has held our entire life together."

Rosa wiped her hands on her apron and stood, placing her basket of beans on the bench. "Come with me, please, Lilia," she said, then turned and went into her house.

Lilia followed her inside, blindingly dark compared to the bright day.

Rosa stepped into her bedroom, saying, "Just a minute," leaving Lilia and Alejandra at the doorway. In a few seconds she returned.

"Let's sit," she said.

Rosa's demeanor encouraged Lilia. How comfortable her presence could be when she was not drinking. This must have been the Rosa of Lilia's mother's childhood.

"What do you know of your father, Lilia?"

The question struck Lilia. Her father had died before he'd married Lilia's mother. She knew nothing more of him. He was not from Puerto Isadore, but from a nearby village. Crucita had never spoken about him, and Lilia's questions had ceased years ago.

"I know little. He and my mother did not marry, and he died before I was born."

"Your father loved your mother, Lilia. But like Héctor, he, too, dreamed of a golden existence in *El Norte*. He chose to leave your mother in hopes of finding a better life for them."

"And for me," Lilia said.

"No, child, not for you. He never knew of you because your mother was unaware of her pregnancy when he and his brother Jorge left Oaxaca for America. We were all friends: Jorge; your father, Teodoro; José; your mother, Zarela; and I. Like Héctor, the two brothers talked foolishly of making their way in a promised land. They left, and your mother never heard from your father again. Soon after your birth—which was the day of your mother's death—this letter arrived from America. Jorge, your father's brother, sent this to me and José. Jorge knew nothing of you or of your mother's passing."

Rosa handed the yellowed envelope to Lilia, and reached for Alejandra. Lilia fished the child from the sling in which she carried her and handed her to Rosa. She took Alejandra outside, and Lilia watched through the open window as Rosa picked flowers and tickled Alejandra's cheek with the pink blossoms.

The postmark on the envelope read Arizona, U.S.A., and the date was the year of Lilia's birth, twenty years earlier. She pulled from the envelope a sheet of folded notebook paper, only slightly less yellowed than the envelope. Scrawled in faded black ink was a letter penned by an uncle she'd not known existed.

My friends Rosa and José,

I write to you so you will know what became of me and Teodoro. I should have written sooner than this, perhaps, but each time I put pen to paper, my stomach churned and my throat parched, and my effort ran dry. But you must know this: I am in El Norte in the place called Arizona. I have found employment building homes, and I have met many others from our country. But I write not so much to tell you of myself, but to tell you of Teodoro, of our journey. And this point is where I have stopped this letter to you one hundred times before.

We chose a dangerous route from Mexico to America because we understood this passage to be less frequented than most by Border Patrol. We crossed on foot through the desert, and I can tell you we experienced hell on earth. We each carried a jug of water on the journey. We'd been told of watering holes for cattle, places along our course we could replenish our water supply. Either they lied to us, or we simply missed these places, for we could not find them.

My friends, the sun beat down harder than any sun I have known. By the second afternoon we had consumed all but one fourth of one jug of water. We carried in a sack some oranges, nuts, and tins of sardines, but what we craved was the water we did not possess. The sun and sand sucked the very liquid from our bones, and I felt my insides turning to sand like the desert floor. Our tongues swelled from dehydration and our feet blistered from the sun-baked wasteland. We both knew we would die in that desert if we did not find a water hole. We pissed in our jugs to drink our own urine.

By the fourth morning, Teodoro vomited and spoke of things I could not see: of boats and the sea and of his beautiful Zarela. His red eyes rolled in his head, and I wondered if I, too, looked so close to death. By the fifth afternoon, I placed Teodoro in the shade of a creosote bush. I knew we could no longer travel in the heat. I placed a urine-soaked cloth on his head in an effort to cool him, and we lay there until the sun set.

We stumbled on in the dark, thinking of the rattlesnakes and scorpions we could not see. In the morning we passed the unmistakable form of a sun-bleached human skull, then we rested in the shade of another bush. I knew then we would die soon, and I was half right. I fell asleep under the bush, and when I awoke, my brother was dead. What could I do? If I used my energy to bury him, I, too, would die there.

I pulled his corpse from under the bush and gathered a small pile of stones, which I stacked in the shape of a cross beside his body. I prayed for his soul, and for forgiveness for my part in my brother's death in this barren hell. In truth, I wondered if God heard prayers from such a place, then I moved on. Within an hour I came to the first watering hole, and I filled my jug and Teodoro's, which I'd carried with me. I drank until my belly inflated like a balloon. The following afternoon I came to a small ranch. The woman there would not employ me, and even raised her shotgun at me. But she told me the way to the nearest town. I considered what I would do if the Border Patrol were to catch me and send me across to Mexico, and I knew I would attempt the journey again, in honor of my brother Teodoro. But the Border Patrol did not catch me, thanks to God. In that border town I took a job washing dishes in a small cantina. After a month I found employment with a house builder, and that is where I have worked these past six months.

I hope you are all well in Puerto Isadore. I could not bear to tell Zarela of Teodoro's death. He loved that girl and spoke until the end of bringing her to America and raising a family there with her. Perhaps the news of his passing would better come from your voice than from me in a letter. You could tell Zarela that my brother spoke of her until he could walk no more and even then, when his parched tongue could not speak and his slow breath came raspy as dry reeds in the wind, I know he loved her still. He attempted the journey for Zarela.

Your friend,

Jorge

LILIA FOLDED the paper and slipped it into its envelope. Through the open window she watched Rosa lifting Alejandra in the breeze.

What effect did Rosa believe the letter would have on Lilia? And why had she not shown her this before now?

Lilia stood and walked outside and, only then, realized tears streaked her cheeks. Crying had become the natural state of her eyes lately.

"This only makes me want to go more," she said to Rosa.

"How could it, Lilia? After all that unnecessary suffering?"

"Because he loved my mother. Because Héctor loves me. Because the men in my life shared that desire: to make a better life for me. Alejandra and I will go, and we will complete the journey my father began before my birth, the journey Alejandra's father has taken for her."

"I see your mind will never change," Rosa said, handing the baby to Lilia.

"No," Lilia said, reaching out to Rosa. "I understand your concern. But we are not so different, you and I. We value our loved ones."

"God bless you, Lilia."

"And you, Rosa."

Rosa nodded, but spoke no more, then returned to her bench and her basket of beans, tossing cracked corn from her apron to the chickens.

Lilia took a last glance at the sea, then headed home to pack a few belongings for the journey she and Alejandra would soon make.

EMANUEL'S UNCLE chewed a cinnamon stick and read a newspaper and did not rise when Emanuel and Lilia entered his house, which smelled not of cinnamon, but of garlic.

"Hello, Uncle. This is Lilia."

The man's teeth were the color of his skin, the color of the cinnamon dangling from his lip as if it were a cigarette. He nodded and smiled a wide, toothy grin, looking at Lilia from her shoes to her face before he spoke. "Lilia. Hello."

"Good afternoon," she said.

"Who is this you have here?" He pointed at the bundle secured to Lilia's chest.

"This is my child, Alejandra."

Emanuel's uncle continued to grin.

"Lilia, this is my Uncle Carlos."

Now Lilia nodded, but said nothing. In her left hand she gripped a small bag containing Alejandra's diapers and other necessities. The strap felt hot and moist against her palm.

"So, we will leave this afternoon. I have two others I am taking this trip. Once they arrive, we will go. If all goes well, we'll get to the border within a few days. From there, I cannot tell you how long we will wait. Certain conditions determine our movements, you understand."

Lilia wished he'd stop smiling. The discolored teeth did not unsettle her as much as the man's slick demeanor. No one should smile so much as this, not when the purpose of their meeting was serious, and life-changing, and dangerous.

He continued, "Do you have questions for me, Lilia?" He stared as if he were looking through her, as if he were thinking thoughts that didn't match his words, thoughts better suited to his ridiculous smile.

"My daughter," Lilia said. "I wonder how we will cross with her."

"I do not cross with babies, but I have a woman who manages such affairs for me. You will meet Matilde. She will handle that job."

A rap at the door interrupted their conversation, and Carlos rose to admit two identical men. Lilia had seen twins before, but never two who looked as much alike as these. They appeared a bit older than Lilia, maybe in their early thirties. Both wore white t-shirts, denim jeans, identical straw hats, and boots. The only perceptible difference was their shirttails. One of the twins wore his shirt tucked into his pants, his belt cinched tight; the other did not, and Lilia wondered if this were intentional, so others could tell them apart.

"We are all here now," Carlos said, by way of introductions.

Emanuel turned to Lilia. "Go with God, Lilia. I wish you happiness with Héctor. I must leave now." He smiled at her, then leaned in and kissed her cheek with dry, rough lips.

She should thank him, she knew, but suddenly she considered Héctor's misgivings about Emanuel, and she froze with self-doubt and fear. He must have seen as much in her expression, and he gripped her shoulders and whispered in her ear. "My uncle is harmless, Lilia, and he will get you what you want. Remember that. You are getting what you asked for." He kissed her again, above her ear.

When he turned and walked out of his uncle's house, Lilia knew she would never see him again. She wondered how much this journey would cost Emanuel, what he had paid his uncle. The twins and Carlos talked among themselves as if she were not in their presence. She ran to the door.

"Emanuel," she called. He was at his car, opening the door, when he turned to her.

"Yes?"

What did she want to say to him?

"Yes, Lilia?" he repeated.

"Thank you," she said so softly she wondered if he heard the words.

"Go, Lilia," he said before slipping into his car. She watched him drive away until a hand touched her back.

"We shall go now," Carlos said.

Her body went rigid, and she tightened an arm around Alejandra.

"This way," Carlos said to Lilia and the two men. He locked the front door and led the three out the back of his house to a pickup truck with a covered bed. "Do you have a preference?" Carlos asked the three travelers and motioned to the truck.

The untucked twin said, "I'll ride up front."

"Very well," Carlos said, opening the back for Lilia, Alejandra, and the other twin. Lilia climbed inside first, followed by the twin.

"We have a long trip. You have what you need here," Carlos said before shutting the back of the truck.

Inside were blankets and a couple of pillows, bottles of water, a crate of oranges, a tin of nuts, some tortillas, and a string of peppers.

"I'm Pedro," the tucked-in twin said.

"I'm Lilia. This is Alejandra."

The twin nodded without expression, and attempted no further conversation. He pulled his hat down over his eyes and slept late into the evening. This suited Lilia. She passed the time dozing, nursing Alejandra, and eventually peeled an orange and sucked its juice.

They stopped only twice for fuel and to relieve themselves before darkness came.

Well into the night, they pulled to the side of the road a third time. Carlos opened the back of the truck. "I need to rest, but we must not stop. You drive awhile," he said to the man in the back, shoving him awake. Carlos gave him a few instructions regarding their direction and highway numbers, then climbed into the back with Lilia as the twin joined his brother up front.

Few cars traveled the roads at this hour, and Lilia could see only darkness. Alejandra stirred on the blanket beside Lilia, and she stroked the child's feet to soothe her. Carlos said nothing, but Lilia imagined his oily smile and his cold eyes watching her, penetrating the darkness as if he were a creature of the night. She curled around Alejandra, her back pressed against the hard side of the truck, creating as much distance as possible from her coyote. The vibration of the truck and the drone of the engine lulled her into a relaxed state of consciousness; she was neither asleep nor alert, her mind drifting on people and places far from where she lay.

Crucita's warm chocolate, always with the right amount of cinnamon. Lilia smelled the cinnamon first. Something was wrong; Crucita was dead. But the cinnamon, Lilia could smell the strange scent of cinnamon. She jerked awake, trying to hold her breath, to stop her heart so that she could listen. The blackness of the night and the rumble of the truck's tires on the road rendered sight and hearing useless, but the smell of sweat and cinnamon swirled around her, sickened her. Her mind understood more than her racing heart could bear.

She sat, shoving her feet, scooting her body into the corner, away from him. "No," she shouted.

His hand came down hard and clumsily like a paw on her shin, and she knew he could see no better than she. She kicked her legs, knowing she had nowhere to go. His second grab came swift and with precision and he caught her firmly by her ankle. He gripped her arm with the other hand and squeezed tight.

"Lilia," he said. "Such a pretty girl, Lilia. Relax."

"What do you want from me? Let go of me," she said and kicked up hard with her free foot. The blow slammed into Carlos's face. Lilia could not see the blood she imagined gushing from his nose.

A fist like a jug smashed into the side of her head, knocking her backward, into the bed of the truck. Another blow came hard into her hip. "Stupid girl. You are so foolish." He grabbed her by the hair and brought her face so close to his she felt his hot spit on her cheeks when he said, "What choice do you have, girl?" Lilia imagined the garlic and cinnamon on his breath seeping into her clothes, into her pores.

What choice did she have? He could kill her now, but she would rather die than give in to him. The side of her head throbbed, and everything spun wildly.

"Get away from me," she said, but her voice sounded weak, small, and not her own.

"I don't like uncooperative girls," he said, but he had shifted, moved away from her. Alejandra began to cry. Then Lilia understood that he had won.

"How about this, Lilia? You learn to enjoy my company, and this baby will continue on our journey. If you remain foolish, then I'll drop this little one off on the side of the road."

"No, please," Lilia begged, sobbing now with the full understanding of the nightmare into which she'd delivered her child and herself. "Don't hurt her, please."

With nowhere to go, no way out, and no notion of where she even was, Lilia closed her eyes and thought of Crucita as Carlos moved to her, pushing his hands into her thighs blindly. Alejandra's crying continued in the corner, and Lilia envisioned the iguana amid radiant, green leaves up above her in the courtyard. When Carlos moved hands like foraging beasts across Lilia's body, her mind reached up, up, over her head, out of herself toward the iguana who sunned each day on the limb outside Lilia's bedroom window.

She stretched toward that sunlit place high above, knowing if she reached far enough she could summon him, could find his mysterious home among the glorious, blazing leaves. And when Carlos pressed his hot mouth to her neck and into her ear, she breathed in not his putrid scent but the bouquet of the blossoms dangling like jewels from the iguana's tree, inhaled them deeply, sharply, escaping to the intoxication of their perfume.

Her pants scraped and bruised her thighs as Carlos shoved them down, but she floated among the leaves, seeking the iguana's lair, wishing to hide there forever. When Carlos pushed himself into her, the burning was the sun, and she clenched her eyes shut and summoned the iguana to protect her, his skin soft and green.

With each heaving of his body, Carlos hummed a tune to himself or to her, she could not know. Lilia closed her heart and ears to all but the iguana's image. She smelled the flowers in the tree, focused on the light reflected in the iguana's eye.

When Carlos's breathing grew heavy and wet in her ear, she sought the soft Pacific breezes rustling the leaves, and she coasted, circling higher and higher above her house and her village until everything became so small and dissolved into nothingness.

When Carlos lifted himself from her, collapsing beside her, she drifted back down toward the iguana's tree, floating above its sanctuary for a long while before sinking into his refuge, safe beneath the cover of verdant leaves and fragrant blossoms. As the snores from Carlos grew loud and steady, she slipped down from the tree and vomited. Shivering, she pulled Alejandra to her and held the child until the night's darkness faded to gray.

In the morning, when they stopped for fuel, Lilia felt Carlos's stare searing her.

"Do you think you get something for nothing?" he said, sitting up, coughing with the first words he'd spoken in hours.

She could not look at him. His smell lingered on her, and she imagined boiling herself in a huge pot, scrubbing him from her; the heat could not get hot enough to melt him away.

"Do you know what my fee is, girl? Have you any idea what Emanuel is paying for you to cross?" He coughed, expelling phlegm onto the blanket beneath him. Taking a stick of cinnamon from his shirt pocket, he continued. "I told the boy he is crazy, but I gave him a deal. I didn't charge him for that baby."

Her body ached, and she sat motionless, her knees pulled to her chest. She wished she were a knot, one no person could ever untie. His voice sickened her, and she felt pure hate for the first time in her life. It rose from her gut and tasted of decay, and she understood how hatred within someone could kill them, like a lethal dose of rot spreading in a body's veins.

"But Emanuel understands I collect my fee from a baby's mother if necessary. Like I said, I don't like uncooperative girls. You'll come around."

They traveled another full day, stopping rarely. The men took turns driving between breaks for fuel. When Carlos next resumed his spot in the back of the truck, Lilia's fears became reality when he moved to her again, this time with an air of tenderness, as if the last time had changed the atmosphere between them. She wanted to spit in his face, but she knew she would regret doing so.

This time she did not move, but let him do what he wanted to do. His attempt at tenderness combined with the light of day made this experience worse than the first. Again she went to the iguana's tree and circled above the sun-drenched leaves until Carlos finished with her. As she floated above the tree she looked for Emanuel on the ground; she wanted to know if he knew what would become of her, if his uncle's plan had been revealed to him already.

Carlos banged on the truck's cab to get the twin to pull over.

"You'll ride up front with me now," he said to Lilia.

She did not argue or even speak but followed him from the back into the front, grasping Alejandra and her small sack of diapers and supplies.

When they neared the border, he drove them into a neighborhood.

"You'll hand off your baby here," Carlos said.

15

THE MODEST house stood tucked among the others on a dusty sidestreet, and Lilia tried to envision the woman inside. The small yard, like those around it, was dry and brown, and the front steps split an unimpressive rock garden, sparse with prickly pear and a barrel cactus. Carlos knocked hard, three times, on the faded gray door. To a passerby, they appeared a family, perhaps on a visit to the grandparents' house. Lilia, hugging Alejandra to her breast and standing behind Carlos, shivered with worry and guilt. A stereo inside played fancy music, music unlike that to which she was accustomed. The door opened a few centimeters, the chain still fastened. When the occupant saw Carlos, she closed the door, unlatched the chain, and reopened, to admit them.

Inside was dark and cool, and before Lilia's eyes adjusted to the low light, she perceived a strange, pungent, earthy smell. She could not determine the scent, a mixture of sweetness and dankness that didn't match the finely appointed interior she could distinguish from where she stood. The rugs, artwork, and comfortable, expensive-looking furniture and tapestries contrasted sharply with the simple exterior of the house. Lilia wondered at the woman's income, the money she earned for illegally taking babies into America.

The woman didn't speak, but Carlos and Lilia, holding Alejandra, followed her deeper into the house. The perilously tall heels of the woman's open-toed sandals clicked across the tile. With a long finger-nail, polished dark purple and matching her lipstick, the woman pressed the knob of the stereo, and an unsettling silence followed. She wore a slim-fitting, short black skirt, unlike the loose, flowing style the girls wore in Lilia's village. Her coarse hair she wore short and styled in dark auburn tufts about her head.

Lilia followed the woman and Carlos through an archway into a sunroom filled with orchids and glass terrariums. The flowers, potted in vessels of various shapes, sizes, and materials, gave the room a humid feel, a distinct contrast from the arid plains of northern Mexico through which Lilia had just traveled. She wished Héctor could see these deli-cate blossoms dangling with such beauty and grace from their narrow stalks. In America, she would tell him of this room of orchids, of their thick glossy leaves and their dainty petals of orange, purple, and yellow. They held more beauty than anything she'd seen in a while, save for her beautiful Alejandra.

Lilia assumed the glass terrariums housed more precious plants until she detected slow movement in one. To her revulsion, she realized the glass boxes tucked among the flowers contained snakes. The woman turned to Lilia and Carlos, and at that moment Lilia first looked upon the woman's face.

Weathered and pock-marked, her visage housed the most striking, pale green eyes Lilia had ever seen. Her eyelids were shadowed the color of a fresh bruise, and Lilia wondered how long it took her to paint her face like this. A small gold stud graced her left nostril, but she wore no other visible jewelry.

"Matilde will get your child to America," Carlos said.

Lilia nodded and gripped her sleeping daughter tighter.

Matilde did not smile when she said by way of a greeting, "I know what I am doing."

Lilia wanted to appreciate Matilde's assurance, the strength she exuded, but the woman's harshness, along with the slow undulation of the snake encased in glass behind her, disturbed Lilia.

As if reading Lilia's mind, Carlos said, "Matilde is a tough one. She possesses the confidence for dealing with Immigration. She'll get your child across."

Lilia extended to Matilde the diaper bag, forcing her gaze away from the serpents.

"Inside you'll find a pacifier and formula," she began, but fell silent when Matilde raised a hand, eyes closed, her mouth twisted as if vomit has risen in her throat.

"Lady," Matilde said, "I have crossed with a baby many times before. Yours is not the first. I know what to do with a bottle, with formula. I can change a shit-filled diaper, and if the child wails, I will plug his mouth with the pacifier."

"My baby is a girl. Her name is Alejandra," Lilia said, determined to speak, though her voice sounded peculiar and flimsy. "You'll find an old shirt of her father's in the bag. The scent of it, of her father, soothes her better than the pacifier sometimes."

Matilda smiled as if to humor Lilia, a smile that said she had received instructions from fifty other young mothers. "Alejandra, is it? Well, not until you get her back. She is Ernesto, the name her papers say. She will be a boy for a while," she said, turning to the nearest snake cage. "Do you like my babies?"

When Lilia didn't speak, Matilde continued, "Perhaps you recognize this species? He is my favorite, very lethal. The coral snake. You are from Oaxaca, yes? You have something in common with this coral snake. He, too, came to me from Oaxaca."

Carlos smiled now, enchanted by Matilde. He seemed unaffected by the musty air that was beginning to choke Lilia.

"If you are thinking the border patrol is going to remove your baby's diaper to see if she is indeed a boy, you can relax," he said, disregarding the snake Matilde gently lifted from a terrarium. "They have no interest in that, though they are perverts, I am sure."

"Have you ever held a snake?" Matilde asked Lilia.

Lilia could not speak but shook her head.

"My snakes protect me. They are better than dogs for that," she said, caressing the snake with a long, purple fingernail.

"This one is Cihuacoatl; she is named after the snake goddess. Perhaps you imagine she is slimy?"

Lilia took a step back, clutching Alejandra.

"Cihuacoatl is sleek and dry. Holding her is a sensual experience too few know."

When Lilia showed no inclination to hold the snake, Matilde smiled wryly and whispered to the snake, returning it to its container. "Another time, perhaps."

Carlos said to Lilia, "Let us go now. We have others to meet."

Matilde reached for Alejandra. Lilia did not release the baby to her, but slipped the blanket from Alejandra's head and buried her face in the infant's thick, black hair, a hint of lavender lingering there from her last bath. Lilia knew she had no choice now if she was to see Héctor again, if Alejandra was to know her father. With more resolve than she had ever known, Lilia handed her sleeping infant to Matilde.

Carlos, walking to the door, said to Matilde, "She will see you in Brownsville, Matilde."

With utmost willpower, Lilia followed Carlos. The malodorous air swirled around Lilia's head, and she slumped to the floor, powerless over the stench, the imminent separation from her baby, and the pain inflicted by Carlos. He lifted Lilia as soon as she dropped, and he repeated, "You will see her again in Brownsville."

Lilia wished to conjure the iguana from her courtyard, to escape this agony and float among the iguana's soothing leaves, but this pain was too much, and no relief came to Lilia. She looked toward Alejandra one last time.

Matilde, holding the baby in one arm, leaned over a waxy, yellow blossom, inhaling its perfume. Carlos urged Lilia toward the door.

When they reached his car, Carlos repeated once more, "You will see her in Brownsville." He turned up the radio and spoke no more.

Lilia watched the scenery pass by her window with eyes too tear-filled to focus and imagined Alejandra waking in that strange, suffocating place with only Matilde to care for her. She knew if she was to survive, to succeed in joining Héctor, she must not think of her child again. She dabbed her eyes with her sleeve, but still she could not prevent her eyes' weeping. The tears subsided only when Lilia pushed her palms into her eye sockets with such force that flashes of pain and light sparked there.

LILIA CROUCHED on the bank of the Rio Grande, waiting in darkness among shapeless trees with Carlos, the twins, and another man and a boy Carlos had met near the river. Lilia could swim, having grown up beside the sea, but she sensed the boy's fear. His father fastened a rope about the boy's waist and looped the other end around his own wrist. Carlos inflated a large trash bag, and gave it to the child to hold as a floatation device.

A full hour yet before daybreak Lilia could barely see the ribbon of murky water stretching before her.

Carlos cautioned them. "Don't take that river lightly. It is far deeper and far stronger than you imagine."

Lilia could make out the boy clutching his father's hand, but she could see little else and wished she could swim the river in daylight instead of at this moonless pre-dawn hour, when everything about her felt strange and hidden.

"Go," Carlos said.

The group scrambled down the muddy bank into the slippery shallows. Weeds brushed Lilia's bare ankles like snakes slithering, parting for her entrance. She recalled Matilde's undulating serpents, and she closed her eyes, forcing herself to press forward. The river was cool and swift, and when Lilia was chest-deep, she swam, visualizing remnants of Carlos gliding from her body like scales.

The others were behind her now. She could barely distinguish the silhouette of a lone tree on the far bank, and it became her focus. She swam toward it, but the current pushed her down the river. Soon she could no longer see the tree but thrust herself toward the bank. She considered the boy, tethered to his father, being dragged over and under and across this river like a fish snagged on some hook.

She crawled up the steep bank, the muck caking her hands and legs. Like a sightless creature emerging into a dark and secretive world, she searched the river for the others, listening. The air smelled and felt the same as on the Mexican side, and she discerned the same discarded cans and man-made debris on this bank as well. How odd that the great land of opportunity existed this mundanely. What had she expected? Trees sagging with ripe fruit? Fountains of cool, fresh drinking water or Coca-Cola? She recalled Héctor's excitement about this place, and she believed if she walked far enough in the light of day, she would discover the greatness of this Estados Unidos de América. She could not believe otherwise.

One of the twins clambered out of the river beside her, but neither the man with his son or the other twin had surfaced. The first twin and Lilia watched and listened. Within moments Lilia perceived the splashing struggles of the man and his boy just a few meters away, and she swam out to them. She reached for the boy's flailing hand and helped him to the shore. The terrified boy's grip hurt her fingers, but Lilia held tight until he released her, safe in the tall grass, where they crouched, waiting.

At the first hint of dawn Lilia noticed the boy's raw skin oozed red in a ring around his hips, belly and lower back where the rope tether had cut into him. Lilia thought of the fish the men caught at the pier in her village: flopping, eyes bulging, lifeblood oozing where hooks ripped flesh. The boy's face revealed his pain, but he barely whimpered. He understood the expense, the seriousness of this endeavor.

They sat in high green-brown grass, scanning the swirling surface in silence, save for their labored breathing. A cool breeze blew, and Lilia hugged her knees to her chest, surveying the distant shoreline where Carlos stood, a small, dark dot on the green edge of her homeland. Carlos waved to them, then slipped beneath foliage and out of her sight. She prayed she would never see him again and that the next coyote she'd face, the one Carlos had arranged in El Norte, would be humane.

The other twin did not emerge, and his brother paced the bank frantically calling to the river. After ten minutes, Lilia and the man and his boy had to proceed, to meet their contact on the American side. The twin would not leave his brother behind, and he jumped and ran along the shore with grief and confusion, crying and cursing and pleading to God. Lilia and the others left him there beside the river, along with the rope and the trash bag that had carried the boy across the water.

They followed the bank to a patch of abandoned cars Carlos had told them to find. The vehicles were strewn about like bones from some forgotten massacre. They were to climb inside, hide, and not show themselves until someone approached and called out the name Juan.

Lilia recalled Carlos's instructions: "You may see others hiding like you. You'll have no need to speak to them, no need to answer when someone approaches and calls out Pedro or José or Jesús. You listen for *Juan*. When you hear this name, you move quickly to him, and he will take you on your way."

Lilia and the father and son scampered into cars, the father and son remaining together.

Lilia, shivering from wet clothes and exertion, chose a car similar to the others: paint long gone, make and model indiscernible, front seat and steering wheel missing. She curled into the back seat. The interior, sun-bleached and ragged, looked to have once been red, and strips hung from its ceiling like a weathered tapestry. The interior smelled of others who'd come before Lilia, a distinct human essence. This car graveyard seemed unlikely cover for those seeking a better life. Where were those who came before her? Did any forget the name they were to listen for? Had one been told to listen for Juan but emerged at the name José? What had happened then? Such foolish questions, she told herself. She thought about the missing twin and prayed he had surfaced down the river, though she knew he had drowned. She wondered which brother remained—tucked or untucked shirttail—and what would become of him.

Weeds grew through the rusted-out floorboard. Tiny purple blossoms at the tips of long, thin stems reached for the morning sunlight streaming through the broken window. Lilia fingered a determined stem, bending the tiny blossom to her nose, but it released no scent. She'd never seen this species in her village, and understood her future would be filled with experiences new and strange.

"Victor." She heard the word clearly and froze. Again, "Victor." The sound was a man's voice, deep, hoarse. Lilia imagined the burly man behind the sound. She imagined she heard the slightest shuffling outside, and she dared not move. Silence resumed. She had heard neither the man's approach nor departure. She had heard nothing save for the calling of the name, but she knew those waiting for Victor had departed. She closed her eyes and thought of her family, though she told herself doing so was pointless and created more pain.

The creaking of the car door centimeters from her face startled Lilia, and she gasped, but did not scream, when a man crawled onto the seat beside her. Their eyes met, and he seemed wary of Lilia, like one who comes upon a snake in the weeds. He was not the twin feared drowned but a dark-eyed stranger wearing gray denim pants and a faded brown t-shirt, both wet, as was his hair. His silent nod said both "I will not hurt you" and "You will not harm me in return." She acquiesced, made room for him. He folded himself onto the seat beside her, careful not to touch her as he pulled the rusted door closed behind him.

They did not speak but remained sequestered, each to a side of the seat like mice caged together for the first time, unsure but aware they were both in new territory. She wondered about his story, his hometown, his family. Did he have children? Was he gentle? Corrupt?

She considered all she would endure to get to America, what others such as this man beside her had to endure. She wished to say to the man that this experience made them see each other the way a dog sees a dog in the street or a bird sees another bird in a tree, but she said nothing and stared at her hands.

She thought of the boy, hidden nearby with his father in some junked car. Lilia imagined the scar he would carry forever, like a ghost belt ringing his waist. She wondered what his wound would represent to him years from now. His bravery? A mistake? A beginning? Or something far more sinister she could not yet imagine? She supposed everyone had scars somewhere, especially those who risk everything. She prayed her choices would not leave permanent scars, either apparent or hidden, on her own child. On herself.

Lilia believed the man beside her would not harm her. How could she know this? Everything now seemed reduced to its base; humanity had been stripped to skin and bone and pounding hearts, to the rise and fall of breasts praying to get beyond this point, to another place. She understood that she and this man awaited their fates, the completion of journeys begun so that one day they would experience the sweetness of hoping for more than their ancestors could have considered.

"Juan." The word broke the silence, and Lilia looked at the man beside her who had also heard the call. This was not the name he awaited. As she nudged the door open, the man nodded farewell to her. She slipped out, careful not to crush the purple flowers that stretched toward the light.

16

THE MILD SUNDAY afternoon hinted only slightly that fall would arrive in the coming weeks, and the breeze on Héctor's face felt cool, invigorating. Jasper had shown up at Pablo's house earlier that day telling the men that Elizabeth wanted them to help Lucas finish off the old hickory he'd begun dismantling the day he'd injured his leg.

"This is important to her, and to him, too," Jasper had said, and so the men obliged, piling into the back of his truck.

"I am worried about my wife," Héctor said to Pablo and Miguel in the back of the truck.

Miguel looked at him, and Héctor saw his own worry reflected in Miguel's eyes. How could any of them know what happened each day in their villages back home? Miguel had no wife, but he had family he'd left behind.

"Your wife is not well?" Miguel asked.

"The last we spoke she wanted to get her own coyote and cross. I told her to wait, that I'd finance a safe way for her."

Pablo spoke now. "Where would she get the money, Héctor?"

"She has an old friend, a man she went to school with, and he has offered to help her. I am uncertain about his intentions or who he is connected to. I told her the idea is crazy."

Pablo whistled and shook his head. "Yes. That is crazy. I hope you talked some sense into her."

Before Héctor could speak, Miguel said, "Shit, man. And your baby, too? Does she realize how evil some of those characters are? Every cocaine mule at the border can offer her help, sure, but they have no interest in helping anyone but themselves. They just want the money. Or worse."

"I tried to tell her as much, and she became angry, insulted. I do not care about her anger, but I worry because I have been unable to contact her again."

Héctor picked at a callus on his palm, but he felt his friends' eyes on him. He loved Lilia because of her strength, but now, for the first time, he resented her determination and headstrong ways because those traits made him appear weak, as if he had no control over his wife.

"What are you thinking?" Miguel said.

Héctor could barely acknowledge the thoughts that had seeped into his consciousness.

He did not look up at Miguel when he answered. "I am worried either she has been harmed by this Emanuel, though I do not think that so likely. Or worse, I fear I have lost her to him." He raised his eyes and studied their faces. "How can a man know when he is here and his wife is there?"

They said nothing for a while.

Miguel broke their silence. "I doubt this Emanuel would take on a woman with a baby. And I doubt you'd have married a woman who'd leave you when you're doing all you can to make her life better. I think you are foolish to worry so about your Lilia. I am betting all is well in your village. She is just sore at your berating. You will speak soon; I am sure."

They pulled up beside the hickory tree to find Lucas and his wife already there. Héctor pushed Lilia and Alejandra from his mind; worrying about them would serve no purpose and would distract him from his work for Lucas. Then he, too, might slice his leg with the chainsaw and be of no use to anyone.

Jasper spoke with Lucas and Elizabeth. They laughed, and Lucas shook his head. Héctor wondered if Lucas felt reluctant to resume the job that had changed everything, but he admired his boss for being here. Lucas could have instructed Héctor to do the job for him. Something about Lucas's desire to finish the job himself gave Héctor strength, though he couldn't name the reason. He admired a man who saw through something he had begun, and he recognized the trait in himself. Somehow, he would keep faith in Lilia because that is the deal they had made when he had left her and Alejandra. He would hold up his end of the bargain, no matter what he imagined was happening in the places he could not see.

Pablo spoke with the gringos and explained to Miguel and Héctor that Lucas would cut a few limbs. They would need to support him. Then, they were to stack the wood into the truck to haul away.

When Jasper cranked the chainsaw, Héctor detected a trace of pleasure in Lucas's expression. The gringo looked relaxed, comfortable among the people surrounding him. Jasper motioned to Héctor and Pablo to come to them. Lucas passed his crutches to Elizabeth, while Jasper handed the chainsaw to Pablo and mouthed a few words to him Héctor could not understand. Jasper moved to Lucas's left side and Héctor stood to his right, and they helped him position himself along side a protruding branch. The two held Lucas as Pablo passed him the chainsaw, careful to maneuver the teeth far from anything. Lucas nodded and accepted the saw. Glancing at Elizabeth, he revved the motor and the teeth whirred. With great concentration he put saw to limb.

Any awkwardness Héctor had felt in holding his boss this way, his hands tight around the man's waist, melted with the realization of the significance this act had for the gringos. He could not know their history, the exact circumstances of Lucas's accident, but he understood this day to be one they needed to see through.

The saw shimmied through the first limb, and Lucas turned to tackle another. Héctor and Jasper moved slowly with him among the hickory's boughs, supporting him where he chose to go. As Lucas proceeded,

Héctor felt his boss's sweat beneath his fingers. After several minutes the shirt was saturated, and Héctor's hands dripped, but still Lucas labored.

When most of the branches had been diminished to portable logs, Lucas cut the motor and wiped his wet brow. He stood in the fresh sawdust, as if assessing his job, for a full minute.

Héctor helped Pablo and Miguel stack the hickory into the truck. As Héctor loaded the wood, he watched two squirrels chasing one another below a nearby oak. Acorns hung in profusion from the limbs, and he imagined the creatures gleeful with full bellies.

Some things in life were simple to comprehend, like a pair of squirrels skirting the trunk of an oak in complete bliss, but other things were so complex, like the need of the gringo to step in among the branches of a dead tree, despite the effort, sweat, and humility the act demanded, or Lilia's need to prove herself, her capabilities, to him no matter the danger.

The squirrels squeaked as one pursued the other into dense foliage, their game of chase nothing more than entertainment, a way to pass the day. They had no other yearning at that moment than to be happy, to delight in each other. Héctor wanted to believe Lilia's desire was not so much to prove herself as to join him. He had to believe that, and he had to forget about Emanuel. Héctor would send money to Lilia as soon as he could. He would take care of her as he had promised, and she would be happy with him.

When Héctor and the others loaded the last of the hickory, Lucas said, "Héctor, can you stay a few minutes? I'll take you home."

Héctor nodded and climbed into the back of Lucas's truck as Jasper, Miguel, and Pablo left. Lucas drove slowly back toward his own house, and Héctor wondered at his conversation with the señora in the truck's cab. Did they speak about the tree? About the weather? He longed to have such mundane talks with Lilia.

When they reached the house of the gringos, Lucas and Héctor walked over to a dilapidated shed at the edge of their yard. A beautiful songbird chirruped on an oak limb above them, and Lucas stopped to watch it.

"That's a beautiful bird. Do you know that one, Héctor?"

The bird was indeed beautiful, such colorful plumage, but no, he did not know this creature. He shook his head.

"A painted bunting. I thought I'd read somewhere you Mexicans cage them, keep them as house birds."

"Is maybe true, Lucas, but not in my home. I no see this beautiful bird before. He is very nice," Héctor said, puzzled at the intensity with which Lucas gazed upon the bird.

"No?" Lucas said, rubbing his chin. "Well, I was sure I read that some place. Be a shame to cage a thing like him anyway. Odd he is here now. Not the right time of year for him. Must be lost."

"My country is big. Maybe in someplace these birds is in the cages, but not in Puerto Isadore."

When Lucas resumed walking toward the shed, the bird flew from the oak, and the men watched him flit into a mass of azalea bushes.

The idea of capturing a bird so striking irritated Héctor; caged animals had always troubled him. Perhaps he'd given Lucas the answer he'd desired. Possibly the American felt as Héctor did and was relieved Héctor knew nothing of capturing such a lovely creature.

How horrible life in a cage would be. In Mexico he'd felt caged himself ever since he'd made the choice to cross. With each step closer to achieving his dream, the cages became increasingly smaller, and he'd had less and less control. He'd felt caged in his big country, then caged in the border house with Miguel, only to feel caged in the truck's sealed undercarriage. But the smaller the cages became, the closer he knew he was getting to his freedom. What a strange journey!

Under the shed was an old white farm truck that looked like it had not functioned in years.

"This is for you, Héctor."

Héctor could not believe the words. "For me?" He said, pointing at his own chest.

Now the cage doors had been flung open; Héctor's freedom continued to unfold in unexpected ways.

"That's right," Lucas said, his shirt sticking to his stomach, still damp from exertion.

"Thank you, *señor*. Is very good truck."

Lucas kicked the front tire. "Yep, it's a good old truck. I'd like to sell it to you. For cheap. One hundred dollars." Before Héctor could respond Lucas added, "You don't have to pay it all now. I'll take a little out of your pay each week until it's paid for."

"Each week is okay. Is very good," Héctor said.

"That's right, and then it'll be your truck. To keep," Lucas said.

Lucas opened the door, pulled the key from under the seat and handed it to Héctor.

"This is for the farm and for the road between your house and here. Not for big roads, Héctor. Do you understand? Drive only around here."

Héctor did understand. A sense of great independence welled in him. No longer would he have to depend on Pablo for transportation. Soon he would find his own house, and Lilia would join him.

He shook Lucas's hand and patted him on the back, saying, "Thank you very much, *señor*. This is very good truck."

"The paint is not good," Lucas said, pointing at a gray, chipped spot on the driver's door. "And the brakes are not great either. Big problem with brakes." He pointed at the brake pedal with the base of his crutch. He hobbled to the back and pointed at a busted taillight. "Needs fixing," he mumbled. Then, pointing at the other taillight, he said, "And that one is no good. Also needs fixing."

"Is okay. I fix," Héctor said, feeling no concern about most of the defects except the brakes. He pointed at the brake pedal and looked at Lucas in hopes of further explanation about the problem. Lucas seemed to understand.

"It's okay," Lucas said. He gave some clarification about the brakes, but Héctor could not comprehend most of the words.

"Need fluid," Lucas said. "They leak. Where's your dictionary?"

Héctor handed the book to Lucas. Lucas explained again, pointing out *leak* and *fluid*, before adding, "It's no problem today, Héctor. Tomorrow I'll tell Pablo. Pablo can translate, okay?"

Héctor nodded, shoving the ragged dictionary into his back pocket. His own truck! He had not anticipated such fortune, and he would not disappoint Lucas. Lilia would be proud when she heard this news.

"Go on, Héctor. I'll see you tomorrow."

Héctor started the dusty, old truck. He had to pump the gas, but in seconds the engine rumbled. He thanked Lucas again before driving toward Pablo's house.

Today had been a good day. He would call Lilia tonight. He would insist Armando find her or send a messenger to find her and bring her to the phone, and he would tell her of his truck and of his love for her and faith in her, and he would ask her to have faith in him. He would promise her he would send for her and Alejandra as soon as he was able.

The sun dipped behind a stand of ancient live oaks at the far end of an empty field as Héctor drove to Pablo's house. He turned the knob on the radio, sure that it would not work, and laughed in surprise when it crackled to life.

The gringo Lucas was a good man, not only for the gift of the truck, but because he noticed the pretty bird in the tree. Héctor could not name exactly why that aspect of his boss's character pleased him, but whatever it was brought to mind the boys in Puerto Isadore and their fighting cocks.

For as long as he could remember the boys in his village would train those roosters on the beach, prodding them, dragging them backwards through the sand by the tail feathers, peppering them with pebbles and shells. They'd laugh at their sport and bet Cokes on whose bird would become the champion fighter. The boys never noticed the beautiful plumage, didn't care that the losing rooster would die. No, an animal, like a person, should be free to roam, to live.

When Héctor pulled into Pablo's yard, Miguel sat reading a sports magazine beneath the oak.

Miguel stood. "Whose truck?" He ran a hand along the hood.

"The gringo gave it to me to use around the farm."

"Not bad," Miguel said. "Why are you so solemn then?"

"My wife, Miguel. Something is wrong. I cannot shake the feeling, you know?"

"You are an old woman, worrying for no reason, Héctor. Perhaps I should get you a cane to walk with, maybe some reading glasses. You will hear from her soon, man."

Héctor had no interest in light conversation. Miguel could not know any more than he if Héctor and Lilia would speak soon. And if they did not, what could he do?

17

LILIA SAT in a large, hot room in a house only several minutes from the river. She thought she could hear the waters of the Rio Grande flowing by, but the windows were closed and hidden beneath dark, mismatched sheets, and Lilia knew she only imagined the sound of rushing water. In one corner, several piles of clothes lay discarded like a forgotten past, all damp, muddy. The room smelled of sweat, of an organic odor, as if dirty animals had bedded here, and a dankness hung about the place despite the bone-dry heat outside.

The coyote opened a jug and took a long swallow before extending the container to Lilia. She had not realized the extent of her thirst until she raised the water to her lips, and then she felt she could drink the contents dry. The coyote watched her, and she passed the jug back to him before her thirst had been satiated. He replaced the top, then walked to the window, inching back the curtains to look outside. Light flashed in through the gap. On their drive to this place, the coyote had delivered the man and boy to a different house, and Lilia wondered if she'd see them again and if the twins somehow had been reunited on the shores of the Rio Grande. Lilia studied the coyote as he examined the world outside, looking, waiting for something or someone.

On one wall hung a metal crucifix, its patina a comforting green. Below it, on a small wooden table, sat two candles, mounded, yellow, and well-used. The coyote didn't speak, and Lilia wondered if he were incapable of speech, a mute. Perhaps his boss had removed his tongue for some betrayal, sliced it out and fed it to a mongrel in the street. But then she recalled how earlier he'd called out for her beside the river, and she felt foolish and childlike in her imaginings.

She looked about her surroundings. The room contained no sets of anything, no pairs, nothing matched anything, save for the two melted candles. The décor was haphazard, arbitrary. Everything sat at odd angles that had no order, no organization, as if the contents of the house were moved often, shuffled at random, by whomever entered. Lilia recognized this as a room for visitors only, not inhabitants, for there hung no family photos on the walls, no albums on the shelves, no school books, or potted plants that would require watering. The furnishings consisted of a couch, a single bed, several folding metal chairs, a card table, a small end table (the one with the candles) and a partition concealing one corner of the room. Several ashtrays brimming with butts represented to Lilia hours of waiting, or anxiety, or nervous anticipation.

When she turned toward the coyote again he stared at her, his face expressionless. He released the curtain, darkening the room, then walked to the center of the room and tugged a dangling cord, illuminating a single bulb hanging from the ceiling. After lighting a cigarette, he tossed his match into an ashtray, and flipped on a lone fan in the corner. Lilia had not noticed the fan until then, but its oscillation, along with the dull glow of the bulb, served only to exacerbate the oppressive heat and mustiness of the place.

From his belt he pulled a knife and from his pocket a small whetstone, and as he slowly dragged the knife across the stone's surface, a smirk tightened his face. His eyes locked with Lilia's until she had to lower her gaze to the dirty floor, a faded yellow linoleum, heavily trafficked, curling up along the wall nearest her. She said nothing but focused on the slow scraping of knife on stone.

"We must cut your hair," he said.

Lilia met his eyes and this time she did not look away. She said nothing for she did not know what to say or how to react to him.

"You do not already know this?" he asked, stepping closer to her.

"No," she said.

"You will see soon enough," he said, shaking his head as if amused. He returned his focus to the sharpening of his knife and in an instant appeared to forget about Lilia.

A vehicle approached and the coyote returned to the window, lifting the curtain only briefly before letting it slip from his fingers. He went to the door and opened it. Several men entered, though they seemed hardly to take notice of Lilia. Within ten minutes two more arrived, and within a half an hour the room was filled with men. Most of them wore damp clothes, and Lilia understood they, too, had crossed the river to arrive in this room.

This place was no one's destination—it contained too little to sustain anything—but more a stepping stone, a place travelers stopped on their way somewhere more promising.

A fat man wearing his long, gray hair in a ponytail and holding a dented metal box called the men to him, one at a time. When he called Lilia, she went to the table behind which he sat and on which he'd placed his file box. He stared at her, studied her features, asked her weight, her height, then flipped through his box. He pulled out a small card, held it up beside Lilia's face, then shook his head, replacing it in the file. He withdrew another, similar card and again held it beside Lilia's face.

This time he nodded, handed the card to Lilia and said, "This is you, now. Go over there to chop and color your hair." He motioned to the partition.

Lilia looked at the license in her hands. For such a small piece of paper and plastic, it felt as substantial and important as anything she'd ever owned.

"Go on now," the man shouted at Lilia.

"Thank you," she said, nodding to him and proceeding where he'd directed her.

She read the name: Beatriz Gómez. All she'd ever been was now replaced, diminished to the memories of those she'd known up to this point. She wondered if anyone would ever call her Lilia again. She wondered if Héctor could call her by her real name, or, if he did so, the nortemericanos would understand she was illegal, that she was not Beatriz Gómez, and they would haul her back to Oaxaca, or worse, to some border town where she knew no one, where men like Carlos lurked. No, she would never be Lilia again. She wondered what Crucita would think of the new name. Not much, she imagined.

Behind the partition, a sink hung loose from the wall, its bowl stained the color of rust. Above the sink, Lilia saw her reflection and wondered who the girl in the mirror had become. The reflection's eyes belonged to someone hardened, someone Lilia no longer knew.

Beside the sink was a cardboard box containing scissors and hair dye, a couple of bars of soap and a dirty rag. Adjacent to the box, a wastebasket half-filled with hair. The voice of the coyote who'd retrieved her from the junked car startled her.

"I cut their hair," he said, looking into a trash bin. "All the girls with long beautiful hair like yours."

She feared he would slash her with his knife, but she prayed he'd refrain with so many others present in the house. Still, she could be sure of nothing.

"Why?" she said.

"The identification cards. A girl would have an easier time passing herself off as another woman if she wore her hair short and colored. You could always tell the Immigration official you'd recently cut it. Do you see? This is just a precaution."

Lilia nodded and picked up the scissors, trying to avoid her own eyes' reflection.

"I can do this for you," he said. "I am good."

"No, I'll do it."

He shrugged his shoulders and disappeared around the partition.

Lilia began chopping her hair in clumps, but the scissors were dull, and she found she had to cut just a few strands at a time. Her hair was barely damp now from her swim in the Rio Grande, and she cupped water in her hands to wet her head. The cutting was easier when the hair was soaked. She tossed the long strands on top of the other hair in the basket, wondering how far from this place those women had gone.

She examined her work in the mirror. The image reminded her of Alejandra's hair, unruly tufts sticking out at odd angles. She felt she should weep in mourning at the loss of the hair Héctor had loved so, but her hard eyes had nothing to offer. If she and her husband were ever reunited, nothing would remain of the wife he knew; Carlos and the coyotes had killed that girl.

She opened the bottle of dye and squirted the contents onto her head. The liquid was the color of marigolds, and it stained her fingers orange as she rubbed it into her scalp.

The coyote appeared behind her in the mirror, watching.

"Not bad. You may have a future as a hair stylist."

He had resumed sharpening his knife on the whetstone, and Lilia wondered if this were a habit or a means of intimidation.

She said, "Do you know when I can see my baby?"

"Today or tonight. Matilde knows where to find you."

Lilia nodded and washed her hands in the sink. The coyote handed her the dirty rag from the box.

"What are your plans? You have a husband in South Carolina, Carlos tells me. You will need to phone him, yes?"

Again she nodded. "Yes. He does not know I crossed." Instantly she wished she'd not offered him that information. He could kill her now, and Héctor would never know what became of her. "I mean he does not know I am across. I need to let him know I have arrived in the United States."

"Of course. Will he come here to retrieve you and your baby?"

"Yes. He will be here soon after I phone him. He is expecting my call," she said.

The coyote laughed. "He will not be here very soon, girl. America is big. South Carolina is far from Texas, where you are. You will have to wait a few days."

Lilia did not expect this, and she wondered if the man spoke the truth to her. "May I call him, please?" she said.

"Come with me," he said, slipping his knife into the sheath strapped to his belt.

She ran the rag over her head, drying the streaks of orange that stained her temples and ears, then followed him to a small kitchen in the back of the house.

"No charges to this phone," he said. He stood in the doorway, turning his back to her. She could not decide if he were standing guard, protecting her, or if he were intent on eavesdropping on the first conversation she'd have with her husband in days. She dialed the number with shaking hands, but hung up before she heard a ring. So much had transpired since she last spoke to Héctor that suddenly she could summon no appropriate words to say to him.

After several minutes of silence, the coyote turned to face her. "Tell him you are in a house in Brownsville, Texas, and that you are safe. Tell him to drive toward Brownsville; it is located on any map of Texas. I have a telephone number for you to give him to call when he gets near." The coyote turned around again and leaned against the door jamb. He plucked his knife from its sheath, and the gritty sound of metal to stone resumed.

She believed now this coyote would not hurt her, and with determination, she dialed the number for Pablo's house in South Carolina.

18

THE WANING workday offered no hint of the dense morning fog that had rolled in off the river hours earlier, settling in the clearing that was the newest field. A silent, temporary visitor, the fog cleared by midmorning, revealing a cloudless sky. The three men stood beside Héctor's truck, looking out over the tilled, black earth and the long snaking lines of irrigation tubing, ready for the young magnolias that would soon arrive by eighteen-wheeler.

Lucas gazed across the field, his eyes bright, clear. Perhaps he imagined the field thick with the dark green foliage of four hundred "Moon Jewel" Southern Magnolias, their blossoms glossy and fragrant. Within weeks, a second field would be planted with just as many.

"You fellows worked hard to get us to this point. The place looks good, doesn't it?"

"Yes," Héctor said. "What is for tomorrow?"

"We got so much done the past two days, we could handle the trees arriving tomorrow, but I don't believe the driver can get here from Florida before the end of the week. Tomorrow we can mow the other fields, prune up some of the crepe myrtles, and fertilize the back field."

"Okay, boss man," Miguel said, nodding. With the impending sale of Jasper's farm, Miguel's duties had dwindled. Lucas had hired him to help prepare for the new magnolias.

Héctor's back ached, and he was glad when Lucas said, "Let's get out of here. Enough working this day. You want to give me a ride to my truck, Héctor?" He motioned to the far end of the field, his own truck nearly hidden in shadows cast by tall pines there.

"Yes," Héctor nodded.

"Miguel, you get up front. I can ride back here," Lucas said, working himself up onto the tailgate.

"You is the boss man, no? You ride in the front, Mister Lucas."

"Go on, get in, Miguel. I'm fine back here," Lucas said.

"Okay, then I is the boss man, now, right Mister Lucas? I can tell Héctor what to do, no? Because you make Miguel the boss man if I ride in the front?"

"Boss him all you want," Lucas said, as Héctor started the engine. The truck ran well, and Héctor hoped Lucas noted the fine care he had taken of it. When they reached the end of the field, now dark in shadows, Lucas thanked him for the ride and said, "Truck looks good, Héctor."

"Yes. I fix the lights in back, and I vacuum two, three times in the week. The brakes is okay because is much, how you say, fluid I put in." He checked the brakes every other day. He understood doing so was a requirement to his keeping the truck.

Héctor had kept this gift from Lucas clean and in good working order. Lucas had promised the old truck would run for ages if Héctor maintained it.

"Well, as long as you keep the fluid in the brakes, you'll be okay," he said, not for the first time. Lucas worried so about everything regarding his farm, from the leaves on the trees, to the soil, the rainfall, to the proper maintenance of everything. He showed particular concern for the old truck's brakes, and so Héctor took extra care with them.

Lucas made his way to his truck, barely a hitch now in his use of the crutches. He paused, swiveling to face Héctor. "Hey! I understand a little house near Jasper's place is soon becoming vacant. I know money's tight for you."

"What is tight money, Lucas?"

"I understand you do not have *mucho* money," Lucas explained. "I talked to Jasper about the house. Elizabeth and I want to help you out with that, help you rent it, get set up on your own for when your wife comes here."

"Is very nice, Lucas. Thank you. Is very good. I like these house."

"You fellows have a good night," he said. "See you in the morning."

As Héctor drove from the dirt road onto the blacktop, a flock of pelicans flew past.

"Look, " Miguel said, pointing. "Count them!"

Héctor slowed to a stop. The birds took several seconds to clear from view, twenty-four of them, all heading in to roost for the evening, their bellies rounded with fish. Héctor had not realized his own hunger until the grumbling in his stomach reminded him of the late hour. This had been a good day; the fields were prepared for the new trees, and Lucas seemed pleased. And, his own house! Lilia would not believe their good fortune. Maybe they would speak tonight, and he would rest afterwards because Lilia would be pleased with him and the slow but steady realization of their dreams.

19

WHEN DARKNESS came, most of the men departed the house. The few that remained slept or mumbled among themselves. The atmosphere was calm, quiet, as if nothing but business should happen here. Lilia sat at the end of a couch, weary and in need of sleep and food, and sick with worry for Alejandra. Lilia wore no watch and had no way of knowing the time unless she asked the coyote, and though he had been kind enough, she preferred not to speak with him. The man in South Carolina had told her to call back later, saying Héctor was not yet in from the fields, but she could only guess how many hours had passed. She feared angering the coyote if she asked to use the phone too frequently or if she pestered him about Matilde and Alejandra.

"You needed to call again, right?" The coyote stood over her. She must have closed her eyes; she had not heard him approach.

He extended a steaming cup to her. "Coffee," he said.

"Yes, I need to call again."

"Go on, then," he said, motioning toward the kitchen.

She stood and walked to the kitchen. A pot steamed on the stove beside a pack of instant coffee. The sight comforted her and struck her as being the only domestic adornments in this house.

She sipped the coffee the coyote had given her. It was warm and bitter with no sugar, but the heat soothed her and would satiate her hunger. She drank half the cup's contents before she dialed the number, and this time, Héctor answered.

"Héctor?" she said, uncertain of where to begin, of what to say. So much had occurred that he could not possibly know, and her throat tightened. Her voice sounded false, odd, as if from the distant end of a tunnel, from a place far from where she stood, and its strangeness frightened her.

"Lilia, tell me you are okay. Are you well? I have tried to phone you for days. Armando said he has not seen you."

"Oh, Héctor." Each time she opened her mouth to speak, emotion choked and silenced her.

"My God, Lilia. Is it Alejandra? Is our baby okay? Speak, please."

His panic forced the words from her throat. "No, Héctor, Alejandra is okay. I think she is okay. Oh, God, where do I begin? Héctor, I have crossed. I am in *Estados Unidos de América*. In a place called Browns-ville, Texas. I am so sorry to defy you, Héctor."

"You are in America? And Alejandra, too?"

She cradled the phone between her ear and shoulder, pushing her fists into her eyes with grief and disgust at herself. "She will arrive here tonight. We could not cross together. Please Héctor, can you come get us? I am so sorry to have gone against your wishes. But I am here, and I need you so very much."

"Dear God, Lilia. How in God's name? So you allowed Emanuel to finance this, to finance your crossing? You could have been killed, Lilia. Where are you now? Who has our baby girl?"

"A woman. Her name is Matilde. She works for Emanuel's uncle." With the thought of Carlos, the coffee churned in her gut. "I am in a house near the border. I have the phone number for you, and when you get near, call, and the coyote will instruct you here."

"Lilia, I do not know what to say to you. My God! You are actually in America. You cannot imagine the thoughts I have had the past few days when I could not find you. And now you are asking me to ask my boss for days off when he needs me. This is crazy. God damned crazy, girl! But I will go to my boss's home now to speak with him, and I will come to you tonight. Lilia, I love you, but I am both angry at you and shocked you are here, in this country. You are hardheaded like your Crucita." He paused, "Have the coyotes mistreated you?"

She started to speak but stopped short with no appropriate answer to give.

"Lilia?" he asked.

"Just come to me as quickly as you can, Héctor. Will you do that?" She lowered her voice when she heard a shuffling behind her. "Please," she said, her voice weakening.

"I will leave tonight, Lilia. I will call you when I get there. Give me the number."

She felt a tension within her slacken, like Héctor had snipped in two a string that had been pulling her shoulder blades together. She gave him the number and hung up with assurances they'd be together soon. He was coming to her. If only Alejandra would arrive unharmed, then the pieces of her world might some how match up again.

Lilia closed her eyes and slumped against the kitchen wall; she'd never known such exhaustion. She brought a hand to her breasts, the skin felt like corded rope, hard and knotted. She massaged the lumps, trying to soften them. They were hot to the touch, throbbing. Lilia knew if she could express just the slightest bit of milk the pressure would lessen. If only Alejandra would arrive soon...

Somewhere nearby a crash and shouting snapped her into full alertness. She wanted to hide but had nowhere to go. Another crash like wood splintering against wood, and the grunts of men exerting great effort or in great pain.

She could not know who fought or who was at fault. She inched slowly to the doorway. The end table lay busted beside the couch. Just as she leaned through the door, the coyote plunged his knife into the neck of a man who earlier had slept in a corner. She believed her weary mind deceived her until the man reached for the knife with both hands before collapsing to the floor. When the coyote jerked the blade from the man's throat, blood spewed like a fountain, speckling everything surrounding the men with slick red dots. With each pump of the man's heart, blood shot up in streams above him, lower and lower until the flow slowed to a trickle and the collar and breast and sleeve of the man's shirt grew crimson. How could blood flow from a body so quickly? The coyote stood over him a full minute, his chest heaving and his breathing audible. The man on the floor did not writhe or thrash in pain. He shifted only slightly then moved no more.

Lilia watched his lifeless face in horror as a blood-tinged bubble rose from the man's mouth, then settled on his lips like a pink glass ball, translucent and fragile. She thought of the delicate Christmas ornaments for sale in the pharmacy during her childhood, how she had admired them so. She wished the thing on the man's lips would burst so she would no longer have to endure the sight.

The coyote kicked the dead man hard in the back, then spat on him, cursing. When the coyote turned, seeing Lilia watching, he said not a word. His eyes glowed like obsidian in the sun, and sweat stained the armpits of his shirt. Lilia had never seen a man with such a look, and she cowered when he brushed past her to wash his knife in the sink.

Lilia could not move, nor could she take her eyes from the lifeless, bloody heap on the floor. The blood pooled around the corpse spreading wider and wider until the skirt of the couch began to absorb it, and she watched with revulsion.

She realized then that none of the others lingered in the house; she and the coyote alone remained with the dead man. Lilia supposed the others had gone on to their destinations, but she must wait for Héctor before she could leave this place. What had the dead man's crime been? She shivered, unable to take her eyes from the black-red pool that had begun to thicken and gel, until a knock at the door startled her.

Matilde? Surely Matilde and Alejandra waited beyond the door. What little air remained in the room escaped at that moment, and Lilia struggled to inhale, to stop the sudden sensation that she was suffocating. She heard herself gasp, wanting to run toward Matilde, despite the dead man's blood that pooled between her and the door.

The coyote cracked the door enough to reveal a slim wedge of night. He spoke to someone outside briefly, a creature of the dark with a man's voice, and then he closed the door and locked it again.

For the slightest moment, Lilia's life had shifted close to normal with the expectation of Alejandra's safe return. But then the full horror of her surroundings engulfed her, and she clenched her teeth and squeezed her arms around herself to keep from crying.

She opened her eyes at the sound of the coyote dragging the dead man toward the door. The man's head hung strangely and the slick, pink bubble was gone from his lips. The coyote had tossed rags into the drying pool of blood, but had yet to wipe up the spoils of his fight.

"I need to leave for a while. Lock the door behind me and don't open it until I return. No one else will come tonight."

Lilia could not look into his face but nodded.

"He tried to cheat me," the coyote said, struggling with the weight of the corpse. "He was no good. Don't think on what you saw. The image will poison a girl like you."

Lilia did feel poisoned, and nothing but holding Alejandra would numb the sting.

The coyote stopped short of the door, catching his breath. "This is not a child's game we play here. Too much is at stake. Do you understand?"

She raised her eyes to his. "Yes," she said.

"I need you to clean that mess while I am gone. More towels and some bleach are in a kitchen cabinet. I should return in half an hour." He spoke matter-of-factly, like a parent commanding a child and expecting no argument. He opened the door, lugging the cheating man's body behind him, and disappeared into the night.

The gore touched everything. Lilia retrieved more rags from the kitchen. She sopped up what she could, but the edges of the pool had begun to thicken and dry. A streak of red extended to the door where the man's body had been dragged. Lilia wet a towel in the sink, then, on hands and knees, scrubbed the evidence of the killing off the floor. The splatter on the couch was more difficult to erase. She soaked a rag in bleach and dabbed at each tiny dot of blood. When she finished, she washed the rags in the sink, emptying the pink water four times before it stayed clear.

She soaked her own hands in bleach then scrubbed them with soap and a rough sponge. Even so, her skin felt stained and toxic. What was the coyote doing with the body? The dead man's family would likely never know what became of him. Lilia wondered about his mother, if she were living and if she had loved him the way Lilia loved Alejandra. And what kind of mother was Lilia to have trusted strangers with her baby?

A new terror seized Lilia, the reality that people did die in this business of crossing into America. She had seen so just now and could not deny the evil. The reality emptied her, left her as hollow as the hull of a corn kernel the ants had eaten. For the first time in her life she acknowledged she could withstand nothing more. If something had happened to Alejandra, Lilia would be weakened beyond healing, like the thinnest husk of grain, its germ within devoured. And she would welcome her demise.

She studied her eyes in the mirror, wondering at the evil her choices had spurred, and she scrubbed her fingers until her own blood colored the sponge.

20

WHEN MIGUEL and Héctor crossed the state line into Texas, they had been driving nearly sixteen hours. As they neared the place called Corpus Christi, Héctor's vision blurred and he struggled to focus on the highway and the signs they passed. He pulled into a truck stop for a few hours' rest and to time their arrival in Brownsville at daybreak. He slept almost as soon as he reclined his seat.

At four a.m., Héctor woke to the sound of a big rig passing by. He jerked awake, afraid he had slept too long. When he started the engine, Miguel stretched and said, "Would you have imagined we'd be back here in Texas so soon?"

"You're a good friend, Miguel," Héctor said, easing onto the highway. "And Pablo, too, for letting me borrow his car."

"Would Lucas not allow you to drive your truck?" Miguel said, retrieving a pack of smokes from his shirt pocket.

"The brakes are not safe. They leak, you know? If I keep up with them—which I do—they are fine, of course. But still, Lucas is a mother hen. A worrier."

Miguel laughed. "I just heard the chicken call the turkey a fowl. You know something about worrying yourself, Héctor."

"My point," Héctor said, shaking his head, "was to express my thanks for your friendship, for your coming with me."

"That's what we do, you know?" Miguel said. "We have been through some things together. You'd get out of working for a couple of days, too, if I needed you." He lit a cigarette and flicked the match out the window. "You don't smoke anymore?"

"I never smoked in my life, except when I crossed the border," Héctor said. "You were my bad influence then."

"I entertain you, friend. Count me as a blessing," Miguel said, blowing a smoke ring.

Héctor had wanted to call the number for Lilia since they'd left South Carolina, but he knew doing so would not bring them together any sooner. Not much longer now and he would touch her warm skin and stroke her long, beautiful hair. How he had missed that.

"My Lilia is beautiful," he said.

"Yes, you have told me this a thousand times from the day we met. I have very high expectations."

"You will not be disappointed. She is the most beautiful girl in the world, and loving, too. She will like you, Miguel. But she is as strong-willed as a billy goat. That trait is not always so good," Héctor said.

"That is just women, Héctor. They are the tougher sex."

"Have you ever been married, Miguel? What do you know about women?"

"I have six sisters. I know plenty about women. They beat my ass. Why do you think I ran away from my country? I could not tolerate the women in my house."

Héctor looked at him, never knowing when Miguel made sport of him. Miguel's grin widened.

"I bet you don't even have a sister, man," Héctor said, eyeing him.

"If I did, I would not let you near her. That is certain."

Héctor pointed to a road sign ahead. "Look. Forty miles to Brownsville." He pulled into a rest area to make the call. Miguel gathered coins from the dashboard to buy them chips and two drinks.

After three rings a man answered, and Héctor was transported to the moment he'd first phoned his own coyote. How long ago that day seemed now.

"I am calling about a woman you have there. My wife, Lilia."

"She is here. Wait."

In seconds Lilia's frail voice greeted him, and, with the coyote muttering directions to her, she instructed Héctor how to find her.

HÉCTOR FOUND the house easily enough. A truck rusted in the driveway and an old car sagged on blocks, nothing noteworthy about the place. But then he knew enough about coyotes to understand the importance of an insignificant appearance.

"Do you want me to go with you?" Miguel asked.

"No, but I want you to keep this for me." Héctor handed him all the money from his wallet. "I brought all I had in case he demands some payment, but I don't want to have any money on me when I go inside."

"I'll be here," Miguel said.

Héctor stepped to the cracked, gray driveway. Brown, dead blades of grass pierced the asphalt in several spots, as if the grass had once had hope but had given up its fight soon after breaking through the surface. The morning was already warm and Héctor lifted his cap to wipe his brow.

As he walked toward the house, the curtain behind a window shifted so slightly he couldn't be sure it had moved at all. Someone watched him approach. He knocked on the door, suddenly wishing he'd packed a knife or a gun in his waistband, though he owned neither.

A man opened the door, but Héctor hardly saw his face. Lilia stepped from behind the coyote and across the threshold, and the man closed the door behind her. When she fell into Héctor's arms, he drew her into him. He tilted her head back to look into her eyes. Her face had aged in the time they'd been apart, her skin sallow, her brow lined, and her beautiful hair! What had she done?

He ran his fingers across her scalp. "What is this?" he said.

"I had no choice. To look like my new identification. I am Beatriz Gómez now," she said, her voice ashamed, sad.

"My beautiful Beatriz," he said. "Where is our baby girl?"

She pulled away from him, and her expression sparked fear and anger within him.

"Where is Alejandra?" he repeated, his fingers sinking into her thin, firm shoulders.

"I don't know," she said, tears streaking her cheeks.

"What?" he demanded, yet Lilia told him nothing.

She sobbed and pulled at her temples, clenching her own hair like a madwoman.

He jerked her arm. "Is she in Mexico?"

Lilia shook her head, choking on the words she would not say.

Never had such rage boiled in Héctor. "Speak, God damn you," he said. "Speak to me about my child, Lilia. Now!"

Héctor searched her face for an answer, for anything, then slapped her hard across her cheek. "Where?"

"I wish I knew. She should be here, but..." Lilia cowered, her hands covered her face.

Never had Héctor stood outside of himself like this. Never had his emotions swung so wildly, and he threw her to the ground at his feet. What could she mean? How could she not know where their daughter was?

"She should be here!" he repeated. "Where the hell is she? Where did you leave her?" He would drill his boot into her ribs if she did not answer him.

"She is with a woman the coyote knows. Matilde. Her name is Matilde," she said, her arms shielding her head from another blow.

Héctor brought his hand to his brow sucking in a gulp of air to clear his head, to understand this news from his wife.

"Easy, easy, friend." The voice was Miguel's. His hand came down hard on Héctor's shoulder. "Come, now, Héctor."

A new rage erupted in Héctor. How dare Miguel interfere in this matter between him and his wife? How dare Miguel tell him a goddamned thing? "This business is not yours," Héctor said, shoving Miguel's hand away.

"No, but I will not sit and watch you beat this woman, Héctor."

Miguel's face bore no trace of its usual lightness. His tone of voice matched his dark expression, and Héctor wanted to knock the look from Miguel's face.

"I do not give a shit if you watch or not. Get back in the car, Miguel," Héctor said, jutting a finger into Miguel's chest.

The door to the house slammed. Héctor jerked around to see the coyote stepping toward them, a raised pistol in his hand.

"Get out of here. Take your nonsense away from this place," he said. His voice was low, steady. He was accustomed to being obeyed, and his gun was cocked.

Héctor turned from the others and walked to the car. What else could he do? He opened the driver's door, sat down, and waited for Lilia and Miguel to get in. The coyote stood watching them, his pistol extended, until Héctor drove from the house. He had no notion of where to go, or how to begin to find the stranger who had Alejandra.

21

HÉCTOR'S DRIVING frightened Lilia, but saying as much to him frightened her more. She moved from Héctor, toward her door.

When Miguel said from the backseat, "You are going to have the police on us quick, Héctor. That will not help this situation," Héctor listened and slowed to a stop on the side of the road.

The morning sun glared through the windshield. Héctor lowered the visor, but that did nothing to lessen the intensity. They must be facing east, and Lilia wondered which direction Alejandra was from here.

Héctor's grip on the steering wheel whitened his knuckles, and Lilia understood what fury simmered within him. She was grateful for Miguel.

"Tell me what to do," Héctor said. "I cannot fix this problem without knowing everything, Lilia. Do you understand this?"

"Yes," she said.

"What has happened?" Miguel said.

"Lilia, tell Miguel. You tell him what has occurred."

In their phone conversations, Héctor had laughed about this Miguel fellow, saying how pleasant he was, and what a friend to Héctor he had become. Lilia trusted he would help them, that he was a kind man.

"Our daughter," she began. "I left Alejandra with a woman on the other side. The coyote Carlos took me to her and said she brings babies across. That is her job, and she is good. That is what he told me." Lilia tried to make this sound feasible, to make her actions seem sensible.

"Go on," Héctor said, not looking at Lilia but staring into his own lap, his fingers still wrapped tight on the steering wheel.

"Alejandra remained with the woman Matilde when the coyote and I left to cross. He told me she would meet me in Brownsville. Within eight hours of my crossing."

"How many hours ago was your crossing, Lilia?"

Lilia had never before heard such disrespect and mockery in Héctor's voice.

"Over twenty-four," she said, her tongue suddenly dry.

"Do you have a number for this woman?" Miguel asked.

Lilia shook her head.

"For your coyote Carlos?"

Again, Lilia shook her head. "No," she whispered.

Héctor punched the steering wheel with such force the horn sounded and startled Lilia, bringing again the fear of the police.

"What do you suggest we do, Lilia? I will do anything to get Alejandra back. You tell me because I do not know any of these people you have taken up with."

He had warned her not to cross on her own, but her pride and determination did not allow her to heed her husband's wisdom. The realization of her poor judgment crushed her now, and she would not turn away if Héctor moved to strike her again.

"I asked the man in the border house, the coyote you saw with the gun, if he had a way to contact Matilde. He said he did not. He said she is always efficient, always timely. He told me to check in with him this evening."

"This is crazy, Lilia. How can he not have a way to contact this woman?"

When Lilia did not answer, Miguel said, "You must know someone else who is acquainted with these people."

"You know Emanuel," Héctor said. "Call him, Lilia. Find out from him how to contact his uncle."

Of course, she must find Emanuel. Never had Lilia felt so incapable and foolish. Worse than foolish, she felt neglectful and bad and deserving of whatever pain befell her from this day forward.

Héctor pulled onto the street, driving slowly to nowhere in particular. "We will find a phone, and you will call Armando's shop, and you will make contact, somehow, with Emanuel."

"Yes," Lilia said, grateful for Héctor's guidance and to be alone no longer.

"There," Miguel said, pointing, "up ahead at the corner is a telephone booth."

Héctor parked the car, studying the lot with the wild look of one who is lost and uncertain of his surroundings. He fished the calling card from his wallet.

"Use this," he said.

Lilia moved from the car and into the booth with speed, worried that an Immigration official or a police officer could notice her. She could not possibly know how an average American woman acted. How could she trust that her actions and appearance were not suspicious? If she were caught here and sent to Mexico, she might never be able to find Alejandra.

She pushed the buttons on the phone as fast as she could without making a mistake. Héctor spoke to Miguel in the car, his hands flashing before him as he spoke, and Lilia did not have to hear the words to understand the topic of their conversation. She prayed to God for Alejandra's safe return as she watched the men, their words rendered silent behind the car's windshield.

After just three rings Armando answered. Lilia took a deep breath. Where to begin?

"Armando, this is Lilia. I need..."

"Hello, Lilia," he interrupted. "Rosa tells me you have gone to America."

"Yes, but I have trouble, Armando. Listen to me, please. I need to find Emanuel. Have you seen him around the village?"

"No, Lilia. I have not seen that clown in a week. I imagine he is back in the city. I hope all is okay with you."

"Please, Armando, find Rosa for me. This is very important. Can you send a runner to her house and have her call me immediately at this number?" She began reading the number to him from the phone.

"Wait, wait a moment, Lilia. Let me write this down. You are so fast, girl. Okay, yes, go now. The number there?"

She read the numbers to him; the necessity of a slow pace agitated her and her voice quivered.

"I have it, Lilia." Armando's cash register clinked and pinged in the background, and she knew he conducted business as he spoke to her.

He could not grasp the seriousness of this, and so she shouted at him, "Armando, my baby is missing. Do you hear me? I have to get in touch with those who can help me get her back. Please send a runner up to Rosa's house now. I will wait at this phone."

"Of course, Lilia. Right now," he said before the line went dead.

Lilia slipped back into the car and relayed to the men the details of her conversation with Armando.

"So we sit here, then," Héctor said.

"Armando will get Rosa to call us on this payphone," she said, motioning toward the booth. "I will tell her to find Emanuel, and she will do so. Emanuel will contact his uncle. Carlos will call Matilde. We will then know where Alejandra is, and we will meet this woman and get our baby back." Lilia stopped to catch her breath. Laying out this plan for Héctor set the details straight in her own head as well.

"Let's hope the process is as simple as that," he said.

"I could eat a truckload," Miguel said. "Food helps any situation. Let's buy something here in this market." His tone was light, and while nothing could lessen the burden Lilia carried, she hoped Miguel's attitude encouraged and comforted Héctor.

Circles of sweat darkened the fabric beneath Héctor's armpits. "Go ahead," he said to Miguel. "I am waiting by the phone." He passed three dollars to Miguel. "Get me a drink and something to eat. Chips or crackers. No matter. You want something, Lilia?"

She could not recall the last food she had eaten, though her worries kept any hunger at a distance. "I guess I will eat something, too," she said

"Go. Help Miguel." He pulled two more dollars from his wallet and pushed the money across the seat to Lilia.

She followed Miguel across the parking lot into the store. A bell tied to the door jangled when they entered. The young clerk behind the counter looked up from the newspaper he read and acknowledged them with a nod.

Lilia smelled the grease and seasonings before she saw the heated trays of chicken and vegetables and American dishes she could not recognize, and her forgotten appetite rolled in hard and complete and hollowed her belly.

Miguel pulled two Coca-Colas from the refrigerated case as Lilia looked over the rack of nuts and chips and cookies and crackers. So many choices! "Do you want a drink, Lilia?" Miguel asked.

"Yes, sure. A Coca-Cola, please," she said, taking a package of salted peanuts for herself.

As they made their way toward the counter and the glass case behind which sat the hot, delicious smelling food, Miguel said, "I must have some of that chicken."

"Chicken, please," he said in English to the clerk.

The clerk spoke back in Spanish, "White or dark meat for you?"

"Three pieces, dark meat is good," Miguel said. Then to Lilia he added, "You will eat a piece, no?

"Thank you, yes. The smell of it makes me hungry," she said.

While the man behind the counter packaged the meat in a small white carton, Lilia wondered if the shopkeepers throughout America could speak both English and Spanish like the man before her. She had not considered this before: the existence of many Spanish-speaking Americans, and the possibility encouraged her.

The clerk rang up the three Cokes, the chicken, Lilia's peanuts, a package of fried pork skins, a bag of pretzels, and a handful of hard candies, then placed them in a paper sack. Lilia handed Miguel her money, and he paid for the items. The food and the Coke would clear her head and soothe her belly. With food, this madness would make more sense. Alejandra would be reunited with Lilia soon, and Héctor would forgive Lilia for her poor judgment. Surely events would unfold to reveal a lightness within them all. Such must be the case because she could not bear to be the cause of such bitterness in Héctor.

She carried the bag as she and Miguel headed for the parking lot, but before the jingling bell on the door faded behind them, Lilia stopped. Héctor stood in the booth, speaking on the phone.

22

WHEN THE PAYPHONE rang, Héctor had been forming a mental list of the logical explanations for the delayed delivery of Alejandra. The sound startled him, though he anticipated the call. He banged his knee on the car's door, jumping to get the phone before the caller hung up.

"Hello?"

A man's voice said, "Lilia, please."

"Armando? This is Héctor."

"Oh, hello, I have not heard from you in a long while. How is America, Héctor?"

Héctor dug his free fist into his temple to keep from punching the glass side of the booth.

"I suppose you know from your conversation with my wife that things are not so good here, Armando. Did you find Rosa?"

"She was not at home, so I left a message with her children. I wrote the number and the information on a piece of paper, and also I told the oldest boy that the message was of great importance. She will call Lilia when she gets home from the pier. That is where the boy said his mother had gone. To get a fish for their dinner."

"Thank you, Armando. We are waiting by the phone. We must hear from her soon."

"Yes, sure, Héctor."

Héctor replaced the receiver. Lilia and Miguel stood beside the car watching him.

Miguel sucked the bone of a chicken.

"Was that Rosa?" Lilia looked hopeful, her eyes wide.

"No. We have to wait here. She will call soon," Héctor said, hoping he spoke the truth.

Lilia extended the bag to Héctor. She had never looked as weary, even in the days after Alejandra's birth, when the baby woke throughout the night, crying for Lilia's breast. Even then, Lilia appeared childlike, brimming with anticipation for whatever life tossed across her path.

Héctor took the bag from her. That Lilia, the girl he had married, the one he had left behind in Mexico, was gone.

"We should get back into the car," he said, opening the Coke. The cold bottle felt good in his hand. He imagined that from a distance one could see the waves of heat radiating from him, the way the sun's rays shimmered off beach sand on the hottest days.

Héctor's heat came not from the sun, but from an unfamiliar rage bubbling inside him, just below his skin, and he did not know how much longer he could contain the fury. Only Alejandra's safe return could quench the burning, and even then, he would never forgive Lilia.

The three sat in the car eating and drinking and waiting. A hot breeze blew across the parking lot, rattling an empty can beside the phone booth. Héctor had nothing to say to Lilia or Miguel, and they ate in silence watching the few cars come and go as customers visited the market. Today should have been a cheerful day, one of the happiest in Héctor's life. He tossed the chicken leg from his window, suddenly hungry for more.

"When does the *gringo* expect you back, Héctor?" Miguel said.

"By the morning. I will call him in a while and tell him I am delayed, and I will hope he does not fire me." Héctor looked at Lilia as he said this, wanting her to understand the depth of her foolishness, the problems that could arise from her choices.

"Lucas is a fair man, I think. He has grown children of his own, no? He will understand, and he will give you a break. Your job will be waiting for you," Miguel said. "My job is not so secure."

Lilia must have believed Miguel would lose his job because of their delay in Texas, and she said, "Oh, this is so very bad. I am sorry. I am so sorry for all of this."

She began to cry, hiding her face behind her hands.

"No, no, lady. My job is going away because my boss is selling his land. He will no longer farm. This is why I could accompany Héctor here. My employer has little work for me now." He leaned across the seat as he said this, as if he wanted Lilia to be sure his words were genuine.

Lilia nodded, her face buried in her hands. Tears dripped between fingers greasy from the chicken. Héctor watched her, and for the first time was moved to comfort her. With her thin body curled into a ball and her small face hidden behind dirty hands, she appeared innocent and frightened. Maybe Lilia felt the weight of her actions. How could she not? How many hours had Lilia spent cuddling Alejandra, studying the curve of the child's nose, each fold of skin, every nail, the smell of her breath. Had the baby eaten enough? Slept enough? Wet and pooped enough? Lilia felt as much pain as Héctor, but their pains differed; hers was washed with guilt, his with anger.

He considered reaching for her, to stroke her arm or thigh, when the phone rang. He handed her his Coke instead, and sprang from the car, spilling onto the ground the bag of pretzels from his lap.

"Hello?"

The man at the other end spoke English in an unfamiliar voice, and Héctor could not understand the words.

"Hello?" Héctor repeated.

The man seemed to ask for a person named Sarah.

"Is no here a Sarah," Héctor said, slamming down the receiver.

Lilia and Miguel watched him from the car. Both wore expressions of disappointment.

"A wrong number," he said to them through their open windows, as if they did not know as much already.

Héctor slipped into his seat, pretzels crunching beneath his boots.

"Look, there," Miguel said, pointing toward the opposite end of the parking lot.

A slow-moving police car pulled in and parked beside the market. A lone man in a uniform stepped from the vehicle, glancing toward the phone booth, toward the three sitting in the car. As the officer entered the store, Lilia said, "Does he carry a gun?"

"Certainly he does. I saw it there, on his hip," Héctor answered, agitated not so much by Lilia's question as by the police officer's arrival. A new worry filled Héctor, a more pressing dread and sense of immediate danger for himself, Lilia, and Miguel.

None of the three spoke for several minutes. Héctor gulped the last of his Coke, thinking, weighing his alternatives, and wondering what the policeman did in the market.

"Maybe we should leave for a while," Miguel said.

"But the phone," Lilia said. "We cannot miss Rosa's call."

Héctor turned toward Lilia. Everything she said irritated him. "We cannot be arrested either, Lilia."

"Perhaps we can drive around just a few moments, giving him time to leave. Then we will return. What do you say?" Miguel spoke the words as if his suggestion were no more than a passing thought, but an urgency in his tone betrayed his courtesy.

Missing Rosa's call would be a great disappointment, but being approached by an American lawman could be far worse.

"You are right," Héctor said.

As Héctor started the engine, the officer exited the store. Héctor drove slowly across the lot, passing the police car. The officer watched them; Héctor saw him in the rearview mirror as they passed.

"We have done nothing wrong," Lilia whispered, looking straight ahead.

"No, we have done nothing wrong, except that we are here without proper papers, and to the gringos, that is a crime." Héctor turned onto the street. A hot wind blew through the car, and for the first time Héctor longed for the breezes of Edisto Island. He realized then that in the brief time he had lived there, he had come to think of that place as home.

"Shit," he mumbled.

Still looking straight ahead, Lilia said, "What, Héctor?"

"He is behind us. That man is following us."

"Maybe he is just traveling in the same direction," Miguel said.

None of them spoke for a full minute. Héctor turned right at a stop sign, hoping the police car would not do the same.

"He turned as well," Héctor said. "Miguel, what do you think we should do?"

As they made their way down the unfamiliar street, scrubby bushes littered with bits of trash gave way to small, square houses, identical in nearly every way except for the cars that occupied the yards or an occasional child playing in the dust. Héctor took another turn, and still, the police car followed.

"This cannot be a coincidence, Miguel. He means to follow us. This lawman suspects something of us." Héctor's shirt clung to his skin and a bitterness filled his mouth, the sweet taste of the Coke long dissolved.

Miguel cleared his throat. "I think you should stop at one of these houses."

"Here?" Héctor said, trying to catch Miguel's face in the mirror. He could never be certain if his friend were earnest.

"Yes, any one of these."

"Are you crazy? These houses belong to gringos. We do not know anyone here," Héctor said. Héctor felt Lilia staring at him, and he knew she, too, judged Miguel's idea unwise.

Lilia turned in her seat to look at Miguel, as if to question his seriousness.

"You and I know that we do not know these people, but the lawman does not. If we stop at a house and proceed as if we belong there, we will look less suspicious than if we continue to drive the streets with no destination."

Héctor considered the idea. Miguel had a strange way of viewing his surroundings and of sizing up a situation. Héctor glanced into the mirror, holding out hope he would not see the white car behind him.

"You are right," he said, believing the policeman intended to follow them until he was given a reason not to do so. "We are sport for this man."

"Are you going to stop at a house?" Lilia's voice came high, and her words were quick, like those spoken by one afraid and cornered.

"Yes," Héctor said. He flipped on his turn signal, slowing before a driveway in which two dark-skinned children skipped ropes beside a red car.

He prayed, "God be with us," but did not realize he had spoken the words aloud until Lilia whispered beside him, "Amen."

23

LILIA TRIED to determine from her side mirror if the policeman continued down the street or if he followed them into the stranger's driveway, but she could not tell. "What do we do here?" she said.

Miguel answered, "Take this," handing Lilia two pieces of the hard candy he had purchased at the market. "These children will trust a woman more than a man."

Lilia took the candies from him and wondered what she would possibly say when the children's mother or father came outside and confronted her.

"If the lawman is watching, he will believe we are not strangers to these people. Smile and be gentle, and offer them the candy, and hug them when they take it from you."

"Okay," she said, afraid and unsure of the wisdom in this plan.

"Jesus," Héctor said, shaking his head. He turned off the car.

The children had stopped skipping rope and stood together, watching them. The younger child, a rail of a boy, stood with one hand on his hip, the other hand dangling his rope as if it were a dead snake. The girl, fat and dirty, looked to Lilia to be about seven years old. Lilia imagined the older child eating the younger child's servings along with her own at meals.

The three opened their doors and exited the car. "Hello," Miguel said, smiling and squatting to look the children in the eyes. "Do you speak Spanish?" he asked.

"Yeah," the boy answered, cocking his head.

"No, you don't," the girl said, looking at the boy. She then said words Lilia could not understand. Lilia imagined somewhere nearby a police car parked, its driver watching this interaction.

Miguel extended a hand toward the boy's rope. "I try?"

The boy giggled and the girl looked doubtful when her brother extended the rope to Miguel.

Miguel began to skip the rope, fumbling and tripping the second time the rope passed under his feet. The children laughed, and Miguel continued.

The girl jutted her hand toward Héctor, mumbling English words and clearly wanting Héctor to skip her rope.

"Do it," Miguel instructed. "And offer them the treats, Lilia," he whispered, still twirling the rope and jumping.

Lilia held out the candy to the children. They eyed her only a moment before the girl snatched both from Lilia's palm. When the boy protested, Miguel fished another couple of pieces from his pocket for the boy. The children opened the wrappers, popping the sweets into their mouths, and continued to giggle at the strange men hopping ropes before them.

Perhaps this plan of Miguel's worked. The police car had not pulled into the yard behind them, and, if the policeman were watching, the children appeared comfortable in their presence.

Lilia had never known Héctor to skip rope and the sight amused her. His heavy boots clopped against the pavement as if he were a lame cow. The children must have thought as much, and they doubled over in laughter. Miguel, after a few failed attempts, mastered the skill and began counting in Spanish his successful jumps.

The little girl knew the words and chanted the numbers with him.

"Hello?" a woman shouted to them in English from the door of the house. Dread filled Lilia. Perhaps this lady would call the police about the strangers in her yard.

Miguel handed his rope to the girl and stepped toward the woman, smiling and waving and greeting her with foreign words.

Lilia smiled, too, wishing she could speak to this woman in a familiar tongue, one that would signal a sameness between them instead of their obvious difference.

As Miguel spoke, Lilia and Héctor stood behind him, and the woman called the children to her. The boy trotted to her, but the girl stayed put until the mother shouted at her with a tone of voice any child knew meant "now."

As Miguel spoke, the woman nodded and pointed, as if she were giving directions.

"*Gracias*, thank you," he said, then mumbled to Lilia and Héctor to return to the car.

The three waved goodbye to the woman, who stood with hands on hips, and to the children, who waved back with great energy and happiness. The sun scorched everything here and, already now at mid-morning, sat high in the sky. Lilia guessed the afternoon heat would be unbearable in this border town.

"Is he gone?" Héctor said, his breathing loud as they slipped into their seats.

"Seems to be," Miguel said. "You need to work on your rope-jumping, man."

A wave of relief fell over Lilia and she smiled, eager to get back to the payphone, to get on with finding Alejandra.

"You are the only man I know who could pull that craziness off, Miguel. How do you know how to jump a rope?"

"Sisters," he said, offering the bag of pork skins across the seat to Lilia.

She took one from the bag and bit into the brown, salty rind. "What did you say to their mother?"

"I asked directions to the nearest church."

"Thank you for choosing church. Knowing you, I am surprised you did not ask the location of the nearest brothel or liquor store." Héctor smiled as he backed from the driveway. His smile comforted Lilia; she had not seen much of it in too long.

"Perhaps we are fortunate I do not know the English words for prostitutes and booze."

Héctor flipped on the radio and put the car in gear, heading the direction from which they had traveled earlier.

"So we return now to the market and wait at the phone?" Lilia asked, washing away the briny taste of the pork with her last swig of Coke.

"Goddamn this! He is back there. He waited. He is at the goddamned stop sign," Héctor shouted.

On impulse, Lilia turned in her seat, her legs sticking to the hot vinyl. The police car was easing from the grassy shoulder, as if he had been parked at the intersection, waiting.

Miguel said nothing, but his sigh was audible as he slumped.

Héctor's face twisted, and Lilia imagined his thoughts at this moment, his lifelong dream teetering on a sharp edge. And Alejandra. How would Lilia ever find Alejandra if she and Héctor were returned to Mexico and Matilde had crossed into America with their baby?

"He has turned on his lights, Miguel. He wants me to stop."

"Well, then stop the damned car, Héctor," Miguel said, his voice defeated, garbled through his hands that covered his face.

A pounding in Lilia's chest rose into her ears. "Dear God," she said, seizing Héctor's shoulder, studying his profile for assurance this situation was not the nightmare it seemed.

He slowed the car to a stop without looking at Lilia, without saying a word. The hot air that had been blowing through the windows had not seemed comfortable or cooling until the car stopped and the wind ceased. Then the inside of the car became stifling, a space void of air suitable for breathing, and in the wind's place spread thick, lifeless heat and dread so real Lilia believed she could smell it among them.

"He is coming," Héctor said, watching the lawman's approach in the side mirror.

Suddenly the full volume of the Coke filled Lilia's bladder, and she feared she could not contain this urge to urinate. She squeezed her legs together as Héctor's open window darkened with the policeman's arrival. His girth was that of three men and rimmed his belt as if it were on the brink of spilling, like a wave about to topple.

"*Habla Englais?*" he said with a thick American accent, stooping to reveal his round face, half covered by the lenses of very dark sunglasses.

"Yes, a little," Héctor said.

"All three, out. Now," he said.

Héctor repeated the demand to Lilia in Spanish, and as she scrambled to obey, a trickle of her urine escaped. She stepped from the car, squeezing her legs and bottom as hard as she could, like her life and Alejandra's depended on her self control.

24

WHEN THE LAWMAN asked Héctor for his driver's license, Héctor believed he was minutes away from his return to Oaxaca.

"Yes. I have license," he said, withdrawing the plastic card from his wallet.

"South Carolina?" The lawman asked, studying Héctor's identification. He pointed at the car. "This your vehicle?"

Héctor did not know the word *vehicle* but understood the question. "No, is the car of my friend. He is in South Carolina." Héctor spoke the truth, and as long as he spoke the truth, he felt a sense of security. Any moment he would be asked a question that would force him to lie, and he would not trust himself then. He was not a skilled liar, and surely his eyes, a twitch of his lips, the cock of his chin, something would reveal the truth.

The lawman turned to Miguel. "Where's your identification?"

Héctor understood then the depth of their troubles. The lawman would have no need to see the license of anyone but the driver unless he suspected them all of a crime. When Miguel handed the man his identification, the officer studied it only a moment before he asked Lilia for her license. Panic seized Héctor. When he had greeted her at the border house, Lilia had said her new identity was Beatriz, but she did not mention the quality of her identification. Her expression now was one of despair and confusion.

She slipped the card from her back pocket and extended it to the officer.

He held the three licenses in his thick fingers as if he were playing a card game and sizing up the hand he had been dealt, glancing repeatedly from each card to the three faces in the car.

"You Isadore?" he said, looking at Héctor.

"Yes, is me."

"How long you been in this country, Isadore?"

"Is a few months. Some months," Héctor said.

"You live in South Carolina?"

"Is my job in South Carolina. These is my friends," he said, pointing at Lilia and Miguel, and realizing with horror that he had no idea of the information on Lilia's card other than her name.

"What about you? You work in South Carolina, too?"

"Yes," Miguel said.

"What brings you three to Texas?" the lawman asked, adjusting his glasses.

"Is trip for to visit my cousin in Houston. We are now to travel back to South Carolina."

"Houston?"

"Yes, is very nice, Houston," Héctor said.

"How about you? You live in South Carolina, too?" The lawman spoke to Lilia.

Héctor said to her in Spanish, "He asks if you are from South Carolina, Beatriz."

"No," she said.

"Her English is not so good," Héctor said, trying to smile.

"Says here she's from Colorado."

"I do not know her very long. I think she lived there one time but now no is living there." Héctor shrugged and looked at Miguel.

"I see," the officer said, looking at his watch. He looked in either direction down the street. Héctor followed the lawman's gaze. "I'm going to have to fine you," the lawman said.

"What is *fine*? I do not know this word, mister," Héctor said, worried his poor English would make him suspicious to the officer.

"How much money do you have on your body and in this car?"

Nearly all the money Héctor owned was in his wallet. He had brought it to Brownsville in case Lilia's coyote demanded payment from him.

Héctor opened the wallet to reveal six hundred dollars. "Is all my money. Is no money in the car."

The man took the money, folded it, and slipped the wad into his front shirt pocket. His shirt was tight across his broad chest. He was like a sausage stuffed in its casing. Again the lawman looked up and down the road. "What about you? I'll need to fine you, too."

Miguel pulled his pockets inside out to reveal several coins and a crumpled one-dollar bill. "Is all my money here."

The lawman took the bill but not the coins. "She have any money?" he said, pointing at Lilia.

Héctor said in Spanish, "Beatriz, he wants any money you have."

She shook her head, pulling two coins from her pocket.

"I must search your vehicle now for anything you may have hidden here."

Héctor stepped away from the car and watched the man search beneath the floor mats, under the seats, and inside the ashtray.

"Okay, now. You three need to get on back to South Carolina," the policeman said, pulling his meaty hand from under the driver's seat. The officer wore a shiny, golden wristwatch, perhaps purchased with fines collected from drivers such as Héctor.

Héctor nodded. "Yes, okay, thank you," he said when the officer returned the three licenses to him. "We go to South Carolina now."

The officer nodded once, said nothing more, then turned and walked to his car. His form brought to mind characters in comic books Héctor had seen in Oaxaca City: broad-shouldered, fleshy, and almost laughable. The lawman walked with bowed legs, as if his days were spent on horseback, though, clearly, they were not. His rounded belly revealed a physical softness, and Héctor hated that his presence demanded their obedience. Regardless of the man's doughy gut, he had the power to fine them, though Héctor could not be sure what their crime had been.

The three returned to their car, and, with a signal from the policeman, pulled onto the street and continued in the direction they had been heading.

"I told him we would return to South Carolina now," Héctor said.

"But we cannot," Lilia said, her voice rising. "We have to wait here for Alejandra."

"Of course we do," Miguel said.

"I know that," Héctor said, annoyed with their stating of the obvious. "But we cannot return to the payphone at that market. If he catches us again, we will be in jail or in Mexico before nightfall."

"But Rosa's call?" Lilia said.

"We cannot receive her call there. I will phone Armando again from a different place. We will find a bigger, busier market where we will not stand out."

Neither Miguel nor Lilia responded, and their silence emboldened Héctor. They listened to him. Alejandra was his child, by God. Only he could straighten out the ridiculous web in which her mother had snared her.

He checked his speed to be certain he drove under the limit. The gas gauge registered a full tank. "I have no money to get us home. I do not know how the hell we will buy gas. Jesus help us," he said.

"We have no problems with that," Miguel said.

"No?" Héctor said. "Did that fat goat leave us any money?"

"Have a pork skin," Miguel said, extending the crumpled bag across the front seat.

Héctor said nothing. He had lost all spirit for Miguel's games.

"Go on," Miguel urged.

When Héctor knocked the bag from Miguel's fingers, a few of the brown rinds and crumbs fell to the seat between Héctor and Lilia, and along with them lay a one hundred dollar bill.

Lilia picked up the money and held it for Héctor to see.

"I shoved that into the bottom of the bag when he stopped us. I know enough not to trust a policeman."

"Well," Héctor said, the money only a vague relief when so many other worries pressed down on him. "We are lucky that swollen goat did not swallow the bag and the bill in one greasy gulp."

Lilia swept the crumbs and the curls of pork skins into the bag and returned it and the bill to Miguel.

"You should keep this in case your trick is necessary again," she said.

They drove for fifteen minutes before they found a large shopping center. The lot sprawled before them, and Héctor imagined the whole of his village fitting there. So many cars and shopping carts and people in one vicinity. And the store itself: what could a business sell that would require such space? Five pay telephones lined the wall near the entrance.

"I will call Armando," Héctor said, parking between two large American vehicles that dwarfed his small car. Watching the many people coming and going, he said, "This place is better than before anyway." He wanted to sound confident, but he was unsure of anything.

25

LILIA KNEW she should hurry through the store to get back to the men outside, but the size and the bright lights dazzled her, and she felt like a child witnessing something strange and magical for the first time. She moved among men and women, small children, and babies in strollers, and, somehow, none of them seemed to notice the grandness of their surroundings. Lilia felt as if she had been cast back into her childhood, to a place and time when the adults found fascination in nothing, when Lilia could spend long minutes studying the sheen of a rooster's feather in the rain or the way the fish flapping on the pier turned from blue and green and silvery-pink to a dull gray within moments of being caught and hauled from their watery home.

She made her way to the women's toilets in the back of the store. Even there the clean, white walls, the floor, and the sinks sparkled and smelled of cleaning fluid, so unlike the facilities in her village—dark and smelling of damp earth.

When she had relieved herself, she washed her hands, holding her fingers to her nose to inhale the fresh scent of the soap. She counted four toilets, each concealed in its own stall. She wanted to linger here in this large fancy place but exited quickly when an old woman entered.

Outside, Héctor stood in the booth, waiting on Rosa's call.

"Any news?" she said.

"Armando ran to Rosa's house to give her this number and to explain our change in location, but I cannot know how long the process will take," he said. "Go on back to the car."

Héctor's anger had shifted to rigid authority. He no longer looked at her with disgust but with an expression of dominance and self-reliance, as if he alone could control this situation. His eyes mirrored her own powerlessness, and she obeyed him and returned to the car.

Miguel lay in the back, his cap over his face.

"Everything okay?"

"Yes. Maybe Rosa will call back soon," she said, lying down in the front seat, closing her eyes.

"Sure. She will call," he said, like a dull parent pacifying a nervous child.

She could not be sure how long she slept then, but she awoke to the sound of the back door opening. Héctor and Miguel were trading places.

She sat up. The slant of the sun told her the hour was well into the afternoon. "No word?" she asked.

"Nothing."

"Are you hungry? I could get us something in that store," she said.

"No. We should not spend our money too easily, Lilia," he said.

"I suppose so. You should walk through that market even if you have nothing to purchase. A person could get lost in there."

"Are you trying to lose me, too, then?"

His words stung, though his tone was flat, with no hint of sarcasm. She stared at him, unsure what to say.

"We will get something to eat at nightfall," he said. "This place is open all hours, which is good. Plenty of activity to make us invisible."

She watched Miguel and hoped to see him answer Rosa's call. He sat alone on a bench between the phone and a multi-colored, child-size carousel. None of the patrons shuffling in and out of the store stopped to use the phones. Many of the people had a skin tone like hers and

Héctor's, but the crowd consisted equally of white and black faces as well. Never had Lilia seen such a mixture of people. Watching them would be an efficient way to learn about the habits and behaviors of norteamericanos.

THE CALL came on Lilia's shift. The men had gone into the store to use the toilets and to buy some supper. Lilia had only been sitting on the bench about five minutes when the telephone rang.

"Yes?" she said, jerking the phone from its cradle.

"Lilia?"

"Yes, yes! Rosa! This is Lilia. I am so glad this is you."

"This morning Armando gave me a different number, and I called you right away. Over and over again I called that number, but no one would answer. And Armando says Alejandra is missing. Is this true? Tell me what is happening there, Lilia."

"We had to move. Rosa, I need to find Emanuel. His uncle was my coyote, and only he can tell me where Alejandra may be."

Lilia was overcome then by the complexity of her situation. Summarizing for Rosa all that had occurred would be impossible, and even relaying the most important details seemed very difficult.

"I have not seen Emanuel since you left, Lilia."

"Rosa. Listen to me, please. Emanuel's uncle is the only person who knows the woman who has Alejandra. Without Carlos, I have no way to find my baby." Saying this aloud was like swallowing a sharp blade, and the pain of the truth brought fat tears to her eyes.

"Lilia, of course I will help you as best I can. I will find Emanuel, though I am sure he is back in the city now. Where are you?" Rosa said.

"We—Héctor and his friend Miguel and I—are in the town of Brownsville in Texas. But this is not where we are to live. Héctor has us a home in South Carolina, far from here. Soon we will need to travel there for Héctor's job and because we will run out of money."

"Oh, Lilia. What have you gotten yourself into?"

Of course Rosa would make her way to that, to judging Lilia and questioning her choice to cross. Rosa could not help herself, and perhaps she was right. Things were falling to pieces more quickly than Lilia could make sense of them.

"Do you have a pen and paper, Rosa? Take down a number. This is the telephone number for the house in South Carolina. We cannot wait indefinitely in this place, so if you contact Emanuel, have him call us at this number I am giving you. We will be there within a day or so."

Lilia gave Rosa the number and had her repeat it back to her. The men finished their business in the store and came to Lilia, listening to her end the conversation with Rosa.

"She is going to find Emanuel, but she thinks he is back in Oaxaca City. I gave her the number of the house in South Carolina and asked her to have Emanuel call us there. I know we cannot remain here."

"No, we need to head back to my job. Giving her Pablo's number in South Carolina was the right thing to do."

These were the kindest words Héctor had spoken to Lilia in hours.

"The shadows are growing long, Héctor. Will you take me back to the border house now, to see if Matilde has arrived with Alejandra?"

"Let us go," he said, motioning toward the car.

Lilia could have never directed them back to the house of the coyote. She had lost all sense of direction the moment the policeman had begun following them that morning. But Héctor was wise and observant, and with only one wrong turn, they returned to the border house as the day's last light faded to gray.

"I'll do this by myself. He will not harm me, but I am not sure about his patience with men, with you," she said in a whisper, which she realized was unnecessary and ridiculous.

"Are you sure?" Héctor said.

"Yes," Lilia said, but her body betrayed her words with shakiness and prickly dampness.

She walked to the door telling herself she walked toward Alejandra, that the baby girl lay resting just beyond those darkened windows, and though her legs felt no more solid than bathwater, she knocked hard on the door and waited, determined.

He cracked the door just wide enough for Lilia to see an eye, dark and serious, and she knew at once that this man was the same coyote she had left that morning. When he saw her he looked past her into the yard, at the car.

Satisfied with what he saw, the coyote nodded and let her in, shutting and locking the door before either of them spoke.

A man in a yellow straw hat sat in a chair reading a newspaper. He glanced quickly at Lilia, then returned to his reading as if Lilia's arrival held little interest for him.

"I do not have your child," the coyote said.

Lilia felt herself sinking, her legs losing whatever fiber they once held. She leaned against the door, determined to make sense of this, to make the world believable again.

"Where? What . . . ?" She could not form a solid thought worth speaking.

"I do not know where they are. I have not spoken to the woman who has your baby," he said.

"Why is she late? Where could she be?"

"Girl, I cannot answer that any more than you can," he said.

He wore a blue shirt now. What color had he worn this morning? She could not remember the shirt, just the blood. The blood had spattered his dark shirt. Now she recalled the shirt. It had been green or brown, some dark color on which the blood appeared not red, but just dark, darker than the color of the fabric it dotted.

"Do you hear me?" he said, stepping toward her. "I do not think the woman is coming."

Lilia wanted to slap him, to hurt him.

"Why do you say this?"

"Matilde is always on time, always reliable. I believe something has happened to delay her indefinitely."

"What does that mean, *delay her indefinitely*?" Lilia searched his expressionless eyes for answers they would not reveal.

"Something has happened," he said.

The man in the chair flipped to a new page in the newspaper, as if the world were not falling apart around them. Her life had become like a strong, eye-burning onion, and each hour another layer peeled away from its core. And what was her core? What was inside that would not give way? Nothing. Soon the last bit of her being would dissolve, leaving an ugly, wretched pulp where she had once been.

"Like what?" she said, forcing herself to ask a question she knew would offer unbearable answers.

He glared at her.

"I must know. I cannot abandon her. Please help me find my child."

She felt the final scraps of herself slipping, melting into mush. Perhaps she was indeed becoming Beatriz, just a ghost of a person who once was.

When Lilia was certain he would help no more, the coyote said, "Maybe she was caught. If she confessed the baby was not hers and did not offer up your name, the American authorities will put the baby in foster care. That scenario is not bad. At least your child will be housed and fed."

"What else?" she asked, determined.

"You do not want to know the bad possibilities, girl. Bad things happen. You saw as much here last night. I told you, what we do is not a game."

Her belly churned at the mention of the murder she had witnessed only a day earlier, and in that moment, she looked away from him, unable to stomach the eyes of a killer.

"You know about the bad. They could have been attacked; Matilde could be dead and your baby sold. They could have been in a car accident. A thousand scenarios, girl. A thousand scenarios. I have nothing more to offer you."

"Do you have a phone number for her? A way to contact her?" Lilia's mind skipped like a stone across water; her time with this man, her only solid link to Matilde, was slipping.

"Of course. And I have called her."

When Lilia looked at him he must have sensed her doubt. "Yes, I have called her several times at her home in Mexico, which is the only number I have for her. The line rings and rings. She is not there, girl."

"May I have the number?"

Again he glared at her, and she wondered if she had crossed some uncrossable line.

This time she did not lower her eyes, but stared back at him, waiting.

"Shit, girl, take the goddamned number. It won't do you any good."

He stepped to the kitchen and returned with a pad of paper on which he scrawled a telephone number he said belonged to Matilde.

"I have to get my child back. I will leave with you a phone number for me in South Carolina. And if she arrives or you hear from Matilde, have her call this number for me. Please."

He stared at her.

She took the pad and pen from him and wrote Pablo's telephone number from memory. Handing it to him, she said, "Thank you."

As she followed him to the door, he said, "This is a rough path you have chosen to travel. Turning back is not possible now, girl."

She nodded but could think of nothing to say, and so she walked out the door. She heard the lock click behind her, felt herself pause while her eyes adjusted to the blackness that had descended. She understood she was splintering. She was no longer one Lilia, but something breaking into immeasurable, unrecognizable parts.

Everywhere the insects and frogs had tuned up. Why did they chirrup and croak and click like that? Were the sounds she heard the creatures of the night or parts of herself, flying away from her, crashing into trees and rocks and everything? Her body stood there, but the rest of her, the invisible part, looked on from a distance, no longer connected to the girl Héctor surely watched from the car. She hoped if she listened hard enough she could hear the familiar, guttural voice of an iguana, could hear its call to her, and she would be transported to a place where the pieces of herself linked together again properly.

What sounds did Alejandra hear this evening? Could she somehow hear her mother shattering? Could she feel the shards? Had they pierced her yet?

As Lilia's eyes focused, quick white pricks of light teased her, and she marveled that one could catch tiny glimpses of oneself breaking off and floating away like that. Or were they just fireflies? In Puerto Isadore their lights sparked more green than these.

Once, only once, in her childhood had Lilia seen the phenomenon along a riverbank. She was alone, collecting reeds to make baskets, when she witnessed a swarm of fireflies, lighting in unison, a natural synchronization. Together the insects hovered briefly, then moved down the bank, disappearing into the jungle. She thought then that if their lights were sound they would be a glorious choir.

But these American fireflies' glints held no rhythm, no togetherness. They flickered like a thousand bone-white moons or lost souls, each seeking its own orbit, disconnected from the others.

The distance to the car where Héctor sat seemed a million miles, and Lilia felt incapable of the journey, of the conversation that lay ahead.

26

"HELLO?"

"*Hola, señora*? I am Héctor here."

"Hey, Héctor. How are you? Everything all right?"

"Is okay, *señora*. I am in Texas. I am coming to the work in South Carolina in tomorrow. I know these new trees are coming soon there, and I will be at the work. Is okay?"

"Sure, sure. That's fine. We'll need you back soon for those trees. Have you met your wife and child yet?"

"Is not so good news. Is very bad because my wife she is here, but my child is no here. Is not no where."

"Héctor, I do not understand. Where is your child?"

"Is difficult, Mrs. Elizabeth. I am very sad. We do not understand these either. The man who is help for my wife to get here say maybe my baby, she is, how you say? Lose?"

"Lost?"

"Yes, *sí*, is lost my baby."

"Is your wife okay?"

"She is no injury or nothing, she is cry and very sad at these. We no understand what to do. We drive in these night to South Carolina no with our baby."

"Well, Héctor. I don't know what to say."

"No, *señora*, I know neither. The man say to my wife is maybe my baby is in the foster care in the Texas state. You know what is these?"

"Foster care?"

"*Sí.* The man he say is maybe the place is where my baby is lose."

"Who is this man, Héctor? Does he speak English? Would you like me to call him?"

"No, is no good, Mrs. Elizabeth, because is no good for these man to speak to American."

"Could the baby have been kidnapped, Héctor?"

"What is you say kidnapped?"

"Stolen. Sold. Taken for money by bad people. I am afraid some people steal babies to sell on the black market."

"They sell these babies, Mrs. Elizabeth? For the money? No! What is you say these black market?"

"Illegal sale of babies. But surely this hasn't happened to your child, Héctor!"

"No."

"What can I do for you, Héctor?"

"Mrs. Elizabeth, what is the foster care?"

"It's a place for children who need homes when their parents cannot care for them."

"Oh. Is no okay for my baby because I have home. No need for the foster care."

"How could they have gotten your child into foster care, Héctor?"

"I do not know these, Mrs. Elizabeth. The man he say maybe the police or the Immigration man stop the woman with my baby and take my baby from these woman. These woman is no where. Maybe is in Mexico now. Maybe these woman is dead."

"I can call the foster care people in Texas for you. Do you know what city in Texas?"

"Brownsville, Mrs. Elizabeth."

"Well, I cannot call them at this hour, I'm sure. I'll see what I can do. I will call in the morning, okay, Héctor? Tomorrow I will call the foster care people in Brownsville, Texas."

"Is good news. Thank you. These night we drive in the car to the South Carolina. In the night of tomorrow we see you and Lucas."

"You be careful, Héctor. Hey, Héctor? Hold on. Lucas wants to speak to you."

"Is okay. I speak. *Adiós*, Mrs. Elizabeth."

"Goodbye. *Adiós*."

"Hey, Héctor. You coming on back here soon?"

"*Hola*, Lucas. Yes, I say these to Mrs. Elizabeth."

"Well, I have something I want to run by you. To ask you. A deal for you."

"What is these thing?"

"You know, I have several big shipments, truckloads of trees coming."

"*Sí*, Lucas. Is the magnolia trees?"

"That's right. I want to offer you, sell you, forty trees. They're little. Baby trees, see? They'll cover a tenth of an acre. Will cost you two hundred eighty dollars. You understand me?"

"*Sí*, yes, I think so, you is selling to me some of these trees?"

"Just a small portion of what I got coming. But if you stick with me, with the farm, those trees will grow. You can sell them whenever you want."

"*Sí*."

"In three years you can sell the trees for five thousand or more dollars. And if you hold off selling for five years, you can sell them for twelve thousand dollars."

"*Sí*, is so much money!"

"You understand, Héctor? I'll take the payment of two hundred dollars a little bit each week, not much at a time. I want you committed, to stay with the farm for a long time. Do you understand me?"

"Yes, Lucas. Is very much nice thing. Is… how you say… these is too much like a papa to his boy, no? Is very much nice. Thank you, Lucas. Very much. Is good thing for my family."

"Be safe coming back. We'll see you soon."

"*Adiós*, Lucas. Thank you. Thank you very much."

27

"WAKE UP, Lilia. You must see this."

Héctor slowed to a stop and killed the engine, leaving the headlights burning.

"What's wrong?" Lilia said, jerking awake.

"Nothing is wrong," he whispered, glancing at Miguel asleep in the backseat. "Come with me."

He opened his door, and she followed him out of the driver's side. They were beside the river.

"We are in South Carolina, almost to our new home. That is Edisto Island across the water there." He pointed to the far bank, lush and thickly wooded, but invisible on this moonless night.

"Why are we stopping here?"

"Look down the waterway. Do you see that boat?" he said, pointing.

"No," she said.

Of course, he could not make out even the silhouette of the boat either, but its red and green running lights moved steadily toward the bridge, like ghosts hovering above the inky vastness that was the tide.

As he spoke, the warning lights on the bridge's guardrails flashed red, and the bars descended. "You have never seen anything like this, Lilia." Héctor had spoken little to her in the many hours since they had left Texas. He had had nothing to say. But this place was going to be their new homeland, and he wanted Lilia to understand her surroundings.

"What is it?" she said.

"This bridge is too low for the boat to pass underneath. In a moment the bridge will come apart in its center and raise up for the vessel to sail through."

She stared at him in disbelief.

"I knew you would not believe me," he said, frustrated that she continued to doubt him on even the simplest statements.

They watched the river and the boat's slow approach. He could hear the diesel engine's hum now, could smell it on the marshy air. Just as another car arrived and parked behind them, the bridge began to open. The flat road beyond the guardrails raised up before them, illuminated in the car's headlights like something in a strange dream. Lilia gasped as it reached higher and higher until the pavement stood perpendicular to the road on which they stood. Within minutes, the boat passed through, appearing on the other side, and the road sank back to its original place.

"How strange," she said. "The thing is like a giant mouth. Watching it open like that is almost frightening."

"I love to watch the bridge open," he said.

She stared at the boat's lights, shrinking in the growing distance.

"How odd to see the yellow lines of the highway rise and tower over us like that. Is driving an automobile across such a bridge safe?"

The guardrails began to rise, and Héctor and Lilia slipped back into the car. "You know I'd never put anyone in my family in danger." He meant this, but he also could not resist the opportunity to point out their differences in judgment regarding their family's well-being.

Lilia said nothing but watched the boat's retreating lights.

When she shivered, Héctor said, "Are you cold?"

"No," she said. "But I feel peculiar near this bridge. I do not like it, Héctor."

"You'll get used to it," he said.

"I wonder if anyone has ever jumped from it. When you stopped, and I realized we were at a bridge, I wondered if you wanted to toss me from it."

That thought had not occurred to him, of course, but somehow, he found pleasure in her comprehension of the depth of his anger and despair. "As I said, Lilia, I would never put anyone in my family in danger. Stop such talk."

He knew this woman beside him. Knew her better than perhaps anyone else ever had, and he had proven himself to her time after time. And still, she questioned him. Dishonored him. Everything he did he did for her and for their future, and yet she chose to make decisions on her own, and with devastating effects. Perhaps all women were this way. And if so, why would God instill such a fault in such alluring and necessary creatures?

All the way across America, from Brownsville to Edisto Island, Héctor had offered silent prayers to God. He prayed them over and over like a sacred chant rolling on a loop through his head.

God return Alejandra to us safely. God restore Lilia's loyalty and obedience. God heal our union. God heal our family. Please. Please. Please.

He had not told Lilia or Miguel what Elizabeth had said about black market babies, nor had he told them he was praying as he drove; perhaps they took his silence to be anger and bitterness, and if they had, they would not have been incorrect.

Miguel stirred. "Where are we?"

"We are close. Another five minutes," Héctor said.

Miguel had slept since their last break for gas, somewhere in the state of Georgia. Then, as at each stop along their journey, Lilia had called the number for Matilde, and each time her ring went unanswered.

Héctor turned onto the narrow, unlined road that lead to Pablo's place. "We are staying in a house on this lane, Lilia."

Moonlight shot through a gap in the clouds, filtering through the tunnel of giant oaks surrounding them, illuminating a pasture beyond the trees.

Lilia said, "What is that?"

"Cows," Miguel said.

"They look so large. Perhaps the moonlight makes them appear so," she said.

"No. They are big damn cows, biggest I have ever seen, even in daylight," Miguel said. He was always eager to talk, to answer Lilia's questions, and that suited Héctor. He had little conversation in himself now.

"Here we are," Miguel said, as Héctor turned into Pablo's driveway. Pablo and Maritza sat in chairs by the front door, each with a can of beer between their knees. They stood as Héctor parked the car. He had called them this morning, told them about Alejandra, offering the slimmest of details. He closed his eyes and arched his shoulders, stretching. An unexpected stiffness stabbed him between his shoulder blades, and he winced, surprised at his tight muscles. He was in no mood for company, but returning here, to the closest place he had to a home, felt comfortable.

"You're back. Long drive, I know," Pablo said, slapping Héctor on the back. "You need a beer?"

"I do," Héctor said, motioning toward his wife. "This is Lilia."

Pablo took her hand in his. "Welcome."

Héctor feared Pablo and Maritza would mistake Lilia's weak smile for a lack of gratitude. But when Maritza embraced her and said, "Hello, Lilia, welcome," then added, more softly, "I am sorry for your troubles," he knew she understood his wife's posture.

Lilia looked so puny and strange that Héctor felt a momentary urge to shout, "This is not the wife I went to Texas to retrieve! She has become someone I do not know."

Miguel handed Héctor and Lilia each a cold can. "Good to be out of that car," he said, popping the top on his beer. "No more trips to Texas for me for a long while."

Clouds like paste cloaked the moon, and Héctor could barely see the others' faces now. Pablo resumed his seat by the door, and Maritza lead Lilia into the house.

"Sit and drink with me," Pablo said to the men. "Any more word on your baby, Héctor?"

"Nothing," Héctor said, standing. "I have been sitting for goddamned days. My ass cannot sit any more."

Miguel tossed his empty can into a trash barrel and rose to get another beer. The barrel, already brimming with debris, held the can a moment before spilling it to the ground. Pablo rose, grabbing a newspaper from beneath his chair. Wadding and jamming it into the barrel along with Miguel's empty can, he struck a match and lit the paper.

Staring into the blaze, Pablo said, "What are you going to do, Héctor?"

"We have the number for the woman who Lilia left Alejandra with, and we have been calling her, but her phone rings and rings. Mrs. Elizabeth is going to call the foster care people in Texas. Lilia's coyote says maybe if the woman Matilde was captured and returned to Mexico, Immigration would keep my baby."

Pablo shook his head, taking the fresh can of beer Miguel extended to him.

Héctor liked sitting beside the burning trash barrel. "If the woman was caught, and the foster care people have Alejandra, Elizabeth will speak to them. But if she does find Alejandra, I wonder if the officials will return her to us. If we locate her, I wonder if they will force Lilia and me and our child back to Mexico." Héctor's words flowed like water down a hill, fast and unrestrained. "So many damned *ifs*," he said. An ashy patch of newsprint, thin as gauze, broke free from the barrel and drifted up into the night sky. Héctor watched it as if the thing mattered. When the glowing edge faded to nothingness, Héctor's eyes were drawn to the barrel again, waiting on another ember to flutter and waft, weightless as a scent, into the night.

"Lucas and Elizabeth are good Americans. I think they will do right by you, but the others, the officials, are not compassionate sorts. They'll screw your ass, Héctor," Pablo said.

"I should go see Lucas, now. What time is it?"

"Nearly nine," Pablo said, studying his watch in the firelight.

"I want to let them know I am back, and Lilia needs to meet them." He crushed his empty can and dropped it into the dwindling flames, sending a host of tiny, glowing moons toward the heavens. He did not watch them rise, but imagined as he turned that their light would not last past the treetops.

28

AS LILIA and Héctor climbed into Héctor's truck, Pablo said, "Héctor, I hear the Americans are helping you get a house. My friends live there now, but they are moving out soon to work on a farm on Wadmalaw Island. Congratulations."

"Thanks, Pablo. For everything. I know Maritza will be glad to have us out of her hair," he said, starting the engine.

"These are good people you have befriended here," Lilia said.

"Pablo is a good man. So is my boss. And his wife is funny. She laughs from her belly. You need to meet them, and I need to speak to her about helping us recover Alejandra."

Lilia smelled the cool air rushing through Héctor's open window and imagined the trees growing in the darkened fields they passed. Because they traveled at night, she took in her surroundings with the eyes of the blind, intrigued with wonder at the scents and sounds and feel of the place she would now live. So different than Puerto Isadore.

When she thought of home, she envisioned the village in bright colors: the blues of the ocean, the reds, oranges, and yellows of fruits and vegetables for sale in the markets, the greens of the dense foliage that rapped in the breeze against the courtyard walls, creamy white and green bundles of garlic the village boys sold from the backs of their fathers' trucks, the pink bougainvillea blossoms, profuse and hanging like gems adorning every dwelling. But in this place all she knew was shadow and darkness.

When they pulled up to the house of Héctor's boss, Lilia said, "They are wealthy, these people?"

"Yes, compared to anyone we knew in Puerto Isadore, but not so much here. They seem to worry about money, about holding on to their land. This place belonged to their ancestors, and the gringo fears he could lose it."

She said, "Why would they lose the land of their ancestors?"

Héctor shrugged, opening his door. "Vegetable farming is not so good. Pablo's boss is selling his farm because he cannot pay his debts. But my boss is wise, I think. He has switched his farm to trees. The land developers buy the trees, and so my job should be secure. The land of the gringo will be fine."

As they walked up to the Americans' house, Lilia, encouraged by any conversation with her husband, said, "I cannot understand how this works, this business of land and ownership of the land."

Héctor said nothing, and she again felt his coldness toward her.

The woman who opened the door to them broke into a wide grin when she saw them.

She said words Lilia could not understand.

"Hello," Lilia said.

Héctor and the woman spoke, and his ability to communicate in English amazed Lilia.

The woman ushered them onto a porch where a man sat opening shellfish with a knife, tossing the empty shells into a red bucket and dropping the meat into a bowl on the table. The man struggled to stand, and Lilia saw he had but one leg. He, too, spoke foreign words, and Héctor said to Lilia, "He says to you, 'Welcome to America.'"

The man pried open a large shell with his blade and extended the dull gray insides to Héctor. As her husband plopped the slick creature into his mouth, the man began opening another shell. He offered one to

Lilia, though she understood not the words but the gesture of his hands and his facial expression.

She shook her head and said, "No. Thank you, no." When the man smiled, comprehending her English, Lilia exhaled and relaxed the slightest bit.

The woman said words to Héctor that Lilia imagined were the usual pleasantries one said upon welcoming a visitor into one's home. How awkward to stand among others, including one's own husband, and their conversation be completely indecipherable. Lilia busied herself with her ragged thumbnail while the three beside her talked.

As they spoke, Héctor's words grew louder, his tone urgent and his hands animated, and Lilia knew he spoke now of Alejandra and Matilde. The woman nodded, a v forming between her concerned eyes, which remained fixed on Héctor's face. The man continued to open his shell-fish. After many moments of Héctor's uninterrupted explanation, the woman fetched a pencil and paper and jotted a few notes.

"Thank you," Héctor said.

She smiled and said something like "Is okay" and "Is no problem," and Lilia believed this woman would help her get Alejandra back. Héctor must have believed as much, too, because his smile stretched as wide as it had the moment he first saw Lilia at the border house, a smile of genuine relief.

The woman touched Lilia's shoulder and motioned for her to follow. Lilia glanced at Héctor, but he and the man spoke and paid no mind to the women, so she followed the señora. They went into a small room with books and framed photographs lining shelves. The woman pulled an album from the bookshelf and sat, tapping the seat beside her for Lilia. The house smelled of bacon and coffee and cigarettes, though none of those were evident, and a comfortable air filled the place.

The woman opened the album, revealing photos of children and family. She pointed to a faded picture of four people. The woman in the photograph wore her hair in a puff upon her head in a style Lilia had never before seen. She held a small girl in a yellow dress. Beside the woman stood a man, tan with broad shoulders. He held his hand on the white-haired head of a boy, maybe five years of age. The boy held a ball and grinned widely, revealing toothless gums.

"Me," the woman said, tapping a finger on the pretty woman in the photograph.

"*Sí?*" Lilia said, wishing she could say more, such as how lovely the woman looked or how handsome the man beside her appeared.

"My family," the woman said, and Lilia understood. The woman's brow wrinkled.

Then she said slowly, as if unsure of the words, "My *nino* and my *nina*."

The woman's kind face relaxed when Lilia smiled and nodded in comprehension. Lilia studied the picture again and wondered at the ages of the boy and girl now. She guessed the woman beside her to have aged at least thirty years since the picture had been taken.

Together they looked through the pages of the book, and Lilia watched the white-haired boy grow into a young man similar in stature to his father's figure in the first picture. The girl grew, too. Eventually wearing eyeglasses and metal braces on her teeth. In each picture the man had both legs, and Lilia wondered when he'd lost one. The señora seemed to like Lilia, patiently trying to explain photos, though her Spanish was minimal. She could not know how much Lilia appreciated the intimate gesture of sharing private, family photos. The effort was the woman's way of welcoming her into their world when words could not be exchanged.

When they reached the end of the book, Lilia said, "*Gracias.*" The women joined the men on the porch where they appeared to talk of business.

The señora spoke to Héctor, and he translated for Lilia. "She says a church nearby offers classes to teach English as a second language. She asks if you'd like her to sign you up. The classes are on Saturdays."

Lilia wondered if she had a choice since these people employed her husband, but she should learn the language, and so she said to Héctor, "Okay, I suppose." She turned to the señora and nodded, saying, "*Sí, gracias.*"

On their ride home, Héctor said to Lilia, "Lucas says he will employ you. He says five days a week, he can use you. The orders for trees have picked up some because they are advertising their farm in special tree magazines. And also the large shipment of new trees must be planted."

"This is good," she said. "What did she say about Alejandra, about the foster care people in Texas?"

"She will call them tomorrow. If they have Alejandra, she will find her. If they have her, the señora says they will want to reunite her with us because that is their job. Our prayers should be that they indeed have her, Lilia."

"I must believe they have her. And if they do, we will get her back, won't we?"

"Yes, if they do, we will get her back. Mrs. Elizabeth says this is so."

Until she was forced to consider otherwise, Lilia would believe Alejandra rested comfortably in a loving home in Texas, the home of a nice lady like Elizabeth who wanted to find the baby's parents.

Neither spoke for several minutes before Lilia said, "Did you like the taste of the animal from that shell?"

"Yes. You would like it, too. They taste of the sea, salty and fresh."

"Their color is like sick flesh, dull and lifeless. They are not white and flaky like a fish," she said.

To her surprise, he laughed. "No, but I would not eat a flaky oyster, Lilia. Sometimes, you are ridiculous."

When Lilia and Héctor returned to Pablo's house, they found the place quiet and dark, save for a small lamp that burned beside a pallet of blankets and pillows that had been arranged on the floor of the main room for them.

These people wanted to give Héctor and her privacy. Though grateful for their empathy, Lilia dreaded bedtime with Héctor.

She had never hidden anything from him. What Carlos had done to her would remain with Lilia always, and she prayed that in time the sharp edge of the pain would dull. Already, with the disappearance of her daughter, Lilia's thoughts seldom shifted to Carlos, her mind frenzied with worry and longing for Alejandra.

Héctor stood at the kitchen sink, washing his face and hands beneath a slim florescent light. "Mrs. Elizabeth will help us," he said, not looking at Lilia.

She wondered if he were speaking to her, or, more likely, if he spoke to himself, reassuring his own mind.

Lilia had heard people speak of broken hearts, but she had never before known the term to be literal. Her chest ached as if her heart were being pulled apart, as if Alejandra, Héctor, and Carlos had each seized a piece of that fragile muscle that beat in her breast, leaving little to sustain her.

"You always manage to surround yourself with people who embrace you. Elizabeth will help us because she and her husband know they are fortunate to have you here. They will help because of you, Héctor."

He slipped off his shirt and sat on the blanket, the lamp throwing odd shadows toward the ceiling.

"Come here," he said, looking up at her, his face neither angry nor weary, but almost expressionless.

Though she could not hide such a sorrowful experience from Héctor, revealing the truth about Carlos felt impossibly difficult. The grief would torture Héctor, or perhaps he would see the offense as justice for Lilia's part in losing Alejandra. Yet, Héctor must know. She could not be intimate with him until he knew what had happened to her.

She stepped toward him, and Héctor took her hand. She wished she could be more like him, thoroughly good and confident about life; but with Carlos, she had spent time with the devil and so she had changed. He had forever damaged her.

Héctor tugged her hand.

"Héctor, I have to tell you everything about my crossing. Some painful things," she said, holding both his hands now.

"You are here with me in America now, Lilia, and that is a dream I have held for years. When Alejandra is back with us, maybe we will both see all that has happened as being worth the chances we have taken."

Lilia knelt beside him. With one hand he stroked the remnants of her hair, and Lilia wondered if he resented what she had done, the long locks she had cut.

"The man who brought me to the border," she began.

Héctor said, "Emanuel's uncle?"

"I can barely stomach recalling him, but you must know." She looked into his face, half concealed by shadow.

Héctor's eye narrowed, his cheek tightened with the clenching of his teeth, and he glared at her. "Tell me what you mean."

She knelt before him. "He violated me. In a way that cannot be taken back." She dropped her gaze and whispered, "I fear you will not want me, what I am now."

Héctor brought his hands to his temples. "What are you saying? This man is that goddamned Emanuel's uncle? Could Emanuel not know his uncle was a monster?"

"I do not know, Héctor. I am so sorry."

"Sorry? Dear God, Lilia."

She placed her hand on his arm, but he jerked away.

"If I ever encounter Emanuel or his uncle, I swear to you now, I will kill them. I will kill each of them myself. Do you understand me?" His hands gripped her shoulders, and he shook her.

"Yes," she said, afraid he would wake the others.

"Damn this, Lilia. You do not think. You are like old Crucita, stubborn and unwilling to listen to anyone. I warned you; coyotes play a high stakes game."

He spoke the truth; had she listened to Héctor she'd still be in their village with Alejandra, still longing for him as he longed for her, and, eventually, he'd send the money for their crossing. His anger was justified, and she remained before him to bear the brunt.

"You are right," she whispered. "I was foolish to allow Emanuel to fund my crossing, but I wanted to get to you."

"My wife must have faith in me. I always told you I'd bring you and Alejandra here. Did you doubt that?"

"No, I never doubted you. Crucita died, and her passing changed something in me. I lost my reason for staying."

He glared at her with eyes she did not know, and she feared he would strike her. "So, before Crucita died you were undecided about leaving. Is that what you are saying? That you were uncertain if you'd come when I sent for you?"

"No, Héctor. I always knew I'd be reunited with you. But when Crucita passed, my connection to that place diminished. You know her thoughts. She did not approve of our leaving our village, our country."

"This is not the point, Lilia! You knew I would send for you, but you chose to take the future into your own hands, as if crossing were as simple as plucking a low-hanging fruit from a tree. You have no respect for the plans we made, for me."

"Héctor, you know that is not true. Crucita's passing was not the only motivation. Rosa couldn't understand me. She never accepted your reasons for crossing, or my desire to join you. I had nothing left to keep me in Puerto Isadore." Lilia wanted more than anything for him to pull her to him, but he did not.

"You defied me, Lilia. You put yourself and our baby at risk. You got yourself screwed over and you lost our child."

"I never intended to disrespect you, and I love that baby girl more than I have ever loved anything before," she said, wiping tears that blinded her.

He looked as if he could spit in her face, as if she were a diseased mongrel at his feet. When he walked out the door, she followed him, desperate to make amends.

"I traveled here for you," she said.

He stood beside the trash barrel, now dark, its last ember fading hours earlier.

"Lilia, I do not question your motives; I question your judgment," he said.

"Please forgive me, Héctor. Please love me." She began to cry harder, suddenly more afraid of him than when he had struck her. If he said no, she would have nowhere to go.

"God damn this all, Lilia!" He kicked the barrel hard with the side of his bare foot, as if he were booting a ball.

"I am so sorry. I would rather die than hurt Alejandra or you," she said.

"Is that so? Well, Lilia, you are killing me. We have no guarantee the girl is in foster care. Do you know people kidnap babies? Do you know they sell them for money, like pets, like someone taking in animals they find in the street then making a profit from them?"

"What are you saying?"

"I speak the truth, Lilia. Mrs. Elizabeth tells me this. People steal children to sell them."

"This cannot be so, Héctor. How can such evil people exist?" She stared at him, pleading. How foolish she was, how stupid, and naïve. She had been rash in her actions, just as Rosa had warned, with crushing results. "Can this really be true?"

Héctor sat down bent-kneed on the ground, his back against a large tree that loomed above them, and rested his head in his arms. She sat beside him, careful not to touch him. They sat in silence so long she wondered if he had fallen asleep.

How had their lives come to this place, to this point? She had been tempted by Emanuel. She had allowed his hands to grip her legs, his lips to kiss hers. She had trusted him to arrange her crossing, allowed him into her life in a way that destroyed it and the lives of those bound to her. Had she believed, even briefly, during her separation from Héctor that perhaps Emanuel could fulfill her, could make her happy? Or had she never taken him seriously? She could not be sure now, but whatever her reasoning had been, her interactions with him had tainted everything that mattered to her.

Too afraid to wake Héctor, she was considering leaving him there outside when he said, "Nothing is turning out here as I planned."

"Maybe everything will yet," she said.

"I have dreamed of coming here for as long as I can remember. Of bringing my family here." His head remained in his arms, resting on his knees, and his words were muffled.

"I know," she said.

"No, you cannot know, Lilia. You have not wanted anything the way I have wanted this." His words fell soft now and held no trace of anger. They were the words of the defeated.

"Rosa showed me a letter from my father's brother," she said, wanting him to know everything.

"Your father's brother?"

Lilia recounted her father's last days to Héctor, and how the image haunted her.

Before Matilde and Carlos, before the coyote had stabbed the man's neck at the border house, Lilia had been haunted by visions of her unknown father's shriveled body, prone beneath a creosote bush. When she tried to conjure an image of his face, full and handsome, her mind's eye saw only death, lips like dried fish, and an eyeless visage of human leather stretched over bone.

"He did what he did for my mother, and in the doing he lost everything," she said.

Héctor lifted his face, turning to her, his expression hidden in the darkness.

"So maybe you do understand me then. Your father and I are one in the same. We each took a risk for a woman we believed deserved the world."

"And I took a risk for the one I love, too," she said.

Héctor stood. "We should get to bed. The night is late."

She rose and followed him into the still house. Lilia eased, fully clothed, beneath the thin blankets that awaited her and Héctor on the floor. Héctor slipped in beside her.

They did not touch or speak again until the morning.

29

HÉCTOR LISTENED in the darkness, pretending to be asleep, knowing what he would hear, but hoping that this time the sounds would be different. Maybe this morning, when Lilia rose, clutching her thin, yellow robe, and slipped beyond the front door to dial Matilde's number as she had done each of the seven mornings since her arrival, Matilde would answer and say, yes, yes, of course, baby Alejandra is with me, healthy and content.

Within moments, Lilia opened the door, the large oak tree beyond the house silhouetted in the gray light of early dawn. Each morning when Lilia stepped back inside, defeated and increasingly desperate, her phone call unanswered, compassion flickered in Héctor and the urge to hold his wife welled within him. He had yet to pull her close to him, to feel her body the way he used to, the way he had once longed to do. He had urges, but his bitterness over Alejandra's loss dulled them.

Silently, his wife sat in a straight-backed wooden chair and rested her head in her hands. Héctor watched her from the floor where he lay motionless beneath blankets that covered part of his head.

He knew Lilia considered the news this week from Elizabeth, that the foster care people in Texas had no baby fitting Alejandra's description. They would keep Alejandra's information, would keep looking for her.

The woman in Texas was kind and explained that they had hundreds of babies from undocumented aliens; so yesterday, as they fertilized the latest shipment of magnolias, Elizabeth had encouraged Héctor and Lilia to keep faith.

Lilia had proven to be a hard worker, toiling in the fields as a man would toil, helping Maritza with meals and cleaning each evening, and attending with great effort to her lessons from her first English class at the church. She labored to make their fragmented life work, but her effort did not numb Héctor's pain, nor, he believed, did it lessen her own.

Someone stirred in the bedroom Miguel shared with the children, and Lilia stood, wiping her eyes, and stepped to the kitchen to prepare a pot of coffee for them all. Héctor shifted to watch her.

Maritza, Pablo, and Miguel had not mentioned Alejandra since the day after Lilia had arrived, understanding that if Héctor and Lilia had news, they would offer it. Miguel emerged from the bedroom, nodded to Lilia as he passed the kitchen, then stepped outside for his morning cigarette.

Each morning proceeded like this, and just as he could not see Lilia dial Matilde's number, neither could Héctor see Miguel smoke; but sounds and smells drift, and so Héctor understood the practices of each early riser in the small house they shared.

Good Miguel, always trying to lighten everything, to cheer everyone, but how could anyone lighten the loss of a child? Héctor smelled Miguel's smoke and the coffee brewing and thought how close to perfect this could all be. Perhaps Alejandra lived, but not knowing tortured him worse than if her death were certain.

Héctor yawned and stretched, pretending to have just awakened. "Coffee smells good," he said to Lilia.

"It is almost ready," she said, barely glancing in his direction.

If he had anything more to say to her, perhaps he would do so, but nothing more came to him. Often he wished he could extend pleasantries to his wife, simple kindnesses to encourage her, but those had run dry in Brownsville.

He joined Miguel outside.

"Another shipment of the magnolia trees arrives today, no?" Miguel said.

"We're already up to our asses in those trees, but yes, another truck comes from Florida today," Héctor said.

"Well, good for the gringos," Miguel said, tossing his cigarette into the trash barrel.

"Yes, it is good. Lucas should make some decent money, and maybe he will toss some our way." Héctor shivered. "This is the coolest air I have felt," he said.

Pablo, a mug of steaming coffee gripped between both hands, stepped outside and smiled. He shoved one hand into his pocket. "You wait a few more months. Then the weather really turns cold."

Héctor rubbed his hands together. "I need some of that coffee." He could not think about tomorrow, much less about months from now, because his thoughts would turn to Alejandra, and where she would be then, and where the future would carry them all.

Inside, he found Lilia and Maritza talking in the kitchen beside the stove. They ceased their conversation when they saw him, and Lilia poured Héctor a cup from the pot.

When the phone rang, Maritza moved to answer it, and Héctor said, "We need to get going. Another big shipment of trees arrives this morning."

"Lilia, you have a telephone call," Maritza said.

Instead of stepping to take the phone, Lilia froze, staring at Héctor, looking as if she expected him to tell her what to do or who could be on the other end of the line. Maritza jutted the phone between them, and Lilia took it from her.

"Hello?"

Maritza went to tend to the children, now awake and calling to her.

Héctor watched his wife, studying her words, her body, for any indication of release, of joyful news.

"Yes, I am glad Rosa found you," she said.

The caller was Emanuel.

Lilia moved to the chair and sat, then said, "I must contact your uncle. Did Rosa explain this to you?"

Héctor looked at her, wanting to see her face, but she sat hunched, her eyes closed, her shoulders almost to her knees.

Emanuel had better come through.

"What?" she said. "How can this be?" At that moment she looked at Héctor, and the fear in her eyes drew him to her, and he squatted beside her.

"Are you sure? Is this the truth, Emanuel? Do you understand what is happening? God, no, please," she began to weep, and Héctor tried to imagine what news brought the tears.

"When?" she said, almost moaning, clumsily wiping her cheeks. "Okay," she said, ending the conversation. She set the phone on the small table beside the chair and slouched like a plant far too long without water.

"Tell me," Héctor said.

"Carlos is dead," she said, raising her eyes to him. "Carlos is dead, Héctor."

"What happened to that bastard?" Héctor said, still squatting beside her.

"Outside of Mexico City. He was on his way back to Oaxaca when he was killed in some sort of accident."

She did not need to say that their already too few options to get to Matilde and Alejandra were dwindling. Héctor understood and read as much in Lilia's face. If Matilde never answered her telephone, the only possible way of recovering Alejandra, if she were alive, would be through the foster care people in Texas, if they had her. Elizabeth was working on this, making calls, but the process moved so slowly. Héctor wondered if this great America sprawled too big to keep track of itself, like a beast with too many limbs.

Héctor had hated Carlos like he had never hated anyone before, yet the monster's death came as the gravest of blows.

30

LILIA STOOD in darkness beneath the large oak, staring up at a sliver of pale moon dangling like an ornament between branches. The slightest breeze rattled the leaves, and she clinched her robe tight at her neck. Sometimes, she believed she would more likely reach up and pluck the moon from the bones of that tree than hold Alejandra again. Like a prayer, she pushed the buttons on the portable phone, the same way she had begun each day in her new home. Always she counted the rings, and forced herself to hang up after nineteen. Why nineteen? She did not know exactly, but twenty seemed too many. What if Matilde were sleeping, or working in her yard, or feeding her snakes? Sometimes nineteen rings would be necessary for one to get to the phone, and so she counted.

But something happened.

No rings sounded, just a strange beep. Lilia hung up. How could she have called the wrong number? Again she dialed the numbers, but slower this time, watching her fingers. Her heart beat fast, and her hands shook, but why? This was nothing, no news, but this was different, and she had had nothing different in many days.

Again, no rings and a recording began. She listened this time. The number had been disconnected. No one lived at this number; this was no residence. But what about the snakes? They lived there, and so did the flowers in the pots. She had been there. The place was real; the smell of it had made her ill. She hung up and dialed again, slower now, concentrating. She watched as her finger selected the numbers, saying each aloud as she dialed.

Again, the recording.

She squeezed the phone, banging it against her thigh, hating it, hating the mechanical voice that answered her calls. This cannot be, she told herself and dialed once more, determined she had made mistakes in her previous attempts.

When Héctor appeared in the doorway, she realized her noise had attracted him, perhaps even awakened him, but she did not care. He had no use for her anymore anyway; because he wore his disgust so plainly she had decided days ago not to look at him even on the rare occasions they spoke.

When the recording came on again, she threw the phone at the tree.

Héctor said nothing until he had picked up the pieces. "What is it, Lilia?"

She shook her head. "Every morning I call Matilde's number," she said, staring at the chipped place on the tree where the phone had smashed against it.

"I know," he said.

"She never answers, but I try because I imagine she is away and will be home soon. I have had to believe that, you know?"

"Yes," he said.

"This morning, her line is dead. It won't ring. The phone tells me I am calling a place that does not exist." She wanted to take the phone from him so that she could throw it again, harder this time, smashing it to bits so small it could never hurt her again.

Héctor exhaled. What could he say? Their lives were tumbling like the dominoes the old, drunk men played on the pier in their village: one painful event leading to another and another and another until nothing was left standing.

Lilia's hope was the last viable part of her; without it she would be lifeless. She could not abandon her hope, her belief that goodness would prevail, that her prayers were more than pointless thoughts drifting up to nothingness.

"Maybe the authorities in Texas will call soon," Héctor said.

She looked at him then, but his eyes were on the fading slip of moon. He had said nothing encouraging to her in many days, and she wondered if he intended to comfort her now with his words.

Two weeks had passed since Elizabeth mailed their only photo of Alejandra—a small picture from Héctor's wallet taken the week before he'd left Oaxaca—to the foster care people in Texas. Lilia had brought no pictures of her own from Mexico; the Rio Grande would have likely destroyed them in her crossing anyway.

The knots in Lilia's breasts had softened; her milk was drying up. Though the pain had gone she mourned the loss of her milk, for when Alejandra arrived Lilia would be unable to nurse her.

She wanted to ask Héctor what they would do if the lady in Texas never called, but she could not. The day had begun to break, but it brought no warmth, and she shivered beneath her thin clothes.

"I hope they call soon," he said. She realized then he spoke not to comfort her, but himself.

Héctor had not wanted to part with the one picture he had, and so he had driven into Charleston to have a copy made. He had sent the original to the woman in Texas because it was a clearer likeness. Lilia wished he had made two copies so that she could have one, too, but he had not. Late each night she slipped the photo from his wallet and peeked at it several quiet moments behind the closed bathroom door before drying her eyes and easing it back in place and herself back beneath the blankets beside Héctor.

She realized now that everything depended on that original picture, now sitting some place in Texas. Of course, Héctor knew this, too. No words were necessary between them. She walked past him into the house to dress for her day in the fields. What else was she to do?

31

THE COOL MORNING had given way to a milder midday, and Héctor removed his flannel shirt, tossing it onto the seat beside him when he reached the end of a row. He drove the truck slowly up and down between the newly planted "Moon Jewels" while Lilia tossed measured scoops of granular fertilizer from the back of the truck down to the base of each small tree they passed. Occasionally she would tap on the glass and he would stop and wait for her to fix whatever she needed to fix before she would tap the glass again, and he would resume his slow, straight line through the field.

In the distance Miguel stooped at the base of a magnolia and repaired a leak in an irrigation line. The last of the new magnolias had been in the ground a week now. With the intense heat of the summer behind them, the trees would have a few months to grow and establish new roots before the weather turned cold. Lucas explained this to Héctor weeks earlier when the first of the trees arrived.

Héctor liked spending his days outside. He felt grateful that Lucas and Elizabeth were fair and treated him with kindness. He supposed he should also feel fortunate to have his wife there, working alongside him. He knew he should feel as much, but he did not. Instead he went numbly through the motions of his tasks so that he could get to the end of the day, to darkness, to sleep.

He watched Lilia in the mirror leaning over the side of the truck tossing fertilizer just where it needed to be. Her hair had begun to grow, and its beautiful natural color showed at the roots. The dye had faded some, and he would be glad when that physical reminder of her crossing was completely gone.

Lilia tapped on the window. "I am out of fertilizer."

"It is time to break for lunch anyway," he said.

Their conversations now were for practical purposes only, nothing was spoken between them for pleasure or to pass the time. Everything was geared toward work, for survival: *I need more fertilizer. Here is your lunch. Where is the knife? The mower needs fuel.* Never: *You look pretty today. This meal is delicious. Come closer to me. How do you feel? Can I help you?*

Something in him would not let him speak such words to his wife. Part of him wanted to hate her, and, he imagined, she had come to feel the same about him.

He drove to Miguel, who sat in wet grass, straddling a length of black rubber tubing.

"Ready to have lunch?" Héctor said through his open window.

"Good timing," Miguel said. "I cannot do another thing here without a new irrigation head. This one is beyond repair. During lunch may I take your truck to the supply store?"

"Yes, sure. Get in."

Miguel jumped into the bed of the truck, and Héctor turned toward the paved road.

He saw Miguel and Lilia talking, though he could not make out their words. Lilia rarely smiled, and always her shoulders slumped. Héctor supposed if she did not have Miguel and Maritza pulling her into conversations, Lilia would spend her days entirely without speaking.

Sometimes Héctor wished he could forget about Alejandra, could pretend she had never existed. He would imagine he had sent for Lilia, his childless wife, in Puerto Isadore to come to him in America, and that she had crossed safely, and soon they would create their American family with many babies. Sometimes, he would lie awake at night and pray to God to make this so.

When they arrived at the house, Héctor left the truck running for Miguel.

As he and Lilia walked inside for their lunch, he shouted at Miguel, "Take it easy on my truck."

Of course, he kidded Miguel because he had his own vehicle and Miguel did not. He noticed then how dirty the truck was and acknowledged to himself how poorly he had maintained the gift from Lucas since Lilia's arrival, since his world had fractured.

Lilia washed her hands in the kitchen sink before going to the refrigerator to fetch food for their lunch. She heated a skillet and tossed chilies and strips of chicken in hot grease. The smell made Héctor's stomach rumble; no one cooked as well as Lilia, though he had not told her this in a long while. Instead he poured them each a can of cola over ice and sat at the kitchen table. Maritza and her children were away, and the house was unusually still.

"Shit!" Lilia shouted.

He turned to see her sucking on her hand. "I burned myself on the pan."

"Are you okay?" he said.

"Yes," she said, though her expression revealed the truth.

Héctor went to the freezer for an ice cube, which he then folded into a paper towel.

"Here," he said.

She took it from him, and when she pulled the hand from her mouth Héctor saw the burned flesh, already bright red and puffed.

"That looks bad," he said.

She said nothing, did not even wince, but pressed the cold towel to her skin by holding it between her injured hand and her stomach so that she could continue to cook with her free hand.

"Let me finish this," he said.

Without taking her eyes from the pan of meat and peppers she said, "No. I am almost finished."

He nodded. "All right."

She was the toughest, hardest-headed woman he would ever know; he was sure of this. He would never be able to protect her from anything, not even from herself. Somehow he realized then that his inability to do so had crippled him. He watched her there before the hot stove, the ice melting, wetting the front of her shirt, and he felt the distance between them crystallizing, becoming permanent.

She piled their meal onto two plates and set them on the table beside the sweaty glasses of cola.

"Thank you," he said.

She did not meet his glance, but mumbled, "No problem," before eating her food in silence.

Why was everything like this? He wanted to forgive her, to forget and move on, but he could not. And because he could not ever fully forgive Lilia for losing their child, for getting herself raped, he understood that this way of life, this here and now, would be the nature of their existence forever.

When he had finished his lunch, Héctor placed his plate in the kitchen sink and went to the bedroom Miguel shared with the children. He would lie down a few minutes until Miguel returned to take them to the fields.

When loud voices outside the house woke him, an hour had passed on the clock.

Before he could get his boots on, he heard Lilia screaming his name, calling him.

Instantly he thought of Alejandra, and he knew the authorities in Texas had found her dead. He ran from the room in his socks to find Lilia, Lucas, and Elizabeth in the yard beneath the oak.

"What?" he said in Spanish, surprised at his own volume and the panic in his voice.

"I do not know what they tell me," she said, motioning toward the Americans.

"Something has happened. Is it our baby? Ask them, Héctor!"

"What?" Héctor repeated, this time in English to Lucas.

"An accident. At the bridge," Lucas said. "I got a call it was you and

Lilia." He held his hand to his ear as if holding a telephone, but Héctor had understood the words.

"Miguel. Miguel is in my truck," Héctor said, squeezing his temples between his palms, unsure what this could mean.

"Someone saw a vehicle go into the water and recognized it as my old farm truck," Lucas said, heading toward his own pickup. "Come on."

Lilia and Héctor climbed into the back while Lucas and Elizabeth slammed the doors from the front. Héctor had never seen Lucas drive this fast, especially with passengers in the back, barely braking on curves. What could have gone wrong? He knew the answer, knew he had neglected the brakes, had not checked the fluid in weeks because he had not thought about it. He understood something terrible had happened to his friend.

32

THE LIGHTS of two ambulances and a fire truck flashed beside the splintered guard rail of the bridge.

Lucas pulled in close to the rescue vehicles. A small but growing crowd gawked at the edge of the waterway, some pointing at the mangled metal arm that had held the red-and-white striped crossbar, others staring down intently at the swirling gray-green water before them.

"Come on," Héctor said to Lilia as soon as the truck stopped rolling.

Lucas opened his door, surveying the scene a moment, before he muttered, "God damn." He had never looked so somber, and his expression worried Héctor.

Pablo waved to them from the roadside, and Héctor jogged toward him. Lilia followed close behind, exhaling her panic in something like a cry or moan with every step.

"This is bad," Pablo said to them, his brow creased above fearful eyes. "They fished him out before I got here, and they're working on him down there on that boat."

Good Miguel. Maybe he'd been speeding. But probably not. Why would he crash through a guard rail at a drawbridge? Héctor knew what had happened here without having to hear any eyewitness accounts.

Lilia stood close to him, her crossed arms pressed tight to her body as if she were cold, and Héctor recalled the only other time he had stood at this bridge with her. What had she said then? She had shivered that night, too, though the evening had been warm.

More people continued to arrive at the bridge. They didn't know Miguel. Their presence here was uncalled for.

"Miguel," Héctor mumbled to no one in particular, thinking about the brakes on the old white truck, the truck he had loaned Miguel, the truck Héctor was to maintain.

"Why must they gape like that?" he said to Pablo.

"Nothing draws a crowd like a tragedy, even in America," Pablo said, his voice almost a whisper.

When Lucas and Elizabeth reached them, Lucas said, "Tell me what you know, Pablo."

"A farm worker from off the island said the truck did not slow down. He knew the truck was Héctor's. He'd seen this truck before. He said he hoped the driver would jump out, you see? He said the truck crashed through the rails and disappeared over the edge of the road. He said he wanted to do something, but he could only shout out, you know?"

Guilt and anger surged in Héctor. His gut boiled, and he needed to hold fast to something solid. He had been so fastidious, so proud of that truck. This accident happened because of Héctor's negligence.

Pablo continued relaying more details, but Lucas seemed less interested now, as if he believed the remaining details were more for dramatic effect than pertinent information. He knew the gist of what had occurred here. As Pablo spoke, Lucas's eyes met Héctor's. In that moment, Héctor recognized genuine disappointment from his boss. Lucas's skin was so pale he looked as if he would collapse, and Héctor had to look away.

A flotilla of small boats had begun to form in the waterway just beyond the bridge.

Lilia began to sob now.

"The man said he ran to the bridge, wanting to help," Pablo continued. "But he lived his childhood in the city, you know, not by the sea, and so he never learned swimming. He watched the water moving below, you know, praying. Then he said right away some fishermen dove from their boat into the bubbles."

Lilia stared at him numbly, as if Pablo could give her answers to unanswerable questions. Héctor clenched his hands beneath his chin.

"The fishermen came up for a breath and dove down, then came up for breath. The man said to me these men finally came up with Miguel, and other boats came and more men helped, but the man said from where he stood at the bridge Miguel looked bad, like he was not breathing."

A firefighter walked passed them, and Lucas called to him. "I believe that vehicle belonged to me. You got any information?'

"They're bringing in the medivac," the man said. He looked so proud, like a stupid child who enjoyed this excitement.

Lucas nodded to the man, who never broke stride.

"What is medivac, Lucas?" Héctor said.

"A chopper," Lucas said, turning away, walking closer to the guardrail, watching.

"A what?" Héctor asked Pablo.

"A helicopter to get him to the hospital fast."

A dead man did not go to the hospital. This was good information.

Héctor walked closer to the bridge, staring into the waterway below, dreary and the color of ash. An overcast sky had replaced the crisp, blue skies from earlier in the week, and the world appeared to have been drained of color. Boats bobbed beneath the bridge, and in the distance, several more approached.

Was Miguel dead? How cold and gray that water looked, like lead. Where were Miguel's parents? Were they alive? Did they even know where their boy had been living?

Another large boat approached, and Elizabeth pointed at it and spoke soft words to Lucas. The sad look in her eyes put ice in Héctor's belly.

Lucas said to her, "I just don't know, Elizabeth."

"We'll keep praying," she said. "Keep hoping and praying."

She shook her head, covering her mouth with her hand as if the words in her mind were too sad to be spoken, and she had to hold them back with fingers pressed to lips.

Lilia and Pablo stood together at the edge of the riverbank near the other bystanders, watching, waiting. Héctor stood slightly apart from them, anticipating the worst while hanging onto the glimmer of other possibilities.

The stern of the fishing boat below them shifted direction, and, through the muddle of men leaning over, working onboard, Héctor made out Miguel's body sprawled across the bow. The men's heightened intensity in movement and conversation signaled that perhaps hope existed among them, though Héctor couldn't make out their words through the gusty wind.

When the medivac arrived, the pilot set it down at the boat landing, and officials pushed the crowd back. The boat came ashore, and men hoisted Miguel to a gurney. His blue work shirt clung to him oddly, saturated dark with saltwater, as the crew quickly slipped him into the helicopter. Just as suddenly as it had appeared on the horizon, the helicopter disappeared over the distant trees toward Charleston.

Bystanders swirled about the road, the adjacent boat ramp, the bridge, and in the boats on the river below. So many people! They did not know Miguel, at least most of them did not. Why did they insist on gathering here, on pointing and surmising in hushed tones, in running their open palms across the twisted metal, in fingering the splintered wood of the guardrail?

Héctor stared at the spot above the distant trees, imagining he could still see the helicopter, could still hear its roar. He knew Lilia stood beside him; he could sense her there, but he did not see her or hear her. Instead he thought of Miguel's blue shirt, of the strangers touching his friend high above the earth, the medical personnel flying with Miguel to the hospital. He suspected Miguel had never before flown, and a strange sadness sunk into him with the realization that Miguel was probably unconscious, missing his own first flight. Maybe Miguel would never have the opportunity to soar above the trees again.

A touch to Héctor's shoulder. Somehow he knew it was not Lilia. He turned to see her beside him, facing an American man, the one who had tapped him.

"Yes?" Héctor said, dazed and puzzled.

Even before the man spoke, Héctor saw Pablo behind the stranger, moving toward them, panic in his eyes, in his movements. And Héctor knew. Knew a lawman stood before him. The lawman had tapped his shoulder. Héctor stood naked, exposed, trapped. Before the man spoke, Héctor's skin prickled as if he, not Miguel, had plunged into the biting waterway below.

The man opened his palm, revealing a shiny badge, as he spoke. Pablo was beside them then.

The man spoke English words, slow and not unkind-sounding, but Héctor's legs weakened. He understood *Do you speak English?* and *documents* and *please*. The man was asking him for something, extending a hand, a serious expression on his tan, clean-shaven face.

Héctor reached for his wallet. "Yes," he mumbled, though the word came out in a whisper. As he passed his identification card to the man, Lilia exhaled a small whimper. Héctor turned to her, and in her eyes he saw his own fear, the unavoidable clouds darkening, moving over them, whirling. A devastating and imminent storm of disappointment looming toward them both.

The man spoke to Lilia now, his expression fixed, stern. "Do you have papers?"

She nodded, reaching into her pocket, inching closer to Héctor.

"You, too, please," he said to Pablo.

"Sure, yes," Pablo said, moving quickly to comply, though his face seemed small, as if worry had somehow compressed him.

The man fanned the IDs in his fingers, studying them only a moment before he said, "Follow me, please."

No belly fell over this man's belt, no sunglasses hid his blue eyes. He did not swagger or look around to assess his audience. Something about him rang genuine, honest. His purpose was business, and this frightened Héctor more than the pig-like caricature of a lawman back in Texas. This one demanded respect, compliance, because he was doing his job and nothing personal tainted his intent. Héctor could not despise him as he had the man in Brownsville, but he could fear him.

Pablo, Lilia, and he walked alongside the INS man in silence. He wore no uniform and anyone watching would not comprehend the scene. Lucas and Elizabeth stood near the bridge speaking to a woman they seemed to know. Héctor wanted to call to his boss, but what good would that do? Perhaps doing so would put Lucas at risk.

They approached a black, shiny SUV. The lawman opened the back and motioned, "Sit if you'd like." His tone never wavered, and his expression remained genuine and serious. Because he had not commanded them to sit, Héctor remained standing beside the car, so Lilia did as well.

Pablo said, "No, thank you. I am okay." A muscle bulged and tightened above Pablo's jaw, and he stared at the faded gray asphalt of the road. Héctor wanted Pablo to look at him, to meet his eye, to reassure him, but Pablo would not, and then the intensity of their situation fell square and certain upon Héctor.

The wind kicked up, and Lilia tucked a wayward strand of hair behind her ear. The length fell too short to stay in place, but too long not to flap in her eyes. Héctor wished she would stop trying to secure the hair, but she persisted, bringing her fingers to her face every few seconds. White-capped waves danced across the waterway now, making the river look far colder than it probably was, and Héctor shuddered.

The lawman placed a call on a radio, its long cord stretched from the front seat, so that he continued to stand beside his car as he spoke. He talked fast, reading information from each of their documents and studying their faces after he had spoken. Pablo continued to examine the pavement, as if its composition mattered to him.

As he waited for the person on the other end of the radio to respond, the lawman looked at Héctor. "Was he your friend?" He pointed toward the bridge.

"Yes. Very good friend," Héctor said without thinking, without hesitation.

The lawman sucked in his bottom lip and dipped his head in a single nod. "I'm sorry," he said.

Héctor tried to utter a response, but he could think of none, and his reply came as a heavy, girlish sigh. A barge arrived beside the bridge, a huge winch on its deck that would likely haul Héctor's truck from the river bottom.

"Come with me a moment please," the INS man said to Pablo.

The two walked several meters from the car and spoke while looking at Pablo's paperwork.

"He will be okay," Héctor muttered. "He has the right papers."

"But we do not," Lilia said.

"No, we do not," he said.

"What will happen, Héctor?"

He shook his head, staring at the churning whitecaps. His insides felt like lead, and he imagined if he were to split in two, his blood would flow onto the road beneath them as gray and cold as the river that had swallowed Miguel. He sucked in a mouthful of air and said, "They will send us back." He looked at her and repeated the truth. "We will be sent back."

33

LUCAS, ELIZABETH, PABLO, and a young man with orange hair and a fancy suit stood when the guard brought Héctor and Lilia to a small room adjacent to where they had been detained for three hours. The guard shut the door behind him as he left them there. The walls were painted a pale green, unnatural and somehow reminiscent of illness.

The Americans and Pablo stood to greet them. Elizabeth smiled, but her eyes betrayed her, and fresh guilt slammed Héctor.

She hugged Lilia, then Héctor, then turned away and wiped her eyes. Lucas shook Héctor's hand, nodded and winked at Lilia.

"Héctor, Lilia, this is Mr. Hoke LaRoche; he's a lawyer," Lucas said.

Héctor shook the man's hand though he did not know this word, *lawyer*. Small orange freckles dotted the man's pinkish-white skin. Before Héctor could ask the definition of *lawyer*, Pablo translated.

"He understands immigration issues. Lucas called him to see what he can do for you. We just met him here right before they brought you out, and he speaks Spanish."

"I'd like to ask you a few questions to assess how I can best help you," Mr. Hoke LaRoche said in decent Spanish.

"How is Miguel?" Héctor asked. The room in which they sat resembled the one in which he and Miguel had met, save for the ugly paint covering these cinderblocks. The immigration agent who had brought them here described this place as an old jailhouse, now used exclusively as temporary holding for illegal immigrants. The shack at the border had been more pleasant; at least there Héctor had had hope, a chance.

Pablo said, "He's banged up pretty bad, Héctor, but he's alive. He'll be okay."

Héctor wanted to ask more, to say something positive, but words failed him.

Mr. Hoke LaRoche said, "Do you, either of you, have family here?"

"No, no family here," Héctor said.

The lawyer wrote on a yellow pad of paper. "A brother or sister here?"

"No."

"Maybe a parent? Anyone at all related to you in this country?"

"No."

"Because if you could name a relative here, that person could petition for you to stay here."

"We have no relatives here," Héctor said, his agitation growing.

"Have you had any children born here?"

Lilia brought her hands to her face and began to sniffle.

"No," Héctor said.

"How did you enter this country?"

Héctor considered the question.

Mr. Hoke LaRoche continued, "I mean, did you enter with a work visa that has now expired?"

"No."

"Neither of you?"

"No."

The man scribbled more words on his yellow paper. "Did you arrive together?"

"No."

Lilia's sniffling continued, and Elizabeth passed her a wrinkled tissue from her purse.

"So you crossed separately, but neither of you have ever been here legally?"

"That's right."

Mr. Hoke LaRoche ran the long, pinkish fingers of his left hand through his orange hair and exhaled.

Héctor waited for the next question.

The lawyer tapped his pen on the table a few times then brought it to his parted lips, clicking the pen against his top teeth. "Okay," he said. "Not many options here for you. Of course, everyone is allowed due process. But this does not look promising, and if you're indeed deported you'll have to wait a period before you will be allowed to apply to reenter this country."

Elizabeth spoke. "How long?"

"They'll be deported by the U.S. government. When the U.S. deports illegal immigrants, those immigrants have quite a long wait before they may apply to reenter, to *legally* re-enter this country. If they were to have gone back on their own, before being captured, their wait would be less."

"*Would have gone back on their own*, you say?" Lucas said, his voice rising. "That makes no sense."

"Sometimes the government will get wind of an illegal and will send him a letter telling him to leave or suffer government deportation. If he leaves upon receiving that warning, his wait time to apply to reenter the country legally decreases. But if he waits to be deported, the government penalizes him by increasing his wait time in his country of origin."

"How long?" Elizabeth asked.

"Maybe just several years since this is their first and only offense."

No one spoke for a full minute.

"You asked about relatives. Why?" Elizabeth said.

"Well, ma'am, if they had a close relative here, that relative could petition for them to remain here."

"Can no one else petition for them to stay?"

"Perhaps, sometimes, yes."

"Well, Lucas and I are very fond of them. Let us petition for them to stay." Her eyes showed hope, and Héctor wanted to reach for her hand then, as a boy comforts his mother after his foolish behavior has harmed her.

The lawyer answered her in fast-flowing English, then turned to Héctor and explained in Spanish.

"Employers may petition the government, but the hitch is the illegal immigrants must be in their country of origin at the time of the petition."

"So they have to go back before we can fight for them to stay?" Lucas said.

"Yes, basically. And the fee you pay is about two thousand dollars per immigrant."

Héctor stood, pushing his chair away from the table. He looked down at Lilia, who returned his gaze with soft, wet eyes. He looked across the table at Pablo, Lucas, and Elizabeth. No one spoke for several seconds.

"Okay," Héctor said, a tremor in his voice.

They stared at him, their brows creased, their expressions grave. Only the pale young lawyer's forehead remained smooth, tight, his gray eyes waiting to wrap this up.

"I feel thankful for you all, but I am a problem here. These is very difficult." A tear welled in Héctor's right eye, and he angrily brushed it away with his palm. "We have nothing to do but to return to Mexico so in future day we come again to America."

"I am sorry," Mr. Hoke Laroche said. He closed his pad of yellow paper and packed it and his pen in a brown leather bag he pulled from beneath his chair. He zipped the bag and stood. Lilia folded her arms on the table and lowered her head to them. Elizabeth shook her head, over and over, as if in disbelief.

"When will they have to go?" Pablo asked the lawyer.

"I don't know, could be any day, could be a couple weeks. Deportation times vary."

Lucas cleared his throat as if preparing to speak but brought the back of his hand to his mouth instead and rubbed hard against his lips.

"Is essohbee. Goddamn, heh, gringo?" Héctor said, no smile within him to encourage Lucas.

"It is that, Héctor. One hell of an S.O.B."

THE GUARDS kept the men and women in separate sections of the old jail. The men spoke little while they awaited the fates soon to befall them. Their expressions ranged from fearful to weary, but all wore the slumped posture of disenchantment. Though the men's section of the jail appeared full, barely a sound rose from the group save for feet shuffling and an occasional cough.

Perhaps Lilia sat alone somewhere beyond the thick, gray concrete confining Héctor. Or maybe she sat with other women, women from deep in Mexico, who, like Lilia, had lost babies to kidnappers or the foster care system, or other mysterious circumstances. The Lilia he had left behind in Mexico would be frightened here in this place. But so much had happened to his wife since then that she seemed capable only of sadness now. Her sorrow outweighed all other emotions.

After Héctor ate a breakfast of cold eggs and bread, a guard retrieved him. "Visitors," he said. *"Amigos."*

Lucas and Elizabeth waited in the small green room. A female guard delivered Lilia to the room the same time Héctor arrived. When the guards left, Elizabeth slipped Lilia blueberry muffins from her purse, and Lucas passed Héctor an envelope.

"What is these?" Héctor asked.

"Something for you."

Héctor opened the envelope and counted five one hundred dollar bills. "What is these?" he repeated.

Elizabeth waved Héctor's question off with a flick of her wrist. "For you both," she said.

"Just something to get you back here again. You'll always have a job here. You have a field of magnolias that belongs to you, and they belong to you no matter your country of origin." He said *country of origin* in a high, silly voice and shook his head to and fro as he spoke.

Lilia smiled a broken smile, and her response spurred him on.

"Coun-try of or-i-gin!" Lucas shouted, bobbing his head like a hen in search of cracked corn in the dust.

Now Elizabeth and Héctor smiled, too, because none of them had smiled in too long.

"Country of origin, my ass," Lucas said. "You take that and put it away some place safe, and when you are able, you contact us and let us know you're coming back. Your trees and your job will be here."

"Thank you, Lucas," Héctor said.

"We'll come see you again tomorrow," Elizabeth said. "They aren't telling us when you'll be leaving, or how you'll be leaving. These people don't like to tell us anything. But we'll come visit you every morning," she said.

They stayed only ten minutes, and Héctor was glad to see them go. They had little else to say across from one another in the ugly, little room, and he knew the place made Lucas uncomfortable. Like Héctor, Lucas preferred the outdoors, the company of his trees to the bricks and mortar of buildings.

But the next day at sunrise armed guards loaded the immigrants onto a bus. So many guards and so many big, black guns!

Héctor considered saying to Lilia as they walked to their seats, "This is how it was when I crossed. Many men and many guns, only those men were the criminals, those were the ones who broke these guys' laws." Instead he said nothing and moved steadily to the seat to which he was directed. To his surprise, Lilia was allowed to sit beside him, but they—like the rest of the deportees—said nothing until the bus began to move.

Then, as the whirr of the bus's tires rose to a high-pitched hum, Lilia said, "I hope Lucas and Elizabeth do not make the trip to the jail this morning."

"I am sure they will, and by the time they do we will be rolling through the state of Georgia."

She turned and watched the passing landscape through a grimy window. A man across the aisle from them sobbed silently into his cupped hands, and Héctor imagined the man to be leaving behind family and friends.

"Attention. Listen." A guard spoke Spanish into a microphone at the front of the bus.

"Hey! Shut up! This is not a vacation!" he shouted, and all passengers stared at him. "You are being deported from the U.S. for the crime of illegal immigration. You will be boarding a flight to Texas in about twenty minutes. From Texas you'll board buses that will get you back into Mexico. This will be a pleasant enough experience if you each cooperate, move quickly, and do as you're told once we get to the airport."

The man handed the microphone to the bus driver then continued to stand, watching the passengers, their meager belongings clutched to their bellies. He surveyed them as if they would pounce and incite mayhem any moment.

"The airport!" Lilia said, her expression a mixture of fear and amazement.

Lilia's experience with airplanes, like Héctor's, was limited to those that sliced white scars into the high, blue sky above their village, bringing tourists to the fancy resort towns up or down the coast from Puerta Isadore. She had never seen one up close; certainly she had never flown. Still, the chasm stretching between Héctor and his wife reached so deep and so wide that he could barely acknowledge this strange development, and he stared straight ahead at the man with the gun attached to his shoulder.

34

SHE LOOKED at him, but he did not face her. "Héctor, did you hear him? They are putting us on an airplane?"

"Yes. I guess Miguel is not the only one experiencing his first flight this week."

She and Héctor had hardly spoken in months, shifting like ghosts among the trees in the fields and the rooms in their home. So his response now surprised her.

"Are you scared? Of flying, I mean," she whispered.

"No. Are you?"

"A little," she said.

"Don't worry. I'm sure the plane is safe. They wouldn't want us to crash. Then they'd be stuck with us longer, trying to figure out what to do with our bodies."

"With Beatriz Gómez and Isadore Ramírez," she said.

"They have already died," he said. His face was old and tired. "Do you wonder if coming here was the right thing to do?" he asked.

She was not sure why now, at this moment, after all the weeks of indifference, he chose to speak to her, to ask such a question. "That does not matter, really, does it?" she said.

She knew he thought of Miguel, of Carlos, of Matilde, and, of course, always, of Alejandra. Had it just been yesterday that Elizabeth had called the woman in Texas? Yes, only yesterday the nice woman with the foster care people had said, "No, still we have no child like the girl in your photo, but we will keep the photo. We will let you know. We will let you know."

Lilia had wanted to say to Elizabeth, "When? When will she let us know? I can wait if I just know a time, a date. Tell her, ask her. When will she let us know?" But Lilia knew the woman may never let them know anything, especially now.

"I suppose not, but I want to know what you think," he said.

"I do not know, Héctor. The answer seems easy. Of course, I should say yes, that coming here was foolish. We have lost so much."

He turned from her, a hand covering his face.

"I think," she began, lifting her hand, wanting to touch him, though she had not touched him in many weeks. The gesture seemed foreign and she dropped her hands to her lap. "I think if we had not come here, we would be in Puerto Isadore wishing we had. You remember how you were then, your dreams."

"I have been so angry at you, Lilia. I have thought some days that I hated you. Do you know this?" He turned to her now, tears streaking his face.

They sat almost motionless, looking into each other's eyes for a full minute, and she realized then how much time had passed since they had last looked, really looked, at one another.

"You have a right to hate me," she said.

He shook his head. "I could have killed Miguel," he said. "Good Miguel. Funny, harmless, good Miguel. My first friend in this country. Had the fishermen not saved him, he would have drowned. And even so, he is injured, broken and cut and lying in a hospital bed because of me."

"How can you say this, Héctor? You were eating lunch with me. What happened at the bridge was an accident."

"The accident occurred because of the truck, Lilia. My truck. I have been so goddamned angry at you, hating you, so eaten up with misery that I could not even take care of a simple truck. I should have kept up the brakes. Until you got here, I prided myself on maintaining that truck. Until everything in my world shattered, I did right. But I let myself fill up with bitterness, with such resentment, that no room was left for responsibility, for doing what I should do."

Again he looked away from her, as if he could not bear to look at her or to have her look at him.

She knew he spoke the truth, and what could she say? His anger had altered him just as her grief had changed her. Lilia placed her hand on his thigh, just above his knee, a touch so light she was not sure he felt her there until he clasped her fingers tight in his.

She looked out at the buildings passing by and wondered if she would ever be in this place again.

She wished to name this tension between them, to acknowledge their equal contributions to the staggering pain and loss. If she could give voice to the damage their actions had caused, perhaps she would force Héctor to recognize their shared blame, their mutual responsibility for the state of their lives now.

"Our past is painful," she began, faltering, unsure how to proceed without sounding accusatory.

"Not all of it," he said, gazing at the guard up front who now chatted with the driver.

"No, much of our past is my fondest memory, but we are where we are now because of choices we each made, both together and as individuals."

He turned to her with an expression she could not read, and she expected his wrath to surge. When he neither spoke nor pulled his hand from hers, she said, "I could crumble like a clod of dust, Héctor. I feel you could, too."

He nodded. "I don't want that to happen," he said. "To either of us."

"My soul is cracked. I need you to help me maintain what's left," she said.

"The choices we made, we made with the best intentions. I have to believe that, or I will be no good for you, Lilia, and no good to myself. I cannot dwell on the pain anymore or I will, as you say, crumble like a dry clod."

"She may still be near the border, Héctor." That notion, ever-present in Lilia's mind, became words without Lilia making a conscious decision to speak them, and she feared the reality of her continued hopefulness sounded childish.

"I will never abandon hope," he said.

"You have always held fast to your hopes, your dreams. That is your way," she said.

Neither spoke until the bus reached the airport, stopping on the runway beside an enormous plane.

"I have always wanted to fly," he said. "I am glad you will be beside me when I do."

She could think of no response but held fast to his hand as they rose and made their way off the bus.

ACKNOWLEDGEMENTS

To Alejandra and Angel, thank you for trusting me enough to tell me your tales.

To Lanier Thomason, thanks for suffering the pre-dawn crows of Oaxacan roosters and the outcasts of Zipolite Beach.

A sincere thanks to friends who supported me during the writing of this book, particularly Rebecca Ramos, Dorothy Josey, Susie Zurenda, Lisa Atkins, The LTDs, David Dickson, and Gail Galloway Adams. Thanks also to friends Justin and Anna Converse, Susan and Rick Dent, Alex and Jennifer Evins, Billy and Lindsay Webster, Will and Liz Fort, Garrett and Cathy Scott, Stewart and Ann Johnson, Gordon and Molly Sherard, Julian Josey, George and Sissy Stone, Chris and Alice Dorrance, and George Dean and Susu Johnson.

To the world's and my most beloved editor, C. Michael Curtis, thank you for your patience, insight, and friendship.

Enormous thanks to Betsy Teter and the Hub City Writers Project.

Finally, to Mary Eliot, Elizabeth, Will, and Eliot, you are my hope personified. Thank you.

HUB CITY PRESS

Hub City Press is an independent press in Spartanburg, South Carolina, that publishes well-crafted, high-quality works by new and established authors, with an emphasis on the Southern experience. We are committed to high-caliber novels, short stories, poetry, plays, memoir, and works emphasizing regional culture and history. We are particularly interested in books with a strong sense of place.

Hub City Press is an imprint of the non-profit Hub City Writers Project, founded in 1995 to foster a sense of community through the literary arts. Our metaphor of organization purposely looks backward to the nineteenth century when Spartanburg was known as the "hub city," a place where railroads converged and departed.

HUB CITY PRESS FICTION

New Southern Harmonies • Rosa Shand, Scott Gould, Deno Trakas,
George Singleton

Inheritance • Janette Turner Hospital, editor

In Morgan's Shadow • A Hub City Murder Mystery

Comfort & Joy: Nine Stories for Christmas • Kirk Neely

Through the Pale Door • Brian Ray

Expecting Goodness & Other Stories • C. Michael Curtis, editor

My Only Sunshine • Lou Dischler

Mercy Creek • Matt Matthews